Floating Gold

By the same author

Sea Dust
The Twisting Vine
The Black Thread
The Condor's Feather

Floating Gold

Margaret Muir

ROBERT HALE · LONDON

© Margaret Muir 2010
First published in Great Britain 2010

ISBN 978-0-7090-9051-9

Robert Hale Limited
Clerkenwell House
Clerkenwell Green
London EC1R 0HT

www.halebooks.com

ACKNOWLEDGEMENT:

Special thanks go to Susanna Rogers, Marion Collins and Pat
Hornsey for their invaluable input and advice.
Thanks also to Mick Casson, Kulwant Dhillon and Richard
Moore for reading and commenting on the manuscript.
And finally, to my publisher, Mr John Hale, for having
confidence in my work.
I thank you.

Typeset in 10/13pt Palatino
by Derek Doyle & Associates, Shaw Heath
Printed in Great Britain by the MPG Books Group,
Bodmin and King's Lynn

CHAPTER 1

Isle of Wight – July 1802

The human flotsam, lolling in the shallow water near the mouth of the Bembridge River, smelled of fish. Waves washing around the corpse teased it, turning the head this way and that, confusing the sightless eyes; whilst beneath the body the sea hissed, sucking its salt through sand and broken shell. The next incoming wave lifted the corpse and carried it further up the beach, but as the water receded, the man's right arm, as if reluctant to part from its mode of transport, appeared to reach out for it. But the two-faced tide of the English Channel had its own agenda. It had done its duty and, having had no quarrel with the man, had returned him to the land. Now it was time to gather its morning petticoats and withdraw.

Oliver Quintrell stepped closer to the body and removed his hat. It was an automatic gesture performed out of respect for a life departed, yet the sight of the corpse did not stir the slightest quiver of emotion in him. There was no doubt in his mind where the man had come from. The yellowed breeches, stained with the provocative stamp of a black arrow, provided him with that information. The only question the body's presence posed: had the man fallen, jumped, or been thrown from one of the prison hulks anchored in Portsmouth Harbour?

That question would remain unresolved, and in the circumstances any answer would be quite inconsequential. But how the body had drifted from the harbour and floated unnoticed across the busy anchorages of Spithead and St Helens Road intrigued him. No doubt the tide had carried it from the confines of the harbour and spewed it out through the narrow entrance where it had to contend with the fickle currents of the Solent. Whatever factors had transported it, be it

5

wind, current or tide, it was obvious that the corpse had only recently arrived on the beach at Bembridge, where it was to provide a feast for the island's gulls, crows and scavenging foxes.

In Oliver Quintrell's mind only two things were certain – no one would be looking for an escaped prisoner this far from Portsmouth, and no one would be grieving the man's loss.

It being the only item of interest on the beach that morning, the captain tallied his mental observations. For a carcass that was only slightly bloated, the facial features appeared surprisingly normal. The face, streaked by brown hair braided with slivers of green weed, was not unpleasant. The mouth – opened in the final gasping moment of life – showed a full set of teeth. A fuzz of adolescent hair patched the chin, and the skin was virtually unblemished showing no evidence of powder burns. Despite the broad keloid scar almost dissecting his left cheek (testament to a cruel master or defiance of authority), it was evident the escapee was little more than a lad.

Not long dead, Oliver thought. Likely he had swum or been supported on driftwood which had carried him on his watery journey to intended freedom. But the prisoner would have only survived part of the short summer night, succumbing to the sea as the eastern sky glowed in the hour before dawn. In his opinion, as the lad had suffered no submarine disfigurement, his sojourn in the water had been insufficient to marinate his flesh to suit the palates of the local fishes.

Pathetic wretch, he thought. A fool to escape from a prison hulk. On the other hand, he considered a man a coward if he lacked the courage to try to escape from captivity. But on this fine July morning, beside the shimmering stretch of water where the Solent and English Channel coalesced, the death of an escaped prisoner, be he English or French, mattered not a jot.

Closing his eyes for a moment, it was easy for the captain to re-enter the world most familiar to him. He pictured a white beach the morning after a battle. A bay littered with bloated bodies, some washed ashore, others turning in the shallow water like pigs roasting on spits. Carcasses rolling over and over, unable to make landfall. Dead men stripped naked of both clothes and skin. Faceless faces devoid of their human masks. Arms, wrenched from shoulders, scattered haphazardly. Hands poking up through sand. Fingers outstretched in supplication. Severed heads without ears. Human hair blowing in the breeze. The scream of frenzied gulls.

Such an inglorious end stripped a man not only of his raiments but all evidence of nationality, allegiance and rank. For those departed souls there was neither honour nor glory nor recognition – not even a Christian burial. Their mortal remains would be stripped clean by armies of invading crabs. And there were many fat crabs on the beaches that season.

But such florid pictures were spoken little of in the London coffee shops and written of even less in the *Naval Chronicle*. They were the unwritten lines which the astute reader was expected to embellish for himself.

This was the distasteful side of war at sea, but how often over the past nine months had he prayed he could be part of it again. To return to the sea. To sail into the Mediterranean. To navigate the alligator-infested banks of the Indus River. To round the Horn. To experience the thunder of a hundred guns fired in a rippling broadside. To breathe the acrid smoke. To drink a toast to victory. To serve once again in His Majesty's service. But above all, to have a command.

For months now his weekly requests to the Lords of the Admiralty had met with platitudes. His most recent submissions had not even been acknowledged. As he gazed out to the ships at anchor, Oliver knew full well he was not the only captain landlocked since the outbreak of peace. But that fact provided little consolation.

He was thirty-two years of age, boasted the rank of post captain, yet was currently only master of an expanse of deserted beach, in command of a view, and able to navigate nothing more than the pieces of flotsam offered up by the sea.

A wave washing over his shoes soaked his white stockings and returned his thoughts to reality. That his feet were wet was quite inconsequential to him, but the water marks around his ankles were bound to evoke a derisive comment from his wife. How tiresome that type of admonishment was. Such trivial things didn't matter at sea. How often was the weather deck awash? How often did men grapple to stay upright with water washing the length of the ship? Amidst choking smoke, blood and the noise of battle, did a sailor really care about a few inches of seawater? Certainly not!

Oliver shook his head in frustration. Recounting those scenes was the closest he would come to pacing a quarter-deck for the present.

Overhead a pair of gulls distracted him. They reeled and squawked, then hovered; necks outstretched, beaks pointing, legs dangling. They were becoming impatient. The pair had observed the carcass even before the captain had approached. Now their cries were prompting him to move on. They wanted to be first to sample the choicest morsels from the upturned face. Further along the beach, a waiting battalion marched back and forth at the waterline, advancing and retreating with each spill of a wave, awaiting their opportunity.

Though the birds didn't heed the distant sound, from the north came the distinctive echo of a gun salute. Oliver knew one of His Majesty's ships had returned to port. Early that morning he had observed a second rate man-of-war from his bedroom window. From her spread of canvas it had been obvious that the lack of wind and state of the tide was making her passage to Portsmouth difficult.

That particular ship was no longer in view but there was no shortage of vessels in St Helens Road to divert his attention. A fleet of merchantmen was anchored to the north of the river's mouth, little more than a mile away. For more than three weeks Oliver had observed their number swell from a scattered handful to over forty assorted vessels: sloops, snows, brigs, barks, schooners and cutters. To the casual observer, the criss-cross of running and standing rigging presented a cat's cradle of tangled cordage.

It appeared obvious to the captain that they were preparing to sail. Some heading to the West Indies, others the East. Throughout the war the navy had provided escort ships to accompany the convoys but in a time of peace this was no longer deemed necessary. Despite this, a sixty-four-gun man-of-war was anchored at the northern end of the convoy, its tall masts dwarfing those of the other vessels.

There was no question in Oliver's mind that the sailors on board the merchantmen would be content. Many had been pressed into service during the war years and only since the peace had they been able to return to their wealthy employers. Lucky indeed were those sailors. They would be paid full wages, while landlocked naval officers like himself had to subsist on half pay, while the common seamen, littering the alleys and alehouses of every port in England, had to scratch a living as best they could.

The enforced spell of indolence had done little for Oliver but increase his frustrations and add inches to his waistline. His morning stroll, along the beach and around the banks of the Bembridge Estuary, was the only exercise he took. He discounted the games of croquet which his wife prescribed: they did nothing to improve his figure or his temperament.

It was a year since he had been carried ashore to spend three months gazing at the lofty painted ceilings of the Greenwich Seamen's

Hospital. And when at last he was discharged and eager to return to service, the Treaty of Amiens had been signed. This had confounded his frustrations and extended his absence from duty further.

But if Napoleon Bonaparte was proclaimed First Consul for Life, as was expected to happen, the peace would not last. That was not Oliver's personal opinion but the feelings expressed by every officer he spoke to. That afternoon he must pen a letter to the Admiralty. It was almost three weeks since he had last written and it was now time for another request.

The rippling tide hissed and hushed as it turned from its jettisoned cargo and began its slow recoil to the sea, sucking the swollen waters of the Bembridge River with it. By midday all that would remain of the broad estuary would be a narrow freshwater steam serpentining through the layers of silt, which even the wading swans and waterbirds would sink up to their bellies in.

Casting a final long look across the water, Oliver returned his hat and turned from the waterline. On the grass bordering the beach, a man was hurrying towards him. He was running, at times almost stumbling as his feet buried themselves in pockets of soft, dry sand. The captain immediately recognized his steward, not by the velvet raiments which identified him as a household valet but by the ungainly lolloping gait compounded by a slight bowing of the legs – the indelible signature of a seaman.

Increasing his stride, Quintrell mounted the gentle incline to the point where the beach and land converged and tufts of aggressive grasses made their invading stand for possession.

'Captain,' the man hailed, from a distance of almost fifty yards.

'What is it, Casson?'

'Begging your pardon, sir, but I thought you'd want to know,' he called, slowing in an attempt to regain his breath. 'There's a letter at the house for you, Capt'n. Delivered near two hours ago, I'm told.'

'From the Admiralty?'

'Aye, Capt'n, it is. You said you wanted to be told immediately should such a message arrive.'

'Indeed I did.'

As the pair hurried from the beach along the cart-track and up the rise to the white house on the hill, a frown furrowed Quintrell's brow but his manservant did not notice the expression. Casson was lagging behind, partially out of respect, but mainly due to the shortage of air in his lungs rendering him unable to maintain his master's pace.

'Were you not present when this letter was delivered?' Oliver asked, without turning his head.

'No, sir. I was set cleaning the silver. I only learned of it by chance just fifteen minutes ago.'

'Then my wife must have signed for it. Why on earth didn't she instruct you to fetch me immediately?'

The steward's discretion told him a reply was not expected.

Oliver's mind was alive with possibilities. 'Hurry, man, there is no time to waste.'

'You think you might have a ship, sir?'

How could he possibly know the answer to that question until he had read the communication? But it could mean a commission. A ship. A return to service. In what capacity? he wondered.

During his extended sojourn in the Greenwich Hospital, his name had risen rapidly on the post captains' list – a direct result of the deaths of many good men. Since March, however, when the peace treaty was signed, the list's status had changed very little. Now, with so many ships sitting idle, the chances of a command were slim.

Post captains like himself perused the lists with some trepidation, as new names filtered in from the bottom: the nephew of an admiral, the son of a cabinet minister, the grandson of a Fellow of the Royal Society. There were names of men he had never read about in the *Gazette* – young, relatively inexperienced naval officers whose ascent on the promotional ladder had been bolstered not by battle but by the backing of title or money. Peace seemed no detriment to their progress. But for those more familiar names filling the top third of the list, few promotions were being granted. Without war, admirals did not die. Most lived to a ripe old age, languishing in the comfort of prize money and pensions.

Oliver smiled cynically. England could afford to maintain its old men but not its grand old ladies. In the country's present financial state, the government was unable to justify preserving a fleet of redundant fighting ships. Every day saw another distinguished vessel dismasted for conversion to a prison hulk, or more sadly, despatched to the breakers yards. It truly was a travesty.

'If it is the news I have been hoping for, we might both be back at sea before too very long.'

'I pray you're right, Capt'n.'

'No more than I.'

Oliver lengthened his stride with the anticipation of receiving good news. Like a raw midshipman being rowed out to his first ship or a lieutenant receiving his first command, the sense of excitement welled within him.

The shocking alternative could see him banished to a desk job or promoted to port commander of some little-known disease-ravaged harbour on the other side of the globe. He hardly dare consider that possibility. Worse still, he could be notified of an early pension – enforced retirement from the service due to diminished health.

That is balderdash! he told himself. He was fully recovered. Fit to serve. Ready to command.

Casting those thoughts from his mind, he turned back to his servant. 'You will accompany me to London, Casson.'

'Aye aye, Capt'n,' the manservant said, with a renewed bounce in his step. 'Do you think you will get a man-of-war?'

Oliver Quintrell smiled. 'I will settle for a sloop at this stage.'

'Ah, Oliver, you are back.'

The dressmaker attending Mrs Quintrell bobbed a small curtsey.

The captain acknowledged his wife. 'Where is it?' he asked, in a tone which sounded far more scornful than he had intended.

'Where is what, dearest?'

'The letter which arrived here earlier this morning.'

'Oh, I almost forgot,' she said flippantly, as her eyes were drawn to her husband's feet. 'Your shoes, Oliver! They are covered in sand.'

Without altering his expression, the captain considered his reply then consciously withheld his spontaneous response. He did not wish to express himself in a manner he would immediately regret, especially in front of a seamstress.

His wife waved her hand. 'It's over there somewhere. On the side table. I think it's buried under those bolts of material.'

'Thank you,' he said emphatically. 'You must understand, my dear, this communication could be of vital importance to me. To us.'

'Whatever can be of such vital importance to the navy in peacetime?'

Quintrell remained silent as he retrieved the letter which had sunk beneath a sea of blue silk surmounted by a well-endowed pincushion resembling a hedgehog.

His wife turned away from him, tugging at the bodice of her dress. 'A little more fullness here, Sybil.'

Opting for the window seat, Oliver regarded the envelope for a

11

moment then broke the sealing wax.

'I hope you won't mind taking tea alone, dear,' his wife continued. 'I do so want Sybil to finish this for me. Then I must be measured for my new gown.'

He nodded without appearing to listen.

'You haven't forgotten that we are invited to Stamford House on Friday, have you? Also, I accepted an invitation from the Armitages to dine with them on Thursday at eight.'

'Ah,' Quintrell said, as he folded the letter and returned it to its envelope. '*The Economics of Warfare* by Reginald Armitage. He is the only man I know who is convinced he can put a measure on the cost of England's supremacy.'

'Don't be so cynical, dear. Reginald is a charming man. He was educated at Eton and Cambridge and is very well respected. And besides, I have told Felicity that we will be most happy to attend – so the matter is settled.'

'Then I am afraid you will have to attend alone. I shall be unavailable on both occasions.'

Extricating herself from the dressmaker's pins and needles, Victoria Quintrell turned to face her husband, but he was standing with his back to her.

The view from the window had captured his imagination and transported him far from the confines of the drawing room. That particular stretch of sea always intrigued him. It was a body of water which carried no name yet its position was known intimately by every man afloat. This was the point where ships from Portsmouth sailed out from the shelter of the Isle of Wight; where the full force of the westerly wind was first felt. Where ships altered course and the cry 'full and by' reverberated through the rigging. It was the point where the sea swayed to the rhythm of the Atlantic swell.

In the distance Quintrell could see the royals and t'gallants of a ship slowly disappearing beneath the hazy line of the horizon. A merchantman bound for London? A Dutch East Indiaman heading home? A naval frigate? A privateer, perhaps? The distance was too great to identify it and his glass was in the library.

'I am required to attend the Admiralty,' he said, the hint of a smile threatening to curl his lips. 'Ten o'clock in the morning two days from now.'

'At Portsmouth?'

'No, my dear,' he said, with a forgiving shake of the head.

'Admiralty House in Whitehall. Casson will accompany me.' He took out his pocketwatch and opened it. 'I will leave this afternoon and take a boat from Ryde. There is little time to delay. I intend to stay at The George overnight and travel to London on the morrow. I am sure my sister will be only too pleased to accommodate me in the City.' He paused, cleared his throat, then continued in a softer tone. 'Regarding the Armitages and the invitation to Stamford House, you must tender my apologies. I am sorry to disappoint you, my dear, but it is unlikely I will return to Bembridge before Saturday.'

'But Oliver!'

Though the wind hardly rustled the trees on the banks of the Bembridge River, on the north coast at Ryde and across the Mother Bank, it was blowing briskly. As the navy launch headed for Portsmouth, punching its bow into the lively waters of the Solent, Captain Quintrell was not the only one to receive a dousing as the boat sailed towards Portsmouth harbour.

Resting his right forearm across the hat on his lap, Oliver pondered the remnants of his right hand, hidden within a half-empty leather glove. It housed a thumb and forefinger and the malformed knuckle bearing the stumpy remains of his middle digit. Nothing more. Such was the result of direct contact with a four-pound cannon ball. He thanked God it had not carried away his whole arm. Or his head for that matter!

Without removing the glove, he squeezed his thumb and finger together. They were strong. He had made sure of that. He was certain he could grip the rigging on a heeling ship or control a helm in dirty weather. He knew he could draw his sword and hold a pen, a brush and a telescope. But he could not hold his wife.

He pulled the glove off and pondered the thoughts which had troubled him for many months. What was it about his disfigured hand his wife hated? From the moment she first saw it at the Greenwich Seamen's Hospital, it had repelled her. She had said it resembled a talon or a spur. Cruel words which had hurt. Only after some argument had she conceded that it was better than an ungainly hook strapped to a stump, but she disliked it intensely and insisted he cover it at all times.

But the fact it embarrassed her in public was not the end of it. Not since his return home had Oliver been able to touch her, to run his finger through her hair, explore her contours, feel her warmth. The awkwardness of his left hand only accentuated his disability.

He still loved his wife, but by shutting off his touch she was

13

blocking the gangway to his affection. He could not deny that for several months while in hospital his mindless brain had failed to even recognize her, but that had been due to the brain infection and been unintentional on his part. Learning to live without affection was taking a considerable amount of conscious effort. Now when he approached her and she glanced at his hand reproachfully, she would find some minor thing on his person to complain about. There was always something to disparage him for. This time it was his shoes. But far worse than that was in the gloom of their bedchamber, where her skin would tighten to his touch as if some long-legged spider was crawling over her. He needed her intimacy but would not take it unless it was offered freely. How many nights had he stood by the bedroom window gazing out to sea wishing for the confines of his cot? At least there he did not suffer the ignominy of rejection. The fact that time was dulling his own human desires worried him.

On occasions, he had thought to satisfy her by having the unsightly remnants of his hand surgically removed and the cuff of his dresscoat stitched up by his tailor. Now, as the boat entered the confines of Portsmouth Harbour, he was thankful he had not done so.

The array of fighting ships made his spirits soar, and as the launch drifted towards the Hard, the smell of tar and turpentine was succour to his senses. He visualized the guns breeched behind the closed gun ports of a majestic hundred-gun first-rate and for a moment dared wonder if it might be waiting for him.

Tomorrow – London, he thought. And the following day? He would know the answer to that question soon enough.

When the boat ground to a halt on the Hard, Captain Quintrell stepped ashore, followed by his steward. After shaking the water from the hem of his boat cloak, he raked his finger through his hair, replaced his hat and thought about his disfigured hand.

A claw? A talon? A spur? He considered the connotations of his wife's words. The eagle's talon was a perfectly formed weapon for snatching prey. The fighting cock's spur – the ultimate killing device. Both birds were bold and fearless. Both were supremely equipped. One a predator; the other a born fighter.

As they neared the entrance to The George, a young lieutenant stepped aside and saluted. Oliver acknowledged the gesture, touching his bare finger to his hat.

No one had seen him casting his black glove into the sea. And no one would see him wearing it again.

CHAPTER 2

The Admiralty

Oliver Quintrell was restless. He hated the stagnant confines of the Admiralty's waiting room and had chosen to wait in the corridor even though the wooden benches were unpadded and uncomfortable. He would have preferred to pace rather than sit but, with clerks hurrying hither and thither, it was a busy thoroughfare, so he remained seated, his frustrations growing.

His journey to London had been interrupted by several unscheduled stops due to the heavy rain and the necessity of an extra change of horses, but despite the lateness of the hour, his sister had been delighted at his unannounced arrival. After dining late and feeling obliged to consume more than his stomach required, he did not sleep well. A supper of bread and cheese and a glass of milk would have satisfied him well. On enquiry that morning, it appeared his steward had been subjected to a similar fate in the kitchen, but Casson seemed disinclined to complain about the excess, merely stating what a fine meal the cook had prepared.

As Oliver shifted his position on the hard bench, it rocked on the polished floor. The sound echoed. As he readjusted his pose, the noise repeated itself.

Standing guard outside the nearest doorway, one of the marines sniffed continually, like a bloodhound in a rat-infested barn. Occasionally his nasal passages exploded in a mucoid snort, which jerked the other guard from the lethargy into which he was falling. After three such disgusting eruptions, the captain could bear it no longer.

'For goodness sake, man! Stop that!'

The marine responded by snorting loudly without looking in the captain's direction.

At last the double doors swung open and a flurry of footsteps on polished boards announced that the business which had been conducted in that chamber was over. Oliver anticipated that his time had come and rose to his feet.

Three men left the room but the door was quickly closed behind them. Oliver recognized the first of the dignitaries. 'Lord Buckinghamshire,' he said, inclining his head. The man had aged considerably from the young Bevan he had met at a reception several years earlier. Oliver prided himself on his excellent memory for faces though at times names eluded him.

A cordial nod was all he received, followed by a moment's hesitation on the part of the two men walking behind. But nothing further was said and the Secretary of State for War and the Colonies strode off in the direction of Whitehall, followed by the other gentlemen who Oliver did not know. The pair had appeared eager to engage each other in conversation but on seeing the captain they had held their tongues. Whatever subject matter was so compelling to talk about would have to wait until they left the building.

Stretching his legs, Oliver pulled at his neckerchief, which he had fastened too tightly. It was beginning to constrict his throat but now was not the time to loosen the knot. Waiting expectantly, he anticipated his name being called but the doors remained closed.

It was not difficult for him to recall the interior of the room as he had attended the Lords of the Admiralty on four previous occasions. Returning to his seat, he tried to appear relaxed but his pose was unnatural. He checked his watch. Another quarter-hour had elapsed and by now the footsteps were long gone, there were no voices to be heard and even the clerks had stopped their continual ferrying back and forth. Only the sniffing continued.

'Please be seated, Captain.' It was Admiral Viscount St Vincent, First Lord of the Admiralty who greeted him. On his left at the long mahogany table were two other Lords Commissioners. He recognized Captain Sir Thomas Troubridge and Captain John Markham, but on his right were two gentlemen he did not know. Their dress was as dull as the peahen's feathers when compared to that of the cock. Civilians, obviously. Possibly lawyers or ship owners, he thought.

'You may leave us.' St Vincent directed his words to the three marines present. As they filed out, a young blond scribe shuffled nervously to his feet.

'You will remain and record this meeting,' he said, pausing until the door was closed. 'Captain Quintrell, you are well, I trust?'

'Thank you, my lord. I am in exceedingly good health.'

'That is good.' He glanced along the table. 'You no doubt recognized the Secretary for War who just left us.'

'Indeed, I did, my lord.'

'And this gentleman on my right is from the Treasury. And Mr Charles Yorke, the Home Secretary.'

Oliver acknowledged the ministers and the admirals on the viscount's left.

'I apologize for the delay but there has been much to discuss. As you are aware the responsibility of safeguarding England's freedom and keeping her coastline safe from invasion is the role of the Royal Navy. What you may not know is that in achieving this situation, England's financial resources have been stretched to the extreme. In 1799 alone, Mr Pitt had hoped to raise ten million pounds from his new income tax to pay for weapons and equipment, yet the actual receipts fell well short of that by four million pounds.' He paused. 'Another war could be catastrophic from a financial point of view and to this end the country must meet the problem on two fronts. Firstly, unnecessary expenditure must be cut, and secondly new avenues for obtaining revenue must be investigated. Above all, reparation must be made.'

Oliver wondered what role he could play in rectifying England's financial woes.

'Tell me, Captain Quintrell, how did you sustain the injury which halted your naval career?'

'Contact with a four-pound shot, my lord.'

'Rendering you unconscious?'

'Not immediately. That occurred almost a week later.'

'And when you recovered your senses?'

The muscles in his cheeks tensed pulse-like as he clenched his teeth. 'I did not recover my senses for some time.'

'I understand you were returned to England in that unhappy state?'

'Yes, my lord.'

A sheet of paper was handed along the bench, each of the gentlemen taking time to peruse it before passing it on.

Oliver felt the sweat running down his back. So much depended on the success of this interview.

'I understand you have been quite prodigious in your efforts to be granted a commission. You contend that you are fully recovered from your incapacity?'

'Yes, sir.' His lips parted momentarily but he decided to withhold his comment.

'Continue, Captain.'

'My lord, I have been fully recovered and fit to return to sea for many months. And the minor injury to my hand will not limit the performance of my duty, I assure you.'

The First Lord did not look up but referred to another document before him.

'Yes, I notice,' he said, dropping the letter back on the polished surface. 'However, it states here: "*Mental incapacity. Confused cognition. Inflammation of the meninges. Possible permanent damage to the cerebellum.*" Tell me, Captain, are you suffering from permanent brain damage?'

'No, my lord, most definitely not. The head injury was—'

'Thank you, Captain. I have the physician's report in front of me.'

Oliver swallowed. He had promised himself that he would say nothing. He knew that the Board's decision was a foregone conclusion and that he must accept the outcome without argument or redress, but the tone of the interview was giving rise to concern.

'My lords, if you will allow me to speak.' He almost added the words 'in my defence', as the line of questioning was not unlike that of a court-martial. 'I assure you I am fit and well and fully capable of resuming command if the Lords see fit to grant me a ship.'

'I note you were born in 1870, which makes you thirty-two?' The eyes glanced up at him for confirmation.

'Yes, my lord.'

'You have been in the service for only a dozen years which means you did not enter until you were twenty.' His eyebrows rose. 'A little old, was it not?'

'Begging your pardon, my lord, but my father was a ship's captain and I spent a dozen years by his side sailing around the Americas.'

'Ah, yes. An American packet. And how many times have you doubled the Horn?'

'Six times.'

'That voyage does not daunt you?'

'No, my lord.'

'Quintrell. The name is Cornish, is it not?'

'Yes, my lord.'

'Your father's father – what was his occupation?'

'He was a herring fisherman, my lord. He owned his own boat.'

'Captain,' St Vincent said, 'I can see from your expression that you are wondering where this thorough investigation is taking us. Bear with me as I feel it is pertinent.'

To what? Oliver thought. Good God, what was looming? Was he to be retired from the service? Offered a job as lighthouse-keeper on some Scottish island or given the post of overseer on a rotting prison ship? He had heard that there were hulks at Woolwich, Plymouth and Chatham and was familiar with those in Portsmouth harbour. Dead and dying ships. Repositories for the dregs of society. Floating prisons. Eleven in total, lined up in single file – a redundant funeral cortege waiting for another war. He could think of nothing worse.

With his head buzzing from unanswered questions, it was hard to maintain a dignified expression. Only one thing was certain in his mind: he had not been invited to this meeting to receive news of promotion to admiral.

'You have no doubt seen the convoy anchored in St Helens Road?'

'Indeed, sir. More than forty merchant ships.'

'As of this morning, we are informed there are forty-seven vessels and next week they will be joined by another score which are currently gathering at the Nore.'

Oliver was puzzled. Since the peace, the navy was no longer providing escorts to merchant ships.

St Vincent anticipated his enquiry. 'It was posted in the *Gazette* that a small squadron is presently preparing to sail for Kingston. You may also have read that Lord Markingham and a party of diplomats will be sailing to Ceylon to take up their appointments.'

The captain acknowledged this.

'Members of The East India Company Board and several other wealthy traders are also aware of these movements and because of the recent increases in the incidence of piracy, particularly in the North Atlantic, they have requested the Admiralty that their ships be allowed to sail with the naval fleet.'

Oliver waited.

'I should add that this extraordinary requisition was supported by a handsome financial offer which the government, in its present financial position, was not in a position to decline.'

Suddenly a see-saw of possibilities presented itself. Dare he imagine he was to be offered command of a squadron? A promotion to the rank of commodore perhaps? Or command of a second or third-grade ship-of-the-line? His thoughts were cut short.

'Captain Quintrell, you have not held a commission for how long now?'

'Almost a year now, my lord.'

'You do realize that currently we have three-quarters of the Royal Navy's post captains at our disposal, not to mention several Rear Admirals of the Blue who remind us almost daily of their expectations. However,' he said, 'it is your experience, your resourcefulness and your proven ability to handle men under adverse conditions that has brought us to the conclusion that you are the man we will entrust with this particular assignment. You will have your ship, Captain!'

Those words struck like a bolt from the blue: like the call from the masthead when land was sighted after six months at sea; like the taste of fresh water after drinking from a water butt tainted with vinegar; like the final moment of ecstasy lying across a woman's flanks. The words, 'you will have your ship', echoed in his head.

It was a statement which did not require an answer. Oliver wanted to offer his thanks but under the circumstances decided to keep his lips pursed in order to control the corners of his lips, which were intent on providing their own response.

The Sea Lord continued. 'Your ship has been on the stocks at Portsmouth for some weeks. However, I believe the repairs have now been satisfactorily completed.' He turned his head. 'Am I correct?'

'Yes, my lord. Almost two thousand new copper plates have been added to her hull with copper nails at a cost of—'

'Thank you. The cost of repair is irrelevant.' He cleared his throat. '*Elusive* is a thirty-eight-gun frigate.'

Quintrell swallowed.

'I know what you are thinking, Captain, and in light of your previous command, I can understand your disappointment that we are not offering you a ship-of-the-line. In due course you will see the reasons behind our decision. For the present, however, let me say, the vessel we have selected has been chosen not for its size or the number of its guns but for its speed and versatility.'

Oliver tried to halt the flow of thoughts flashing through his head as it appeared that the admiral was adept at intercepting those signals. Instead, his mind flipped back to the beach at Bembridge and the brief conversation he had had with his steward. Flippantly he had said to be granted a sloop would make him happy. But in truth anything less than a sixty-four-gun third-rate would be a disappointment. Yet here he was being offered a frigate: a fifth-grade ship whose command was usually given to a lieutenant. A fifth-grade ship was a mere messenger boy of the fleet. Such a command could be seen as an insult.

'You wish to speak?'

'My lord.' He paused. 'Am I to understand *Elusive* will sail as part of the escort to the merchant fleet?'

Lord St Vincent took a vellum pouch from the admiral on his left and placed it on the table. 'These are your immediate orders, Captain. When the remainder of the merchant fleet arrives from the Nore, you will be ready to sail with them. You will be with them but not of them. Take heed of your orders and follow them to the letter. It is of primary importance that you do not reveal the details to friend or foe. Your ship is well named *Elusive* and once you sail alone, this is the guise you must adopt. We trust you will wear the name like a cloak and become a ghost ship on the sea. Have I made myself clear?'

'Yes, my lord.'

'You have a little less than two weeks to engage your crew and take on supplies. The Port Admiral at Portsmouth will be made aware of your requirements and will give you priority and assistance should you need it.'

Oliver's mind was racing. There would be little time.

'One final item. The Admiralty has taken the liberty of selecting the officer to serve as *Elusive*'s first officer. Lieutenant Simon Parry has an interesting record. You will meet him at the conclusion of this interview. Midshipmen we have aplenty and we will have no difficulty supplying your quota. As to able seamen, I am sure Mr Parry will oversee that matter. However, I must stress the importance of selecting honest and trustworthy men. In peacetime there are many able-bodied seamen eager to sign and willing to serve on anything afloat – therefore, I charge you to choose carefully. The fortunes of England may be affected by the outcome of your voyage.'

'May I ask the destination of the cruise?'

'Your immediate orders are here. You sail with the convoy to Madeira. You will be handed further sealed orders when you anchor in Funchal Road. Those instructions are not to be opened until you reach the fifteenth parallel.'

'Yes, my lord.'

'The content of those orders, which will reveal your final destination, must remain a closely guarded secret. Should you be boarded or taken, those orders must be destroyed. Do you understand?'

'Yes, my lord.'

'Do you have any further questions?'

'No, my lord.'

'Then I wish you Godspeed. Much depends on you.'

Oliver Quintrell stood up and bowed to the Lords of the Admiralty and the other gentlemen in attendance. Stepping forward, he reached out to take the vellum pouch and immediately felt the weight of five pairs of eyes resting on his misshapen hand. But he didn't care. He had his ship.

His last command had been a sixty-four-gun ship-of-the-line and now he was relegated to a frigate. But it was a ship and a command.

The mention of secret orders intrigued him. What would his destination be? He was sailing south to the fifteenth parallel. From there the majority of merchant ships and the West Indian squadron would be heading north-west with the trade winds. Perhaps he would be heading south. The Cape of Good Hope, Cape Horn, Ceylon? he wondered.

The possibility of sailing the South American coastline appealed to him. He knew all the ports from Recife to Rio and Monte Video to Valparaiso. The harbours he had not entered, he knew by reputation. But for now he must take a post-chaise to Portsmouth. There was much to be done – a visit to his tailor, order cigars and honey, then return with all haste to the Isle of Wight and Bembridge to collect his dunnage and attend to many other matters. In the mean time, he would direct Casson to locate his old sailing master, Jack Mundy, and also his gunner and bosun – if those men were still alive. Likely all three warrant officers were landlocked somewhere in the London area. If his memory served him correctly, Mr Mundy attended a church by the Thames at Putney, and the gunner's family had a small cottage near the docks in Chatham.

Even now he could picture himself pacing the quarter-deck; could hear the thrum of the rigging strumming in his ears. He could visualize the sea at night, could trace the staircase to the moon laid out across the water. He could smell the exotic spices of tropical ports and almost feel the damp humidity which enveloped the deck. Then his memory catapulted to Madeira; to silk sheets and the sheen of sweat shining on smooth, glowing skin; to her body rising and falling beneath him, long and slow, like the reaches of the broad Atlantic swell; to the warmth of her lips.

Like the sea itself, her call was magnetic. One day he would see her again.

CHAPTER 3

Mr Parry

'Captain Quintrell?'

The voice shook Oliver back to reality. The naval officer addressing him was impeccably dressed, his uniform taken straight from the cutting room of Cutler and Gross. However, it lacked the perfunctory evidence of tailor's chalk and the aromatic odour of camphor. It also lacked any additional trimmings of gold lace or epaulettes.

'And you, sir, are. . . ?'

'Simon Parry, first lieutenant of the *Elusive*. At your service, Captain.'

There was something vaguely familiar about the face. Had they met before?

The lieutenant inclined his head in an elegant fashion, his gesture lacking any flamboyance but revealing much of his breeding. He maintained the pose for a second but the grace with which he delivered it made the moment appear longer. Then he lifted his face, straightened his neck and, like a recently whittled long bow without a string, stood almost six feet tall; slim, willowy and straight as a die.

After acknowledging the gesture with a quick nod of the head, Oliver inclined his eyes to the man's tidily trimmed hair. It was the shade of a sun-bleached deck, almost white, though Quintrell considered the colour spoke nothing of his age. On the contrary, the premature greying complemented the man's distinguished appearance.

'May I walk with you, Captain?'

'Indeed. I find the corridors of the Admiralty somewhat suffocating.'

As they traversed the well-worn marble and headed towards the grey pavements of Whitehall, the captain was aware of his lieutenant's gait. It was unlike his own. The officer's step was light and smooth and quite different from the ungainly gait of most men of the sea – an unfortunate attribute which attracted the press gangs to recently returned sailors as precociously as flies to a newly slaughtered beast.

He wondered how his lieutenant had coped during his years as a midshipman. No doubt he had served on an admiral's ship, possibly that of a relative. No doubt he had come aboard with a sea chest bursting with private provisions; a quantity sufficient to supply half the crew. Likely he had risen to the rank of lieutenant by favour rather than ability and were it not for the peace he would no doubt have his own command by now.

Quintrell tried to check his cynicism, but he had a festering dislike for patronage and the hypocrisy of the haughty upper class. In his opinion, their behaviour was little different from that of an ordinary seaman, only it was wrapped in frills, bows and flounces, flavoured with fragrances and tied up with a string of titles.

Victoria had accused him of being jealous as he had not been bred to such a life, but Oliver was adamant that was not the case. He could not tolerate affectation or hypocrisy in any man. They were traits which irritated as intensely as hives to a sensitive skin.

It was ironic that the fortunes of war, namely prize money, had made him a wealthy man, so rich, in fact, he could buy himself a country estate if he so wished. But Oliver Quintrell wore the vestiges of wealth as uncomfortably as a hermit crab fitted its discarded shell. His wife, however, whose birthright entitled her to aspire to those ways, revelled in the creature comforts and social status which his fortune guaranteed.

When they stepped out to the street, Whitehall was alive with traffic. Carriages lined both sides of the road, their open doors emitting an assortment of residual odours left by their most recent passengers. On the roadway fresh horse droppings steamed sweetly, reminding them they were far from fresh sea air.

'I thought you would be interested to hear that I have seen *Elusive*, Captain.'

'I was of the understanding that you only received your instructions this morning.'

'That is so. However, I visited Portsmouth two weeks ago and by chance had the opportunity of touring the dockyard with my uncle.'

Port Admiral for a relative? Quintrell wondered. 'Indeed?'

'I noted a frigate undergoing repair. She was still on the stocks and was attracting considerable interest around the harbour.'

'And why is that?'

'Because of the money expended on her in this time of peace. And because of the new copper sheathing. I was told that from Gosport, at a certain hour in the evening, the ship reflected the rays of the setting sun. Some said it looked as though the hull has been dipped in burnished gold.'

'Poetic,' Quintrell said rather scornfully. 'Thank goodness that will not be evident once her bottom is wet. Tell me, Mr Parry, from your observation, had the restoration work been completed?'

'When I saw her, the plating was finished and preparations were being made to launch her and restep the masts. I expect by the time we return to Portsmouth she will be in the water and the work will be complete.'

'And when do you intend to join her?'

'Tomorrow. I intend to travel overnight.' He paused. 'And when might we expect you on board, Captain?'

'Two days from now.' Such a delay was frustrating, but Oliver had little choice. He had business to attend to in London and he must return to Bembridge before taking up his commission. 'However, I shall be passing through Portsmouth tomorrow on my journey home. Be so good as to meet me on the Hard at six o'clock in the afternoon.'

'Tomorrow at six, Captain. I will look forward to it.'

Quintrell arrived at the sea port in the forenoon. The coach ride from London had been tedious and uneventful, setting him down in Portsmouth fifteen minutes earlier than was scheduled. In the afternoon he visited his bank and his tailor and placed orders in several establishments for his private rations. When Casson arrived from London, he would attend to any other items that had been forgotten. There would be ample time, as it would be several days before they would be sailing.

With half an hour to spare, before meeting his lieutenant Oliver strolled through the dockyard area. So much had changed in the months since the war had ended. Now Portsmouth had more sailors lining its wharves than empty casks and barrels. The cobblestones which once rumbled to the sound of gun carriages now ticked with the tap of blind men's sticks and the lampposts provided support for a score of peg-legged beggars. In the local paper he had read that landlocked seamen rivalled pickpockets and prostitutes as the scourge of the town. Such was the legacy of peace.

On the harbour itself, wherries and lighters ferried their wares between ships and jetties, but of the hundreds of victuallers' barges which had once serviced the fighting ships, many had been left to rot in the Gosport mud. The boats and barges which still plied their repetitive trade did so with little of the urgency or expediency required when supplying an active wartime fleet.

Only one first-rate ship was in harbour: a triple-decker carrying over one hundred guns. Beyond her was a frigate, several sloops, ketches and brigs all vying for the broad channels carrying sufficient deep water to keep them afloat.

Dominating the harbour was the line of once-proud fighting ships. Stripped of sails, masts, spars and rigging, the prison hulks stood in single file like a line of Hannibal's elephants – chained together bow to stern, unable to release themselves from the suction of the silt. On deck, the bare carcasses bore only marine signal boxes, while at water level a floating wooden platform skirted each ship creating a curious and almost comical garb. The residual smells, however, which exuded through the bars fixed over the gun ports, were no laughing matter. For the present the prison hulks serviced the needs of London's overcrowded gaols and housed male and female convicts awaiting transportation to the colonies. But there was ample accommodation awaiting Napoleon's men should the tyrant decide to breach the Treaty of Amiens.

For a moment Oliver's mind flashed back to the body on Bembridge Beach, then he blinked, turned his gaze from the all-too-familiar sight and considered the day.

It was near perfect: clear skies and a breeze freshening from the north-west. Ideal conditions for a ship to sail out of the harbour, but for the moment he must bide his time and content himself with a short journey across the Solent to the Isle of Wight and home.

With the majority of his business completed and a navy launch waiting at the gun jetty, he walked smartly across the road to where his lieutenant was waiting for him.

'Mr Parry,' he said.

The lieutenant's eyes did not flinch as he gripped the captain's outstretched hand. There was no evidence of surprise or distaste as his palm wrapped around the appendage, which had the consistency of a dead cockerel's claw.

It is remarkable, Oliver thought, how effectively the upper classes have mastered the ability of appearing oblivious to anything disagreeable. He trusted that this trait would not apply on *Elusive*. A lieutenant must be alert at all times; must be aware of the smallest deviation from normal; must recognize anything unseemly, assess it and act upon it instantly. That was his job.

'Captain, I trust you had a reasonable journey.'

'Reasonable? Yes. But what of *Elusive*? Where is she?'

'Less than half a mile upstream from here. North-west of the Clock.'

From where they were standing on the Hard, the buildings of the Royal Naval Dockyard masked their view.

'You went aboard this morning?'

'At seven o'clock, sir.'

'And your opinion?'

'Sound ship, Captain. Not more than five years old, I would wager. A nice line. However, I hear she was in a sorry state when she was towed in from the Channel. It was argued whether it was best to burn her or repair her. I believe the decision to restore her was justified as there was little damage to the hull. From what I can see the carpenters and riggers have performed an excellent job.'

'And who have you left on board?'

'There are six marines including a sergeant, a ship-keeper and half a dozen carpenters and shipwrights from the dockyard who are still finishing off work below decks. They will be on board for three or maybe four days. And this morning I signed twenty men to help with the victualling. They are all seamen who have served on ships-of-the-line. Four of them were on the same gun crew. There is also a gunner's mate, a bosun's mate, and a cook.'

'Men you know of?'

'No, sir. I chose them from the morning mob milling around the slipway. Quite a large and unruly crowd, and I gather it is the same here every day.'

'In these uncertain times, any chance of a possible berth would travel around the port like wildfire.'

The lieutenant nodded. 'One thing is for certain, there is no longer need for the press.'

'That is good, but I am surprised you only signed twenty men. Have you spoken with the Clerk of the Cheque?'

'I have indeed. He tells me that by tomorrow or the next day we will have the bulk of our men. One hundred and twenty sailors off the

Constantine are being ferried up from Falmouth.'

'*Constantine*. A seventy-four? Served recently in the Mediterranean during the war?'

'That is so. She ran foul of the Scilly Isles and broke up on Bishop Rock more than a week ago.'

'Yes, I heard about it. What on earth was she doing veering so far to the north?'

The lieutenant had no answer.

'The captain will be facing a court-martial.'

Mr Parry paused before answering. 'Indeed. An unfortunate incident.'

'Unfortunate indeed! More likely bad seamanship, Mr Parry. That "unfortunate incident", as you call it, cost the lives of several hundred men. She would have had a muster list of at least six hundred and I expect half of those are probably now bobbing up in the sea around Land's End like a herd of bloated seals.'

Unperturbed, Mr Parry continued. 'I was told that the men who survived are being transported aboard a coastal vessel and if the weather permits will be in Spithead tomorrow. They were given the option of returning to their home but most were anxious to sign.'

'Any warrant officers amongst them?' Oliver asked.

'I will not know until they arrive but I heard that they lost their master, purser and surgeon.'

'So. One hundred and twenty men. And what of the rest? Will you take Portsmouth men?'

'The Clerk of the Cheque advised me that he is sending down a group recently discharged from the Haslar Hospital.'

The captain frowned.

'I am advised that they are fit enough to serve.'

'And I don't doubt that they have served their country well, but on this particular voyage I am not prepared to carry any sailors with deficiencies in either their mental faculties or the number of their limbs. The only purpose I see they serve is to save the nation the cost of their disability pensions. No, Mr Parry, we do not want them. If the Clerk of the Cheque is adamant, I will speak with him myself!' He paused for a moment. 'As to the position of sailing master, gunner and bosun, my steward has remained in London with the sole purpose of locating some men who sailed with me previously. If he is successful, Mr Mundy will be our sailing master. He is an excellent navigator. And with Mr Eccles as bosun, I can assure you we will have a good working ship. Once he locates them, my steward will return with them to Portsmouth with all speed.'

The lieutenant nodded.

'As for the junior officers, the Admiralty assures me they will have no problems filling the midshipman's berth.'

'Excellent.'

Oliver relaxed his expression. 'You have done well, Mr Parry.' The compliment was genuine. He was satisfied with his first lieutenant's achievements in less than a day on board *Elusive*, but that degree of efficiency raised a question in Oliver's mind. Here was a well-bred officer only a few years younger than himself who, besides the apparent benefit of patronage, showed considerable aptitude, initiative and intelligence. So why was he still only a lieutenant?

He thought of his own situation and of the numerous letters he had addressed to the Admiralty which had been unanswered. Yet if a man of Parry's background had written a single letter asking for a commission, the no-doubt crested seal on his envelope would have guaranteed that his correspondence was placed directly into the hands of one of the sea lords.

'Now, you will excuse me, Mr Parry. I must return home with all haste and deliver the news of my commission to my wife.'

'I trust she will be delighted for you, sir.'

A quirky smile crossed Quintrell's lips. No, he thought, she will be less than delighted. In fact she will be quite miffed that her husband will be unable to attend the dinner party at the Armitages'.

'I trust she will be,' Oliver said. 'However, I must be careful to stifle my enthusiasm in case my desire to depart from home and join the ship is misconstrued. The fair sex have the extraordinary ability of viewing news though kaleidoscopic eyes so that the end result, as they see it, is a total distortion to what was originally presented. Would you not agree?'

'I have not had the fortune of marrying.'

The captain wondered about this type of fortune but refrained from continuing the inconsequential conversation.

'I shall come aboard and read my commission tomorrow at four o'clock in the afternoon. One more question, Mr Parry. Do any of the furnishings remain in the main cabin?'

'No, sir. I'm afraid the great cabin is an empty shell. It appears the ship was raked by French guns and the furnishings were reduced to splinters.'

'Thank you, Mr Parry.' Quintrell sniffed the air. The fresh breeze was holding. 'Until eight bells tomorrow afternoon then.'

'Aye aye, Captain.'

The pair parted company, the lieutenant heading down the Hard to the wherry while Oliver headed to the gun jetty where a launch was waiting.

He was tempted to take a boat up the harbour. He wanted to see *Elusive* for himself, but that could wait. She would go down in the water as the victualling continued but nothing would alter her line or beak or stern, and he would see that soon enough.

A group of men smelling of ale and stale smoke stepped aside to let him pass. One of them knuckled his forehead and mumbled the word 'Capt'n' as he walked by. Oliver nodded but his mind was on other things.

It was only in the final moments of their conversation that he had detected a flicker of emotion in his lieutenant's hazel eyes. But like reading signals in a sea fog, the message was difficult to interpret. Was it melancholy? Jealousy? Pride? He thought not. Then perhaps tiredness? But the strange haunting expression had come and gone quicker than a flash of gunpowder.

Whatever lay behind his lieutenant's steady eyes would reveal itself in the course of their voyage. In his experience, the sea was a great unraveller.

CHAPTER 4

Portsmouth

At precisely four in the afternoon, the shrill notes of the bosun's whistles warbled on the placid air of Portsmouth Harbour, announcing unequivocally to every ship anchored within half a mile that the captain was coming aboard.

As he climbed the steps to the awaiting salute, Oliver's expression showed not the slightest hint of the youthful exuberance which was coursing through his veins. It was the same feeling he had experienced as a midshipman, a lieutenant, and as master and commander when he had gone aboard his various ships, and the feeling was more exquisite every time. He wanted to reach out his hand and touch *Elusive*'s hull, but resisted and satisfied himself by merely flaring his nostrils to inhale the smell of fresh paint, tar and turpentine, and the salty scent of the sea.

It was a relief to be back at last, and though the pipes were not entirely appropriate as he had not yet taken up his command he was not about to reprimand his lieutenant for ordering the welcoming gesture.

Within minutes of his arrival, Captain Quintrell had read his commission to the seamen assembled on the deck of His Majesty's frigate, *Elusive*, and once the formalities were completed, he scanned the crew and spoke: 'I trust you men will regard yourself lucky, especially those of you who served on *Constantine*. You are lucky to have survived the sinking of your ship and to have been delivered safely from the sea. You should also regard yourself as lucky to be transferred to this vessel. As you are aware, peacetime has thrown many good seamen into unenviable situations.

'I speak for the officers and myself when I say we too are fortunate to have a crew who have all served previously in His Majesty's Navy. Some of you fought at the Nile, others in the Mediterranean, others with the Channel fleet. I believe those of you who served on *Constantine* did so to the best of your ability under Captain Bransfield.'

He paused and breathed in deeply. 'It is with regret I must inform you that Captain Bransfield departed this life, at his own hand, three days ago.'

The simultaneous sigh of 120 men rolled across the deck. It was like a final rumble of distant thunder long after a storm has passed.

'Captain Bransfield accepted full responsibility for the loss of his ship – as any captain must – but the weight of that burden was too great for him to bear. I ask you to not think ill of him or accuse him of cowardice, and I ask you to remember him in your prayers. Furthermore,' he said, glancing into the rheumy eyes of some of the sailors, 'I ask that the trust and loyalty you showed to your previous captain is transferred to the officers of *Elusive*. And I ask the same of you men from other ships also.

'Finally, let me say, I expect every man, be he able seaman, idler or officer, to be alert at all times. Any man found not discharging his duties to the fullest will suffer the consequences. Furthermore, any man showing disrespect for this ship or its officers will suffer punishment according to the Articles of War.'

Having been reminded of those consequences according to the said Articles at least once every week since the day they entered the service, there was little response from the potted assortment of faces.

'We sail two days from now and in the meantime, there is much work to be done.'

'Enter!' Oliver Quintrell was seated on a three-legged stool at a small circular table barely broad enough to accommodate his leather-bound logbook.

His first lieutenant entered, his head stooped beneath the deck beams.

'Sit down, Mr Parry.'

Crossing to the locker beneath the stern windows, he sat down and waited.

'Mr Parry,' Quintrell said, turning and looking him directly in the eyes, 'in the waist of the ship I distinctly saw one man with a wooden peg strapped to the stump of his amputated leg, and another man with a disfigured face and half of it missing. Did we not speak of the thousands of sailors begging for a berth? Did I not make it clear to you that patients from the Haslar Hospital were not to be signed?'

'Captain, I only accepted four of them, and then only after I had questioned them.'

'And in what unhappy condition do you find the two I did not see?'

'One suffered burns to his torso and the other has lost his left eye.'

'Ha, a good pair of eyes shared between two!'

'If I may speak, Captain. I can assure you all four men are fully recovered and half-vision does not prevent a man from hauling a rope or climbing the rigging. The man with the turned leg assures me he can sew a sail or serve a plate of gruel as quickly as any other. And the man who was burned swears his back is strong. He can heave on the capstan, haul a line, holystone a deck or fill bags of powder as dexterously as any other able-bodied man. If you had seen them, sir, I do not think you would have rejected them. The clerk of the cheque was most insistent I take them. I turned eight men away and obliged him by accepting these four.'

'You obliged him, sir! And what of obliging me?'

'Begging your pardon, Captain, but I was unable to seek your advice and took it on myself to make the decision.'

'You were already aware of my decision, Mr Parry. I stated clearly that I did not want any invalids foisted on us from the Haslar Hospital. Take heed, mister, when I express a decision in future I will expect you to respect it and follow it to the letter. Do I make myself clear?'

'Yes, sir.'

Oliver rose from his chair and glanced out to the dunes of grey mud rising steadily from the bed of the harbour. Between the sandy islands the narrowing channels flowed with only sufficient depth to carry barges and small boats. It would take the incoming tide to refill the empty pound. He was conscious he had not yet checked the tides.

'So, Mr Parry, how many men do we have on board?'

'One hundred and eighty presently and twenty more expected.'

'Two hundred men for a frigate. Adequate, perhaps, but not excessive. A few more would have been preferable. You think that number will suffice?'

'I do, Captain. The reason being, I judge a dozen able seamen from the *Constantine* equal to fifty landsmen any day. The sailors are all fit and willing, and despite their sudden transfer, are eager to get back to sea. It is my opinion, sir, that with a healthy crew and the present peace, we should suffer few losses.'

'Wishful thinking, Mr Parry, and I note you did not include pirate attack, collision, fog or the state of the wind and waves in the vagaries of your equation. Furthermore, there is no guarantee that the Treaty of Amiens will last, and there are still pirates only too willing to snap at the heels of an unruly herd of merchantmen once they poke their noses out into the Atlantic.'

'In my opinion, Captain, two hundred men is a fitting crew for *Elusive*.'

'So be it, Mr Parry, as first lieutenant, the crew is your responsibility. In two days we join Commodore Ingham in St Helens Road and when the merchant fleet is assembled, we sail with them for Madeira. However, I can tell you in confidence, we are not on escort duty, though to all intents and purposes we will appear to be so. It appears the Navy Board has been seduced by a group of wealthy merchants to act as nursemaids.' Oliver recognized the cynical tone in his voice and sighed. 'It peeves me somewhat to say this, but my orders state categorically that we do not commit ourselves to action unless there is no other alternative. We must avoid confrontation like the Yellow Jack. Do you understand?'

'Yes, sir.'

'That is well. Now, I would like to speak with the surgeon as soon as he comes aboard. Let us hope he spends this cruise relaxing over a good book and not battling to stand upright on the blood-soaked sand of the cockpit floor. Would you not agree?'

'Indeed, Captain.'

'Congratulations, Captain. She's a fine ship.' The captain's steward was grinning from ear to ear as he gazed around the cabin with its paucity of furnishings.

Oliver's delighted expression was genuine. 'Good to see you aboard, Casson. Have you just arrived?'

'Not more than five minutes ago, Capt'n. I made myself known to the first lieutenant. He said you wanted to see me right away.'

'I trust you did not come aboard alone.'

'No, sir, I came on with a boatload of middies and their dunnage.'

'Did you find Jack Mundy?'

'Aye, indeed, Capt'n. I took a wherry up the Thames to Putney and asked around. Several folk in the parish knew of him, but not exactly where he was. I was led a merry dance trying to find him but eventually tracked him down. What a stroke of luck – I found him as he was on his way to the docks to sign on an Indiaman. Another half-day and he'd have been gone. He's following in the next boat with the surgeon who we came across waiting on the gun jetty.'

'Good man, Casson. I knew I could depend on you. And what of the other men you were looking for?'

'I couldn't find the gunner, Capt'n, though I did try.'

'Not to worry about him. We have a couple of gunner's mates from the *Constantine*. I will get Mr Parry to suggest one of them to be stepped up. And what of the bosun?'

'I found out where he lived but his wife swore she's not seen him in three years and didn't rightly know if he was dead or alive. By chance, I came across another man on the docks who had just collected his warrant. He has over twenty years' service as bosun on both merchant and king's ships. I brought him along. Mr Taplin, his name is.'

'Thank you, Casson, you did well. And tomorrow you will take a launch to Ryde and find out what has happened to my furniture. You must agree it is rather barren in here.'

'I can't say as how I'd noticed, Capt'n.'

Oliver smiled. 'It will also give you the opportunity to collect your own dunnage. I'm sure you will be looking forward to being back in ship's rig again.'

'Too right, Capt'n.'

On board, Mr Parry was reviewing the six recently-arrived midshipmen. They were lined up on the quarter-deck and although the angle of *Elusive*'s deck was swaying less than a few degrees from the horizontal, two of the young men appeared to be having difficulty maintaining their balance.

'Stand still, you there!'

The lieutenant ran an experienced eye over all six. As usual, though their dress was identical, the men within the uniforms were all quite different.

The first in line could not be described as plump. He was without doubt fat and his ageing uniform bore witness to his excess appetite. The peace had not been good for his figure. Mr Parry ascertained that his name was Peter Wood – nickname, Pud, and that he had sat for the examination for lieutenant the previous year.

'And passed?'

'Yes, sir,' he said, a flush of red rising over his rounded cheeks.

Simon Parry tutted. With few ships-of-the-line in commission, it seemed odd to him that the Admiralty continued to examine young midshipmen when there were no positions available for them. He moved on.

Next was an untidy-looking fellow. His neck-cloth was askew and a length of his hair had come adrift from its ribbon. By all appearances, he would have been more at home in a stable than on the deck of one of His Majesty's frigates, and when he announced his father ran a string of cabs in Camberwell, the lieutenant was not surprised. His name was Reginald Mollard and he had a sharp look about him. Parry made a mental note that this man would need watching.

The third in line was an older fellow. Quite old. Too old, in fact, for a midshipman.

'Your name?'

' 'azzlewood, sir.' The midshipman raised his hat as he answered.

'How long have you been in the service, Hazzlewood?'

'Fifteen years, sir.'

'Do you have problems with geometry?'

'Yes, sir, and algebra too.'

'Can you maintain the log-board?'

'Certainly can, sir.'

'Good.' He moved on. 'And your name?' the lieutenant prompted, to a much younger man whose very stance was quite superior to the rest.

'Biggleswade-Smythe, sir.'

'Ah. The Right Honourable Algernon Biggleswade-Smythe?'

'That is correct, sir.'

'Let me welcome you aboard *Elusive*, young man.'

The midshipman smiled. 'Thank you, sir. I'm very pleased to be here. My father said—'

'On this ship whatever your father said will be of little account. From now on you will be addressed as Mr Smith. I presume from the state of your uniform that you have just entered the service.'

'Yes, sir.'

'And no doubt you will tell me that you excel in geometry and algebra.'

'Yes, sir. And trigonometry also, sir,' he replied confidently.

Mr Parry moved along.

'And you, sir?'

'Tully, sir. Ben Tully, sir. Twelve years in the service – three before the mast, two years as bosun's mate and seven as master's mate.'

'Hm. And what inspired you to re-enter the service as a midshipman?'

'I came by some money, sir, when an old uncle died, so here I am as a middie. I intend to make sailing master one day, if I can.'

'Interesting.'

'And you?'

The last man in line had his head bowed.

'Look at me when I am speaking to you!'

'Sorry, sir.' Lifting his head, the young man revealed a disturbing twitch which affected the left side of his cheek. Unfortunately the muscle spasm gave the impression that he was winking at the lieutenant. Simon watched for a moment. The effect seemed to amuse Mr Mollard. Again he made a mental note.

'And what brought you to *Elusive*?'

'Spell in the Haslar Hospital, sir. I got a splinter in my leg.'

The lieutenant resisted asking the man what relationship there was between the splinter in his leg and the facial spasm. However, having watched the junior officers come aboard, he was satisfied the young man showed no evidence of a limp so there was no need for further questioning regarding the injury.

'Name?'

'Daniel Green. Passed for lieutenant. Sat at the same time as Mr Wood, sir.'

Green was the last in line.

'So, gentlemen, we have two amongst you who have passed the examination but have not yet moved up in the ranks. It would appear, therefore, that Mr Hazzlewood scores seniority with his fifteen years of service. I might add, fifteen years in His Majesty's Navy as a midshipman is a long time.' He shot a glance at Mollard, who seemed amused by the statement. 'Do not misunderstand what I am saying – that length of time carries a certain order of distinction. It means that the officer has seen action and managed to survive.

'I wonder if you will survive,' he said, looking directly at the Right Honourable gentleman. 'Do not be discouraged, Mr Smith, we can put your expertise in arithmetic to good use. One of your duties from now on will be to assist Mr Hazzlewood with his lessons so that the next time he sits for the examination he will pass. And you, Mr Hazzlewood, are charged with teaching Mr Smith how to heave the log and mark the speed and course on the log-board.

'Mr Tully it is your job to introduce Mr Mollard and Mr Smith to the 360-degree view from the cross-trees. And you'll get a taste of the bosun's cane if you let either of them fall. Mr Wood and Mr Green, I will find something suitable for you two in due course.

'Now, gentlemen, if there are no questions, you will follow me and I will introduce you to the midshipman's berth, which will be your home for at least six months.'

'No second lieutenant come aboard yet?' the captain asked, as he watched the deck activity from the quarter-deck.

'Not so far, sir.'

'A frigate such as this usually carries two or three lieutenants, does it not, Mr Parry?'

Simon nodded.

'Then it would be appropriate to appoint two of the midshipmen to the ranks of acting second and third lieutenant. Tell me something of the young officers the Admiralty has blessed us with.'

'Six midshipmen, Captain. There are two who have passed for lieutenant, two men who know the ropes and have experience but may never make it past the examining board, and two others who have never sailed before – one is a young gentleman and the other a character who I feel may need to take lessons in acceptable behaviour.'

'We are indeed blessed! So the likely choice for positions would go to the first two.'

Simon shook his head. 'They would expect the promotion to go their way but I am not entirely sure they have the correct qualities of leadership. I would prefer to establish the calibre of these men first before making a recommendation.'

'I leave that matter in your hands, Mr Parry, but I suggest you do not delay too long. You will advise me as soon as you have come to a decision.'

Simon acknowledged the captain's caution and excused himself, wandering forward to where a group of men were tidying the lines on the larboard side.

Oliver pondered over the man the Admiralty had appointed as his first and, so far, only lieutenant. Perhaps because Parry had entered the ranks under some form of patronage, he was sympathetic with the inadequacies of fellows of a similar background. He hoped that this would not lead to any special treatment or privileges.

But the captain's view on the matter was firmly fixed. No amount of private tutoring in Latin, algorithms or philosophy could prepare a young gentleman for a life at sea. In his opinion, the best midshipmen came from lads who had grown up on the sea from a very early age; boys who had served with their fathers, as he had done, on a merchant ship, attending classes in navigation each winter when the ship was out of the water. In his estimation, lads from this type of upbringing were worthy of donning the garb of midshipman plus they were familiar with discipline and with being disciplined.

He had to admit that over time most of the pink-faced, velvet-palmed young gentlemen made useful middies and later lieutenants and eventually commanders. Many went on to become post captains, some even admirals, though he believed in many cases their rapid ascendance through the ranks was accelerated by patronage rather than any physical demonstrations of leadership, seamanship or valour.

But, indeed, if those gentlemen rose up the promotional ladder by way of ability, then the additional background of breeding usually stood them in good stead. He had noted from his own experience that a well-educated officer, who was also a gentleman, was often less ruthless and cruel than a man who had been deprived or beaten as a child. Added to that, the ratings responded better to the lash of an eloquent tongue then the scratchings of the cat at the gratings. Oliver knew that not all men would subscribe to his views, and his findings did not always apply, but it was a general rule which he believed in.

It was eight bells of the forenoon watch and the young midshipmen were at lessons with their sextants. On deck the marine struck *Elusive*'s series of chimes and Oliver listened and waited. In an instant, as if called to attention by some unseen baton, all the king's ships on the harbour began their ritual call. Like church bells within stone spires, the brass bells tolled from the wooden deck-belfries, calling the seamen to their regular duties. *Ding ding. Ding ding. Ding ding. Ding ding.* Eight bells. As one ship's bell finished, another echoed the chimes, then another joined in, and another.

Quintrell listened to the naval madrigal which was played in full every four hours around every fleet in every port and roadstead in England and abroad. What a wonderfully reassuring chorus it was!

If ever a senior officer had to watch every man-jack of his crew, it was on a newly commissioned ship as she prepared to sail out of Portsmouth harbour. Both Captain Quintrell and Mr Parry knew that as every ship proceeded to sea there were fisher-folk on the jetties watching; wives and sweethearts, merchants and beggars too. But they were of no consequence. It was the unseen eyes, peering from the windows of the Royal Dockyard offices, that they had to be wary of.

As most of *Elusive*'s crew had sailed together on the *Constantine*, Mr Parry divided them equally; half to starboard and half to larboard watch. The remaining men were split indiscriminately. Over the next few days there would be ample opportunity for them to prove their worth and for him to recognize the malingerers.

With the primary urgency having been one of victualling, there had been little time to test the crew's skills in ship handling. *Elusive* was a different class of ship to the one wrecked off the Scillies, but the lieutenant was confident the divisions of topmen from the *Constantine* would have no problems.

Oliver Quintrell was relieved there were no lubbers on board; men who didn't know a halyard from a brace. His junior officers, however, were a different matter. He didn't know how the midshipmen would perform. These men were his responsibility whereas the working crew of the vessel was the responsibility of the first lieutenant – yet Simon Parry was equally unknown to him as far as seamanship was concerned. Sailing out to Spithead would be a test of his lieutenant's ability. He hoped he would be equal to the task.

The high of the tide had passed and the strange second high, which was often experienced in Portsmouth harbour, had followed shortly after. Oliver had learned of it early in his career; an unusual phenomenon caused by the tide in the English Channel flowing around the Solent from both the east and west of the Isle of Wight. But now the ebb had begun and they were waiting for the first-rate to weigh anchor before them.

From *Elusive*'s deck, Oliver listened as orders were issued for the ship to be made ready to sail. On deck, scores of idlers clustered around the pin-rails while dozens of men scampered up the ratlines and spilled along the yards.

Studying the sailors' movements, he followed their feet as they glided blindly along the foot-ropes, watched their nimble fingers unfastening the gaskets. He watched, as without a word being spoken, without a glance at the man next to him, and with the ease of an albatross laying effortlessly on the wind, the topmen rested their chests on the yardarms and worked in total unison. The captain admired their grace. The *Constantines* were a pleasure to observe.

It would be soon enough, once they were clear of land, to send unproven men aloft, but Quintrell had made it clear he would tolerate no accidents at this stage; certainly not before they were well clear of Portsmouth harbour.

With a light breeze blowing from the west-north-west, all that remained was to wait for the man-of-war to weigh. She was moored only a cable length away.

'Silence!' Mr Parry called. 'Wait for the order.'

After a quick word with one of the sailors, he strolled purposefully back to join the captain and Mr Mundy. Also on the poop deck were three of the midshipmen who Mr Parry had decided it judicious to keep out of harm's way.

'Ready to weigh anchor, Captain,' he said.

Quintrell again studied the activity onboard the first-rate ship-of-the-line, watched the sailors from the 800 crew move about the web of rigging like bees over a honeycomb. There were few sounds save the rattle of canvas, squeaking of lines through blocks and the patter of feet on the decking. Every man knew his duty and performed it without question.

How different, he thought, to the French ships he had come alongside – the shouts, the banter, the arguments. Such a cacophony of noise the foreigners made, he wondered how an order was ever heard.

The calls on the man-of-war rang out loud and clear. More canvas was loosed. The capstan was turned and slowly the anchor, dripping with mud, was wound from the harbour bed. For a moment, as if considering its direction, the great ship started to drift back then almost as quickly, with the helm hard over, the staysails luffed and filled, bringing the head of the hundred-gun warship around.

With her topsails taut and her forecourse loosed, the first-rate was underway, assisted by the fast out-flowing tidal current. Prompted by the movement of the man-of-war, the barges, wherries, yachts and bum boats scattered in all directions. They knew better than to get beneath her bow as she commenced her slow passage out of the harbour.

'Take her out, Mr Parry!'

'Aye aye, Captain,' he said, touching his hat and stepping forward. 'Weigh anchor! Loose topsails! Ready on tacks and sheets! Man the braces!'

The messages were quickly relayed along the ship and the task of getting the frigate underway began.

As the capstan creaked and the falling squares flapped like the wings of a flock of angry geese, *Elusive*'s anchor was sucked from the silt of the harbour bottom. The iron pick broke the surface. The rudder responded. The staysails filled and firmed and the frigate's head came around. Creaking and groaning, *Elusive* slowly made way, and as more sail rattled down and was sheeted home she took her position behind the first-rate. With the wind in her sails, the hundred-gun ship swam ahead, making four of five knots. On deck, Captain Quintrell inhaled deeply, showing no signs of the satisfaction he was currently feeling.

'Give her space to breathe,' Oliver said, gazing admiringly at the magnificent man-of-war sailing out ahead of them.

Elusive followed in her wake while several smaller ships formed a procession behind, all waiting their turn to sail through Portsmouth's narrow entrance and out onto the Spithead roadstead. Like a swan leading a clutch of cygnets, the majestic triple-decker moved gracefully down the harbour. As she sailed past two ageing French corvettes anchored in the shallows, the disrobed foreign prizes rocked on the rippling wake, dipping their yards respectfully to the might of the Royal Navy as it glided by.

CHAPTER 5

Buckler's Hard

It was five weeks since the summer solstice and the days still broke early at Buckler's Hard on the banks of the Beaulieu River.

Being an early riser meant Will Ethridge had half an hour to himself before work began at the shipyard. It was a habit he had acquired from his father and grandfather, and Will followed their example in more ways than one.

Walking briskly through the small village, with its row of tall, redbrick terrace houses on either side, he headed down the inclined track. Ahead on the Hard's slipways were the hulls of two new ships, their massive bulk hiding the rising sun and casting long shadows across the riverbank.

The *Starling* had been almost completed to the level of work required by the yard. Very soon she would be slipped into the river, floated down to the Solent and from there towed to Portsmouth for fitting out. In the dockyards of the Royal Navy the masts would be stepped, ballast layered in the hull, standing rigging fitted and the iron cannons and carronades mounted onto the gun deck. Only then would she assume the guise of a naval vessel.

Rising tall beside *Starling* was the undignified skeleton of *Euryalus*. With her inside as clean as a scrubbed half-barrel, the wooden shell lacked any indication that in the coming year she would be commissioned as a thirty-six-gun fighting ship.

In his lifetime Will had seen several famous ships launched on the Beaulieu River. From the very first time he had been allowed to visit the yard with his grandfather, he remembered every ship which had been constructed there. He even recalled some of the ancient oaks

43

which had been carted in from the New Forest to build them.

How could he forget the day the *Sheerness* was put in the water? He remembered how wildly she had swayed on the slipway, how every man in the yard had held his breath for fear the hull would topple, turning twelve months' work into splinters. How the sounds had stuck in his head – the unnerving squeal of timber on timber as she slid slowly into the water, stern first. The thunder of chains. The splash. The rippling waves which radiated right across the river. The cries of relief and the resounding cheers as the small boats warped her around and moored her to the jetty. Despite having neither masts nor rigging, she already had the makings of a fine ship.

As a small boy, he had watched his uncle at work painstakingly carving the ship's ornate figurehead. In awe, he had asked permission to climb up and touch the dove cupped in the woman's outstretched hand. The carved wooden bird had looked so lifelike, he had enquired if it was real.

Though he had never seen a cannon or carronade at close quarters, Will had seen *Illustrious* at its launching on Portsmouth harbour. That occasion was the fondest in his memory and he often recounted the day when the master shipwright took the estate's carpenters and wrights, together with their families, to witness the official launching of His Majesty's latest warship.

What an event that was! The long journey on the back of the timber cart. The harbour at Portsmouth filled with ships of every size and description. The pomp and ceremony and music. He had never seen so many people, heard so much noise or seen such a kaleidoscope of colour – the signal flags and pennants flying from every ship; the marines' scarlet uniforms and the gold lace glimmering from the naval officers' blue uniforms. There was such an assortment of hats and powdered wigs, frills and flowing gowns. Everyone was dressed for the occasion – including the ship itself. A few months in the Royal Dockyard had transformed His Majesty's ship *Illustrious* from the plain wooden hull which had floated from the Beaulieu River to a magnificent fighting vessel – a seventy-four-gun ship-of-the-line. She was fully rigged and ready for battle. What a sight to behold!

Though his favourite would always be *Illustrious*, Will often considered some of the other ships his family had had a hand in building. Names like *Agamemnon*, *Gladiator*, *Hannibal* and *Indefatigable* came to mind – ships which had been built around the time he was born. And though he had never seen them, like everyone else in the village, he was always eager to hear news of their exploits during the long years of war with France. The shipwrights of Buckler's Hard held a special place in their hearts for the hulls they had shaped, and if any one of them was lost at sea it was grieved as deeply as a son or brother who failed to return home from battle.

Will was proud in the knowledge that his father, grandfather and great-grandfather had helped build some of the best ships in the British fleet, for though the Royal Navy built fine ships, it was widely accepted that those launched from the slipways of private yards were equally as good, if not better.

His grandfather, Tobias, said it was because old Lord Montagu, the First Earl of Beaulieu, was such a good man and because the shipwrights' skill had been passed down from generation to generation. He said the men took pride in their craft and were equally proud to be part of the Montagu Estate. In the Royal Dockyards things were different. Shipwrights and carpenters came and went, and in times of war some left their benches to sign as carpenters on fighting ships. But sadly, the old man said, many good men never returned from the sea.

Having grown up on the Beaulieu River, Will's only wish was to be as skilled as his grandfather, the man who had raised him after his father died. Tobias Ethridge had lived and breathed timber all his life and swore he would not stop working until the day he died. Now, his back was bent like a sapling in a strong wind, he had lost the strength in his arms, and his elbows were worn out from the constant blows of the adze. Despite that, everyone on the estate respected and admired him almost as much as they respected Mr Edward Adams, master shipwright at Buckler's Hard.

Now, with little more than a few months of his apprenticeship remaining, Will's ambition to be a shipwright was almost achieved.

As he passed through the shadow of the two great hulls, Will glanced back up the hill. His grandfather had started early, carving a frame from the limb of an oak bough which had been specially selected when it was still growing in the forest. Knowing he had little time for himself, Will ran across the grass to the bank near the old jetty where his handmade boat was sitting. It was a small clinker-built craft made from the offcuts of the finest timber; the chips – the discarded lengths which the shipwrights were allowed to help themselves to. Most men converted their chips into furniture: beds, tables, chairs and chests. In Tobias's case, it was small boats. Over the years Will had helped his grandfather build three. This one he had made on his own.

He had completed the caulking the previous Sunday and today he wanted to slide his boat into the water. Once the planks swelled he would find out how satisfactorily he had sealed it.

With the tide almost full, it was only a matter of pushing his craft a few yards down the grassy slope to launch it into the river. It was not difficult. The ground was soft. Will was strong and once its nose poked into the shallow water it floated from the bank just like the hull of a great fighting ship.

Guiding it round in a full circle, he edged its bow onto the muddy bank and settled it gently. Already drops of water had oozed between the lower planks and trickled to the bottom, but that was to be expected and Will felt satisfied.

'William! William! Come quick!'

He looked up. The cry was urgent. Something was badly amiss.

'What is it?' he yelled.

'It's Tobias! He's hurt bad.'

Dropping the rope on the riverbank, Will ran from the water's edge, up from the old jetty, beneath the shadows cast by the hulls and across the yard to the piles of seasoned logs – the area where selected timbers were shaped into members for the new ships. It was here his grandfather usually worked. Tobias's skill with the adze was envied by all the apprentices at Buckler's Hard and this was where Will had seen him working only ten minutes earlier. It was where a group of the men were now gathered.

Between their legs was the crumpled figure of a man, his back propped against a section of tree trunk. Will knew it was his grandfather.

The yard was silent. It was still early. The familiar daily sounds had not yet begun – the saws were silent in the pits, the squeal of ropes through tackle blocks and the sound of hammers and the calls of the wrights had not yet commenced. But had it happened later in the day, it was still likely the yard would have been silenced by an accident such as this.

'Grandfather!' Will yelled.

'Go get your ma, Will,' the blacksmith said softly. 'Tell her to bring some cloths.'

'Is he all right?'

One glance at the old man and the adze lying on the ground beside him told him he had cause for alarm. The greyish pallor of the old man's skin and the pool of dark blood confirmed the fact.

'Do as you're bid, lad. Go get your ma.'

It was an uphill dash from the shipyard and as he ran Will shouted for his mother, his cries bringing wives from their kitchens, men from their breakfast tables and children's faces to the upstairs windows. Accidents happened at times, even at Buckler's Hard. Less than six months ago the lashings of the scaffold securing the parapet around the top of the ship's hull had worked loose. Several planks had fallen, taking two men to the ground over thirty feet below. One man had died that day and the other never worked again. That had been a bad day on the Montagu Estate.

Alerted by his cries, Will's mother called from the doorstep. 'What's wrong, son? Is it your grandad?'

'He's cut his leg real bad. You've to get some bandages.'

He waited impatiently for his mother, quickly grabbed the cloths she'd selected and ran ahead of her down the street. By now, the crowd had grown. Everyone was concerned for old Tobias as he was well liked and had had a hand in teaching most of the shipwrights in the yard.

As Mr Adams, the master shipwright, stepped through his garden gate and strode towards the group, most of the men moved off, drifting in the direction of the wood stores or sawpits, the majority heading for the hulls supported on the sturdy stocks on the slipway. The long ladders leaning against them swayed precariously as the shipwrights climbed silently, balancing lengths of timber on their shoulders.

'Let me see him,' Will's mother cried, to the group still hovering around.

'Move along, men. Time for work,' Mr Adams said. 'He's in good hands.'

'It's nowt but a nick. I don't know why everyone's fussing so.' Tobias smiled at his daughter, though Will noticed a flickering in his grandfather's eye like that of a man with a great tiredness washing over him.

Without lifting the bloodied neck-square which was covering the inside of his calf, Will's mother knew that the cut was deep. A pool of blood the size of a dinner plate had already turned to blackened jelly at her feet.

'Near chopped his bloody leg off,' a voice whispered.

'Away with you!' Will's mother cried, ripping a broad rent in the old man's breeches and peeling off the sodden rags. Blood ran from the wound thick and fast, spilling over the flap of skin and sinew which was hanging from the bone. She lifted it back carefully and covered it with the clean rags, binding them on with a length of linen. By the time she had finished her hands were red and sticky.

'You're not going to die, Grandfather, are you?'

'No, lad, not for a while yet.' But the old man's eyes were drooping. 'Did you drop her in like you said you would?'

'I did that.'

'Did she take much water?'

'Not much,' Will said, 'just a cupful. Floated real well, she did.' Then he remembered he hadn't pushed his boat out of the water, but he was certain it would be fine. The tide had been high and once it started to ebb it would leave his craft sitting high and dry on the bank. For the present it could wait. He could not leave his grandfather.

Though the call went out for a cart, before it arrived Will took the old man in his arms and carried him home. Old Tobias weighed little more than seven stone.

It was not until half an hour later that Will was free to head back to the yard to start work for the day. He knew he was going to be late. He'd had to run with a message for the manor to send for the doctor; had to bring in extra kindling; drag a mattress to the downstairs room for his grandfather to sleep on. He should have started work at six and felt guilty as he ran past Mr Adams' house. By rights he should have gone straight to work but before that he wanted to make sure his boat was secure.

The shipyard now rang with the sound of a dozen woodpeckers trapped in a wooden box. In a few weeks the *Starling* would be launched and that would be the last the men of the yard would see of her. *Euryalus*, however, still needed much work to be done on her. Sitting proud on the slipway, she resembled the carcass of a beached whale, her ribs poking up into the clear morning sky.

At the jetty, a small schooner was docking to offload a consignment of West Indian mahogany and as it was sitting high in the water, Will knew that the tide had come well up, in fact higher than it had been earlier and much higher than he had expected.

Running past the schooner as fast as he could, he could see that the grassy bank was empty. In the shallows where his boat had been, a pair of herons plodded through the water, plucking their stilt-like legs from the silt.

The tips of the birds' wings dipped in the river as they took flight at the cry from the schooner's deck. 'She's out there!' the captain shouted, pointing to the bend in the Beaulieu River where it made its sweeping downstream curve on its journey to the sea.

Will saw his boat. It was in the centre of the channel and was being carried downstream. The tide was strong and the ebb-flow swifter than a man could walk. If he tried to swim out to it he would never catch it. There was no way of retrieving it from where he was.

His conscience pricked him as he glanced up to the shipyard. He thought of his mother and grandfather. The accident had been bad enough but losing the boat would make matters worse. There was no time to stop and tell anyone what he was about to do and he would have to suffer the consequences when he returned. At the moment his aim was to retrieve his possession. He had spent six months constructing it and it was worth a good amount. And if his grandfather was unfit to work again, his mother would need the extra money.

Without further thought, Will set off along the bank. If he cut across the wooded headland he would save time and if he was lucky the current should carry his boat around the sweeping bend and return it to his side. He ran, jumping over fallen branches, sliding in the boggy streams. He'd forgotten how many twists the path took and as the undergrowth thickened he lost sight of the river. He prayed that his boat hadn't beached itself on the opposite bank.

Emerging into the open, he was able to see far downstream. In the distance was the mouth of the Beaulieu where its wide estuary discharged its waters into the Solent. The sand bars which ran across it were submerged to reveal a broad expanse of sea. Upstream from him, his boat was slewing sideways on the current but heading in his direction. Tearing off his shirt and boots, he waded into the river and when it was up to his waist he flung himself headlong into the water.

It was cold and brackish but even near the bank the outflowing tide was carrying him downstream. Kicking as hard as he could, he made for the middle and, keeping his eyes on his boat, paddled towards it. Grabbing the gunnel without tipping the boat over, he carefully hauled himself into it.

Exhausted and out of breath, Will laid on his back in the bottom, feeling relieved and pleased with his efforts. Recovering his breath, he watched the seagulls wheeling overhead and tried to forget about the trouble he would be in when he got back. However, he still had to find some way to return his boat to the yard.

When he sat upright, he was shocked. He didn't recognize the stretch of water he was on. The alder trees had gone. Now the banks were swampy and low and the river's width was the broadest he had ever seen. His boat had been drifting rapidly and it was still moving.

Sloshing about beneath his feet were four inches of water. His grandfather had warned him to expect some seepage until the planks had swelled, but Will was worried because if more water squeezed in, he had nothing but his hands to bail with.

Kneeling uncomfortably, he realized he had neither rudder nor oars; in fact, there was not even a thwart to sit on or use as a paddle. His boat was being washed downstream, and there was nothing he could do to stop it. Shifting to the stern, he leaned over and dipped his open hand in the river in an effort to steer towards the shore. But the boat was in the grip of the tide and with the wind behind it, its course was set. Across the Solent was the coast of the Isle of Wight and that was the direction the boat was heading.

A flush of panic flared though him. He could jump out and swim to the shore but it was a long way and the current was stronger than anything he had felt before. Then he recollected a warning the old fisherman had once given: 'Beware the Solent. It can travel with the speed of a whale and once you are caught on its back, it will carry you out to sea!'

CHAPTER 6

St Helens Road

Sailing out onto the Solent under single-reefed topsails, *Elusive*'s bow soon encountered the bearded waves whipped by the northerly breeze. On the poop deck the youngest midshipmen were gazing at the grey buildings of the naval establishment, their attention drawn to a group of marines on the saluting platform.

'Are you on watch, Mr Green?'

The midshipman's eye twitched involuntarily. 'No, Mr Parry, sir.'

'Then I suggest you remove yourself from the poop deck or keep your eyes to the ship. Or perhaps you'd prefer to spend the next watch sitting in the foretop.'

'No, Mr Parry, sir.'

'Then let me see you behaving like a foremast-jack again and I swear I will have the sail-maker sew you a pair of canvas blinkers which you will wear whenever you are on watch.'

Mr Smith was unable to hold back a snigger.

'Report to me at the beginning of the middle watch, mister. A night in the rigging might wipe the smile off your face!'

The young gentleman bristled under the collar of his white-trimmed jacket. He was unused to such a reprimand.

'Aye aye, sir,' he said reluctantly, glancing around to see how many eyes were on him. But the sailors coiling ropes were not interested in the antics of the new middies.

South of Spithead the untidy convoy of merchant ships, lying in the lee of the Isle of Wight, was clearly visible. There were several more vessels than when the captain had crossed the Solent from home. They had arrived in the last two days having sailed from the Thames and the

Nore. As the combined fleet of merchant and navy ships were not due to sail for three days, it was possible more merchant vessels would join the fleet. Considering the number of ships, Oliver expected the fleet to divide when it reached the tropics, half going west and the others heading east.

The naval squadron designated as a courtesy escort consisted officially of five ships. The largest was the first-rate which had sailed out of the harbour before them. She was the triple-decked hundred-gun man-of-war and was heading to join the two sixty-four-gun third-rates and two frigates already anchored at St Helens Road.

Elusive was sailing with them but under her own orders.

'Take her south into the Channel, Mr Parry; I would like to see how she behaves.' For Oliver it was an opportunity to not only put his ship to the test, but also his officers and crew.

'Aye, aye, Captain.'

Sailing before the wind, *Elusive* pounded south, skirting the anchored fleet, heading into the choppy waters of the Channel – the place he pondered on from his bedroom window. From the poop deck he cast a fleeting glance to a white speck of a house on the headland, the most easterly point of the Isle of Wight. He wondered if his wife would be at the window watching. Unlikely, he thought.

Leaving the lee of the island, the ship encountered the rolling remnants of the Atlantic swell, which surged constantly along the length of the English Channel.

'After such an absence, you do not know how good it is to be at sea,' Oliver said.

'Believe me, sir,' said Mr Parry, 'I do.'

There were many things about his first lieutenant that he did not know but he would find out in the next few days or weeks. 'The ship is yours, Mr Parry. When you are ready, bring her around.'

'Aye aye, Captain. All hands!' he called. 'Prepare to wear ship!'

The lieutenant's voice carried to the fo'c'sle, though with seemingly little exertion from his throat or chest. The order was quickly repeated along the deck to the men in the bow preparing to sheet the staysails across. On the larboard braces a group stood ready, waiting for the order to haul. On the starboard side it only required one pair of hands to ease each of the lines.

From what he had seen of his first officer, the way he carried out his orders, the way he related to the crew and the junior officers, he appeared quite satisfactory. So far, he conceded that the Admiralty had made a good choice. He could have fared a lot worse. During the course of his career, he had suffered some questionable officers, yet he had always endeavoured to hone them into shape.

Over the last twelve months, he had noted from the *Gazette* that some officers who had served with him in the past had risen to greater things – midshipmen to lieutenants, lieutenants to commanders, and a few had even stepped to post captain, the same rank as himself. But some deserving names had been omitted; seamen who died of dysentery or yellow fever or in battle, sailors who departed this world without recognition or even a decent burial. The Lords of the Admiralty had eyes and ears in many unlikely places but unfortunately they could not be everywhere.

Sea battles were not fought merely for the sake of an anecdote to relate over the dinner table or for a few lines recorded in a book which would have little significance to subsequent generations. Sea battles were fought for king and country and most men gave their lives willingly to keep England free from invasion.

'Ready on the helm! Larboard braces – haul away! Staysails – wait for the call!'

Elusive heeled gracefully as the frigate began its three-mile arc in the English Channel, bringing it around in almost a full circle to point its beak back towards Portsmouth Castle.

'When you have completed the turn, come up into the wind and anchor in the roadstead in the lee of the fleet. I suggest we keep our distance, Mr Parry. I don't want to get tangled with any erratic merchantmen should they decide to start playing foolish games.'

On deck, the carpenter and bosun stood by the gunnels. Like the captain, both men wanted to witness the ship wearing, to see the main, topsail and t'gallant yards on the fore and main masts moving in unison as the ship slowly turned. They were eager to hear the sounds of the ship, the squeaks and creaks of the spars and see the free-flowing run of the running rigging. Also on deck, throughout the manoeuvre, was the sail-maker. He'd been studying the sails since the first staysail had been run up in the harbour. Every inch of canvas was new and noisy and with their fresh covering of gum they appeared grey in colour. Soon salt air, sun and rain would wash and bleach them to a more respectable hue. Now, with every sail stretched tight as a drum-skin, the sail-maker was satisfied.

Half an hour later, the order to drop anchor was called. The sails were hauled up and the job of furling them sent a column of sailors scurrying out along the yards.

'Pass word to the gunner to have his division ready. The powder will be coming on board later this afternoon. And make it known there will be a hundred lashes to any man caught smoking above or below deck until every smidgin of gunpowder has been swabbed from the ships' timbers.'

'Aye aye, Captain.'

'Handsomely now, Mr Trickett, I want each and every barrel dusted down before it is hoisted onboard. And get those buckets topped up and the men ready! I'll not have one grain of powder on the deck!'

'Aye aye, Mr Parry.'

'You men don't just stand there. Mops and buckets. You there, ready with the fenders! Get that tackle secured properly. And you two – down into the tender when she's alongside and lend a hand to load those barrels!'

'You heard what Mr Parry said,' the gunner shouted. 'Anyone with so much as a broken pipe in his pocket will wish he had been blown to kingdom come before I've done with him.'

'Mr Mollard and Mr Smith, if you please,' the lieutenant called. 'Get a pump up on deck. Learn how it operates.'

The two midshipmen looked quizzically at each other.

'Don't just gawp, go do it.'

'Aye aye, sir,' Mollard said, pushing the young gentleman ahead of him as they headed down the companionway ladder to the waist, bewildered looks on both their faces.

'Mr Mundy, would you be so kind as to show these two gentlemen where the pump is, and I suggest you let them have a hand in operating it.'

The sailing master grasped the lieutenant's meaning and repressed the desire to smile.

'Just don't damp their spirits too much!'

'Aye aye, sir.'

'And Mr Trickett, let me know when the powder and shot are all on board. I will inspect the magazine and powder room when you have everything stowed.'

The gunner's mate nodded as he knuckled his forehead.

From the cabin window, Oliver Quintrell could see nothing but sky and sea. As *Elusive* had no corner gallery windows, his uninterrupted view was to the south only – to the choppy water of the English Channel. It was as if the fifty merchantmen and the naval vessels, anchored on her larboard side, did not exist. How good it was to be back at sea. Yet as the ship rolled and pitched, Oliver found the motion slightly uncomfortable. How different the sensation to that of a ship running before the wind; something he had not felt for quite some time. But it would not take him long to adjust.

Sitting down on one of the upholstered chairs at his polished dining table, Quintrell nodded to himself. Never had the sea looked so sweet.

'Begging your pardon, Capt'n,' the steward said, poking his head unannounced around the door. 'Can I get you anything?'

'Coffee, Casson. A nice cup of coffee. Thank you. And would you pass word for Mr Sparrow – I would like to speak to him.'

It was fifteen minutes before the carpenter knocked on the door.

'Beg pardon, Capt'n. One of the shelves in the powder room broke and I had to shore it up. Didn't dare put an 'ammer to a nail in there, so I lashed it up. Mark my words, it won't shift now. It's right nice and firm.'

'Tell me, Mr Sparrow, did you serve under Captain Bransfield on the *Constantine*?'

'No, sir, I hear tell the carpenter went down with the ship. I served on *Illustrious* till she was lost in '94, then seven years on the Calcutta station. If you'll pardon me for saying, sir, I was hoping to get a higher rate with this warrant, but that didn't happen and the letter from the Navy Board said I was to join *Elusive*. So here I am.'

'We may all wish for a higher rate, Mr Sparrow, but in times like these we must be satisfied that at least we are afloat.'

'Don't get me wrong, Capt'n, I'm not disappointed. It'll be an honour to serve with you.'

'Well, if you perform you duties well, I will add my recommendation for you to get a better rate with your next warrant.'

'Thank you, Capt'n. I'd much appreciate a good word when the time comes.'

'Early days yet, and it will be many months before we are back in Portsmouth. Tell me, are you a married man, Mr Sparrow?'

'Yes, sir. Three little ones. Two girls and a lad. But they're grown up now. Brought up by their aunt, they were, as my missus died years ago.'

'I'm sorry to hear that.'

'No need be, Capt'n, they're big enough to fend for themselves now.'
The captain smiled politely.

'Regarding the water level in the well – keep me informed should there be any significant increase at any time of the day or night. Do you understand?'

'Aye, Capt'n.'

'And what of the men assigned to you? Are they satisfactory?'
The carpenter's head wavered.

'Speak freely, man. I'm not a mind reader.'

'I have my reservations about the mates, and the man who claims he's a carpenter has yet to prove it. But it's early days yet.'

'Indeed it is, Mr Sparrow, for all of us.'

The carpenter nodded, screwing his hat around in his hand. 'If that's all, Capt'n, I'd best get back, just in case they have any more problems below. I'd not like to see anyone swinging an 'ammer in the magazine.'

Oliver Quintrell raised his eyebrows as the middle-aged man lifted his leathery knuckles to his forehead and closed the cabin door gently as he went out.

'Boat, heading this way.'

'Where away?' Mr Parry called.

'Three points off the starboard bow.'

An officer, wearing his boat cloak, sat in the stern-sheets. His sea chest, which was resting in the bow, was taking a wetting from the spray. A hail from the boat indicated it was headed for the frigate.

'Hands to sway up the dunnage,' the bosun called. At the same time a rope ladder was rolled down over the side.

'Come aboard, sir?' the midshipman asked, as he stepped onto the deck. He tipped his hat to Mr Parry but ignored the other officers in similar uniforms to his own.

'I had not been advised by the captain that the Admiralty was allocating any further officers to *Elusive*. Your name?'

'Jeremy Nightingale, sir. Midshipman.' He proffered an envelope which had been concealed in the large pocket of the lining of his boat cloak.

Parry looked at the familiar anchor seal pressed into the red sealing wax.

'You realize we are sailing tomorrow?'

'Yes, sir.'

'Wait here, Mr Nightingale.' Mr Parry headed aft.

Standing alone on the quarter-deck, the newest crew member showed nothing of embarrassment and though the deck pitched and rolled his balance was as solid as the stays themselves. While some of the sailors studied him, Mr Tully acknowledged him in a friendly fashion then supervised as the bosun's men lowered a net to the boat to collect the newest officer's dunnage.

'Come in!' Oliver called. 'Ah, Mr Parry.'

'Midshipman just came aboard, sir. A Mr Nightingale. Were we expecting an additional officer?'

'Not that I am aware. Perhaps he had requested a transfer from one of the other navy ships. I presume he presented his papers to you when he came aboard.'

'Yes, sir. I have them here.'

While the captain read through the documents, the first lieutenant cast his eyes around the room. Since his previous visit the cabin had taken on the appearance of a gentleman's habitation. A double line of books graced the shelves of the dark oak bookcase. From the condition of the leather they appeared to have been well read.

Several open charts rested on the elegant dining table, a pair of carved ebony elephants serving as paperweights. Only five of the upholstered chairs remained at the table; the captain was sitting on the other at his writing desk. The locker beneath the stern windows where he had previously sat was decked with velvet cushions. The blue velvet matched the indigo of the chairs. A square of carpet, which still shone with the sheen of Indian silk, graced the centre of the floor.

'These papers appear to be in order so if you are satisfied, Mr Parry, I suggest our new officer is accommodated in the midshipman's berth. In due course I will speak to Mr Nightingale. It will be interesting to discover the level of his seamanship. Advise me, if you will?'

'Aye, Captain.'

'And Simon,'

'Yes, sir.'

'Would you care to join me for dinner this evening?'

'Thank you, sir, it will be my pleasure.'

'Up you go,' Mr Hazzlewood said, almost apologetically. 'Mr Parry's orders.'

Apart from the experienced midshipman, who had been given the duty of overseeing the punishment, there were few sailors on deck to witness the proceedings; most were in the waist playing cribbage or dominoes or just sucking on an empty pipe and gazing at the stars.

'If you find yourself nodding, I suggest you take your neckerchief off and lash your leg to the rigging. Don't want you falling off now, do we, Mr Smith?'

The young gentleman, little more than fourteen years old, looked anxious.

Mr Tully found the punishment amusing. He doubted the Right Honourable gentleman even went to his bedroom alone at night and certainly not without a lamp to light his way. Climbing ratlines, which dissolved into the black night sky, would be something the young gentleman had never dreamed of, not even in his worst nightmares.

'Up, now! Climb!' Mr Hazzlewood ordered, ignoring the pleading glance and the line of wetness shining on the boy's cheek. The wind would soon dry that. Fortunately the young gent's new uniform had dried out after its encounter with the water pump earlier in the day.

'You'll be fine, it's quite safe. You're in luck. There's barely a breeze. Save your prayers till you're sent up there when it's howling a gale.'

With that consolation in mind, Mr Smith started his climb, looking down occasionally and not knowing if he was being threatened or encouraged by the wave of Mr Hazzlewood's hand. Lying so close to the ratlines, his buttons dragged on every single foot-rope as he climbed to the lubbers' hole high above the deck.

'Everything all right, Mr Hazzlewood?'

'Yes, Mr Parry. Thank you, sir. Wasn't expecting to see you on deck.'

'Couldn't sleep,' the lieutenant admitted. 'Noisy blighters, those merchantmen. Kept me awake.' Simon Parry looked across the water. Between *Elusive* and the Isle of Wight more than 200 lanterns twinkled on gently swaying masts. Besides the sounds of drunken mirth and singing, the plaintive chords of an accordion and the scratchings of a fiddle drifted over the waters of St Helens Road.

Running his eyes up the shrouds, the lieutenant was unable to see the young man who had disappeared through the lubbers' hole at the futtocks.

'Is Mr Smith up there?'

'Yes, sir. Just gone aloft.'

'Keep an eye on him, Mr Hazzlewood, but no mollycoddling. I understand his father is a cabinet minister and I wouldn't like to send word to London that we lost his youngest son overboard on his first night at sea.'

'Aye, aye, Mr Parry.'

'Carry on, Mr Hazzlewood.'

'Thank you, sir.

'Mr Hazzlewood! Mr Hazzlewood!'

'Mr Smith, stop that noise. If you want to attract attention on the deck you call "Deck" or "Ahoy below".'

'Ahoy deck, Mr Hazzlewood.'

'For goodness' sake, what is it, Mr Smith? You cannot come down yet. It's not even three bells.'

'I can see a small boat and someone on board is waving. I think he is trying to attract attention.'

'Where away?'

'There!' cried the young gentleman. But the direction his arm was pointing was lost amongst the tangle of shadows and rigging.

'Where?' called the midshipman. 'I need proper directions. Stem? Stern? Starboard? Beam?'

'A bit to starboard of the stem. The boat is coming right at us.'

The midshipman on deck turned to one of the sailors. 'You there, get up top and see what the idiot is talking about. And you – go wake whoever is supposed to be on watch in the bow. If you find a man asleep I'll have his name and report him to the lieutenant.'

In less than a minute a cry came from the mast. 'Deck there. Two points off the starboard bow. Small boat. One man aboard. No sail or oars that I can see. He's hailing and drifting in this direction. He'll hit us broadside on if he holds his course.'

By this time the men of the watch and a few others had gathered on the deck.

'Just as well it's not a fire ship!' one said.

'That's enough of that talk, Smithers,' said Mr Parry, as he approached. 'Mr Hazzlewood, pass word to the captain – small boat approaching!'

'Yes, sir.'

'You men, ready with lines and grapples but do nothing till you get the order.'

The calls on deck drew others from the mess to investigate what was happening.

Oliver Quintrell joined his lieutenant. 'What do we have, Mr Parry?'

'Boat, sir. Seems to be adrift. Floating this way. I have the men ready with lines.'

'How many crew?'

'Just one, sir. He looks rather helpless.'

'If he don't sit down he's liable to tip himself out, the way he's got it swaying,' a voice remarked.

From the deck, the boat, bobbing on the choppy water, was barely visible in the darkness, but the man's bare torso reflected the ghostly pallor of the rising moon.

'Your orders, Captain?'

Oliver scanned the sea around them, checking that there were no other suspicious or unwanted craft nearby. But the only vessels in the vicinity were the merchant ships and all their small boats were stowed. 'If it rubs up against us, fish it out, Mr Parry. Another jolly-boat may come in handy. And when you get the man aboard, enter his name in the ship's log. Our first prize of the cruise, it would seem,' he joked. 'Let me know when you have the boat secured on deck.'

'Aye aye, Captain.'

'Look lively, you men. Ready with the grapples. And try not to sink it.'

'Look what I reeled in!' shouted one of the seamen. 'I caught me a fish.'

'Quiet there, Froyle. You men get the boat hoisted and get that man something to wear.'

Bare feet pattered across the deck. The ship's timbers creaked. It was a mild night and the late summer breeze had dropped to almost nothing. Across the water the fleet of seventy ships lolled lazily from their anchor cables. Moonlight reflected off every cap, plate and metal fitting and the waters of St Helens Road twinkled beneath a thousand dancing lights.

As Will Ethridge climbed aboard, a blanket was flung around his shoulders. He shook uncontrollably – not only from the chill of his journey, but from his growing fear and apprehension. It was not the ship or his predicament which concerned him but the anguish he knew his mother would be suffering. With little hope of an immediate return home, he was angry with himself for getting into such a situation. Moments later, his small wooden craft was hoisted on board and flipped over. Will watched in silence as the saltwater which had seeped into its hull washed across the deck and was returned to the sea through the scuppers.

'Handy little boat,' the bosun said.

'Who'd ya pinch it off?' Smithers asked.

'Fancied yourself as a tar, did you?'

'A pair of oars might have come in handy!' Froyle added.

'He don't need oars. He's got long arms.'

The men's joshing stopped when Mr Hazzlewood walked over. 'Shut your traps, all of you. What's your name, lad?'

'Will, sir. William Ethridge.'

'And where have you come from, Willie lad?'

'Buckler's Hard.'

'And where's that when it's out?'

'Beaulieu River, sir, and I've got to get back there and take the boat back.'

'Pinched it, did you? Felon, is you? Do you know what they do with thieves on a ship, lad? They hang 'em from the yardarm by their fingers, then they cut 'em off one by one, and when the last one goes – splash!'

'One more word from you, Smithers, and you'll be taking your turn at the gratings! Don't take no notice of him, lad.'

Will's face was white in the moon's glow.

'Don't worry, lad, we'll get you fixed up with some clothes and a hammock and show you where you can sleep.'

'But I've got to get back to Buckler's Hard.'

'Buckler's Hard,' whispered Smithers to one of the other men. 'Only thing that's hard on here is hard tack, he'll get more of that than he bargained for in the next few months.'

The midshipman did not hear the comment.

'My mother will be worried stiff,' Will said. 'When will I be allowed to go home?'

Smithers smirked at his mate. 'I reckon if he's lucky in five or six years' time. Depending on what the Frogs decide to do. It could be longer. You could try swimming home if you wanted but the penalty for running is they hang you.'

'I said shut your mouth, Smithers. Don't you take no notice of what he says, Willie lad. Here, take a sup of this.' Mr Hazzlewood handed him a steaming pot that had been sent up from the galley.

Will poured the contents down his throat without hardly swallowing or tasting it. The events which had taken place that morning at the shipyard seemed like days ago. 'Thank you,' he said, gazing up to the rigging above his head.

'I bet you have never stood on a ship like this before, lad.'

'I have that. I've stood on the weather, deck of a man-of-war.'

Everyone went quiet and the smile disappeared from Mr Hazzlewood's face. 'Well, you're certainly no sailor and I don't take kindly to liars.'

'I'm not lying, sir. I come from Buckler's Hard. That's where they build ships like this and some even bigger. I've seen them grow from the keel up. I've worked on them. Helped build them. I've put the planks on them. Seen the figureheads carved. I've hammered thousands of trunnels in decks far bigger than this. But I ain't never been aboard a fully rigged ship before.'

'Well, now you are here, you'll find there's no way of going back. How old are you, Will, lad?'

'Near twenty-one, sir.'

'And what do you do when you're not trying to navigate a boat?'

'I'm apprenticed to Mr Edward Adams, master shipwright at Buckler's Hard.'

'You're a chippie's lad, then.' Mr Hazzlewood turned to the group of seamen. 'You, Froyle, be useful, go tell Mr Sparrow to come up on deck. Tell him we've got a new chippie aboard.'

'Enter.'

After removing his hat, the midshipman attempted to straighten his hair. As he entered the captain's cabin his eyes darted covetously around the room though his head did not move an inch.

'What is it, Mr Mollard?'

'Mr Parry sends his respects, Captain, and said to tell you that the small boat is secured.'

'Good. And the man also, I presume.'

'Aye, Capt'n, but he ain't really a man. Not much more than a lad, though he's long-legged and gangly, a bit like a young horse.'

'Does this colt have a name? And tell me, what delivered him to us in that rudderless coracle?'

'The men have dubbed him "Fish", because they caught him on the grapple. Like a fish on a hook – if you gets my meaning, Capt'n.'

'Yes, Mr Mollard, you do not need to explain further.'

'Anyway, he says his name's Will – William Ethridge – and he says he comes from Buckler's Hard. Says the boat belongs to him and says he built it.'

'Indeed.'

'I told him straight off what the penalties was for stealing one of His Majesty's ships but he swore he didn't steal it. A taste of the bosun's cane would squeeze the truth out of him, I reckon.'

'Like dunking a witch in a duck pond to rid a village of a plague of grasshoppers?'

The midshipman from the streets of London scratched his head. 'Beg pardon, sir?'

'Could it be perhaps that this "Fish" is speaking the truth?'

The midshipman shrugged his shoulders in response.

'Thank you, Mr Mollard, that will be all.'

'Tell me about the midshipmen,' Oliver asked, as he refilled his lieutenant's glass from the Waterford decanter. 'Has any one of them got the makings of a second lieutenant?'

'Early days, sir, but I am being mindful.'

'And the prize taken last night?' he said, with a glint in his eye.

'If only they were all so easy to win!' Simon Parry said, savouring the aroma of the brandy before taking a sip. 'A fine wine,' he added.

'Yes, that is one thing the French do well. But what of the youth on board?'

'He's a man, sir. Full twenty years of age but he lacks the gall of a common sailor so he seems younger.'

'And the seaworthiness of the boat?'

'He claims he built it himself but I'm not entirely convinced of that. It certainly looks and smells new from the state of the timber. It's lacking a rudder and rowlocks and is in need of paint or varnish, but otherwise it's a serviceable craft. I've spoken with Mr Sparrow and he said he will attend to it.'

Oliver leaned back in his chair, enjoying the wine. 'I suggest you ask the carpenter to speak with him. I'd like to know if there is any truth in his story.'

CHAPTER 7

Mr Sparrow

The shrill of the whistles greeted Captain Quintrell on his return from the admiral's ship. Stepping on deck, he raised his hat to the quarter-deck.

'Welcome back, Captain.'

'Humph. I will speak to you in my cabin, Mr Parry.'

The lieutenant turned to Mr Nightingale. 'This is your watch, is it not?'

'Yes, sir.'

'Make sure the captain's boat is swayed up and properly secured.' After advising the sailing master that he was leaving the deck, Mr Parry made his way to the captain's cabin.

'Sit down, Simon,' Oliver said.

'I trust you enjoyed a good dinner, sir.'

Oliver huffed. 'Stuffed quail. A little dry but otherwise an excellent meal. However, the subsequent converse—'

The lieutenant waited while Oliver composed his thoughts.

'Damn the man. Until I boarded his ship, I was content. Content with my commission, content with the composition of my crew. My only concerns were that the vessel was seaworthy and that we would proceed from harbour without incident, which we did. I had my current orders and a pouch of sealed instructions, and all was well with the world.'

'And now, if I might venture to enquire?'

'A direct conflict of orders, damn it.'

The door opened and Casson appeared, balancing two bone-china cups on a silver tray.

'Can I get you anything else, Capt'n?' the steward enquired as he placed the tray on the table.

'Thank you, Casson. That is quite sufficient.'

Oliver sniffed the rich aroma and relaxed back into his chair.

'I shall explain my frustrations as best I can. Firstly, like you and every man aboard, I do not know our final destination, or the purpose of this cruise. My orders are cloaked in secrecy and also some degree of urgency. We are to sail at the same time as Admiral Ingram's squadron and the fleet of merchantmen and make for Madeira with minimal delay. From there we all head south to the fifteenth parallel.'

'With a large fleet, delays could be inevitable. I have known it take a convoy over twenty days to clear the Channel, partly because of bad weather and partly due to the state of the merchant vessels. I believe they were eventually ordered back into port until the weather cleared.'

'That cannot be allowed to happen! Our voyage is of the utmost importance to the Admiralty and, it is suggested, to the future of the country – though I fail to fathom how. Let me explain my concerns. In my conversation with the commodore over dinner this evening, I discovered that he assumes *Elusive* is part of the naval escort and therefore directly under his command.' He paused. 'Yet his orders contravene my written orders from the Admiralty.'

'I'm not sure I understand, sir.'

'My orders are to make for Madeira without delay and from there to the tropics. We are to sail with the merchant fleet but not as an escort ship. They state categorically that we are to avoid confrontation and not enter into any engagement with enemy forces. The commodore, however, who I had assumed would know something of our mission, insists *Elusive* must act under his direct orders and he was not prepared to listen to my argument.'

'That could prove a dilemma should any action present itself.'

'Indeed. Should I avoid conflict, I will be deemed a coward by both my men and the commodore and could likely face a court-martial for disobeying orders. Contrarily, if I follow instructions from Admiral Ingram and engage with an enemy, whosoever that may be, I will be disobeying the orders of the Admiralty. Whatever way I chose, my fate is sealed. Do you have any comment, Simon? Speak freely.'

The lieutenant was hesitant. 'A convoy carrying valuable cargo is always a temptation to privateers, not to mention pirates, false lights and similar malevolencies. I hear the Barbary pirates have become increasingly bold of late, attacking ships in the Bay of Biscay and as far west as Madeira and the Canary Islands. Hence the reason the rich merchants have requested a naval escort. But a secret mission dedicated to a single ship – a frigate to boot – that is unusual, to say the least.'

'I also speculated about that,' Quintrell mused, looking down at his hand missing three of its fingers. 'All I know is that we are attached to this convoy like some useless sixth digit and if we suffer any damage which delays us, all will be lost.'

'Perhaps we should consider the advantages of our present situation.'

'Indeed. We are only thirty-eight guns and alone we may be vulnerable. However, I think no right-minded pirate or privateer would consider engaging such a large fleet especially with the combined cannon fire of a hundred-gun man-of-war and two sixty-fours plus two other frigates besides ourself. In that regard, clearing the Channel should not be a problem.'

'But the convoy can only travel at the speed of the slowest vessel,' Simon added.

'Then we must pray for sound ships and fair winds which will deliver us with all haste to Madeira and thence clear of the Canary Islands to the tropics where we will bid this wretched fleet farewell.' He drank his coffee, leaving only the dark dregs in the bottom of his cup.

'Thank you, Simon; I believe I will sleep well. The fleet sails tomorrow at nine o'clock. We will replenish our water in Funchal.' He smiled. 'There is some excellent venison on that island and fruit of every variety but I trust our stay is no more than three days. However, that decision will rest with the commodore.'

'Ample time, I would think, sir.'

'When we are there, I intend to go ashore for a few hours.'

'Aye aye, sir.'

'But on the morrow we will discover if *Elusive* is equal to our expectations.'

Eight bells summonsed the ship's company to breakfast. By nine o'clock scores of sails were unfurled and shaken out by the topmastmen who decorated the yardarms like wooden pegs and Spithead assumed the appearance of a giant's washday. All that was lacking was the wind to blow the squares of canvas, but little moved in the vapour-heavy morning air save the idlers on the ships' decks busily performing their regular morning rituals.

Noon came and the fleet of merchant ships were still swaying idly from their anchor cables. Only the lightest breeze could be felt in St Helens Road. Occasionally it lifted a vessel's flaccid sails and teased them for a while before dropping them against the silent masts. Then suddenly the wind freshened, blowing crisp salt air across the Channel towards the flowered fields of Normandy.

The noisy clapping of a thousand sails and the creaking of moving timber woke the listless crews. An hour later a dull thud and a puff of smoke rose from the signal gun on the deck of the flagship announcing to the convoy that it was time to weigh anchor.

'Don't trust those merchantmen, Mr Parry. If I am not wrong, they will be as unpredictable as rabbits on a common. I suggest you give them a wide berth.'

'Aye, aye, sir.'

'Take her to sea, Mr Parry.'

'Anchor aweigh! Let fly the topsails!'

Like ribbons unwinding from around a maypole, the fleet of closely packed vessels slowly began drifting apart. After falling back, the breeze tantalized the sails before catching the rattling canvas and punching it out. Like ripples flowing out from a stone dropped on a pond, the distance between the vessels slowly widened.

'Set the courses!'

At the pin-rails scores of sailors hung bodily from lines, hauling them home before securing them around the smooth belaying pins.

On the quarter-deck, Mr Mundy, the sailing master, studied the event through the lens of his telescope. But a glass was not necessary to notice that three of the merchant ships had already come to grief. Turning recklessly in front of a brig, a schooner had climbed onto its deck. A bark had joined the ménage-à-trois and no amount of cries and abuse was about to dislodge them.

Quintrell shook his head.

'Keep us well to the south, Mr Parry. Out of harm's way.'

'Aye aye, Captain. South by west, helmsman. And Mr Nightingale, report any signals from the flagship, immediately. Or from any other ship for that matter.'

'Yes, sir.'

'Mr Tully, I want you to go aloft. I want to be advised of anything afloat in the channel that is not part of this convoy.' The midshipman who had served before the mast was happy to scurry up the ratlines.

With the commodore's hundred-gunner in the van, followed closely in her wake by one of the sixty-fours, the merchant ships fanned out behind them like a flock of uncoordinated ducklings. And while the fighting ships sailed smoothly, throwing up little spume, the smaller craft bounced and pounded into the increasing swell. *Elusive*'s bow hit each successive rolling wave with a resounding thwack and a stream of spray shot across the fo'c'sle. But the mist was fine and was blown off the larboard bow before it had chance to reach the foremast. With seventy hulls raking the waves, the sea's surface turned into a bubbling cauldron of saltwater.

Two hours later the tail of the convoy stretched back as far as the eye could see, and the signal from the flagship to close up had little effect on consolidating the group.

'Deck, there! Ship off the larboard beam.'

'How does she bear?'

'Can't rightly tell, sir. Can only see her t'gallants. But from the angle of her sail, I'd say she's on the same course as us. Probably running along the coast of Brittany.'

'Can you see her colours, Mr Tully?'

'No, sir. She's not flying any.'

'Thank you, Mr Tully. Keep a close eye on her. I want to know if she changes course. And Mr Nightingale, signal the flagship of her presence.'

'Aye aye, sir.'

'Come in – you don't have to knock.' Mr Sparrow stroked the plane along the length of timber, smoothed his hand over its surface and angled the piece of cedar towards the light to examine its shape. Then he glanced up at the tall, slim silhouette in the darkened doorway.

It was always gloomy on the orlop deck but the carpenter's workshop was lit by a couple of lanterns, one hanging over each end of the workbench. The lamps swayed rhythmically, casting shadows on the ruffled sea of curled shavings scattered across the bench. The carpenter's shop was of substantial size. Bigger than the bosun's lockers and larger than the cooper's domain. Even bigger than the galley.

'Come in. I'll not bite you,' the carpenter called. 'You're not on watch right now, are you?'

'No, why's that?'

'You'd be in trouble if you were caught below decks when your watch is on. You should know that by now.'

Will nodded. Hearing the Yorkshire accent reminded him of an old fisherman who used to sail up the Beaulieu River and moor his boat at the jetty at Buckler's Hard. He arrived every Saturday afternoon regular as clockwork to sell his catch to the villagers. He usually did a good trade and Will's mother was one of his customers. What stuck in his mind were the yarns the fisherman used to spin. He hailed from Whitby originally, a fishing village in the north where the fisher-folk made their living from herring or whales. The old man had been a whaler in his younger days and told tales of days spent following the pods and of harpooning the massive sea creatures. He told how the boats were often dragged for miles until the beast was dead. He talked about seals too; of how the snow was red with blood by the time they had finished a kill.

Being born on the Montagu Estate, Will had never seen much snow, or blood for that matter, but the thought reminded him of the jelly-like pool which had oozed from his grandfather's leg. He shuddered involuntarily.

'I was told you wanted to see me, sir.'

Percy Sparrow wiped a dusty palm across his brow then rubbed his hands down his leather apron. 'That's right. You feeling better than when you was brought on board?'

'Aye, sir.'

'Nay lad, you don't need say "aye" or "sir" to me. A simple "yes" or "no" will do.'

Will nodded.

'That's a tidy little craft you was in. I hear you claim you built it, but there's them on board who think you're stringing a yarn.'

'I'm not, sir. Honest. I made it with my own hands, though I got some help from my grandfather.'

'Ah, so he's a boat builder, is he?'

'Shipwright, sir, like my father was, only he's dead. But I'm going to be a shipwright too,' he said proudly. 'My seven years is up in a few months' time.'

The carpenter huffed. 'You'll be lucky to get out of His Majesty's service if the war with the Frogs starts again. How old are you?'

'Near twenty-one, sir. I was took on when I was fourteen.'

'Twenty-one, eh? You're not pulling my tit, are you?'

'No, sir.'

The carpenter glanced along his bench to the tools hanging on the wall. 'Pass me a two-inch auger and an 'alf-inch maul.'

Will looked around. The augers was easy to locate though there were several in various sizes. The mauls, however, were stored in a box in the corner but it didn't take him long to locate the right one and present the tools to the craftsman.

'Put 'em back,' Mr Sparrow said. 'I believe you. I got a couple of hands sent to me as carpenter's mates. Dead wood they are, both of them. One can't read a twelve-inch rule and no wonder – his eyes are fixed in two different directions. I wager he'll never saw a straight line. The other fellow tells me he's a good man on the end of a saw. Spent most of his time in the bottom of a pit, no doubt. Trouble is, he does nowt but snivel and sneeze when he's in here. He'll drive me batty if I have to listen to him snuffling all day.'

Scooping up a handful of shavings, the carpenter dropped them into a half-barrel almost full of sawdust. 'Maybe they'll rate you as acting carpenter's mate if I ask. I'll put the word to Mr Parry and see if we can't get you allocated to me. More money for you down here – that's if your wages aren't claimed by your master on shore.'

Will looked puzzled.

'That's the rule, lad. If you're indentured when you come aboard, then whatever you earn can be claimed by your master, if he has a mind to. There's nowt no one can do about it, not unless they change the laws.'

'Don't seem right somehow.'

'There's a lot that don't seem right, especially when you're on one of His Majesty's ships. But I'll tell you this, if you work down here with me there'll be no watches cos you'll be what's known as an idler. You'll work daytime from eight in the morning till eight at night and that's all. Unless of course there's a call for all hands, then you go where you're put. Bad weather will probably find you on a pump or swinging on a line. And if we get into a fight you might find yourself in the magazine or helping on a gun or carting bodies to the cockpit.' He looked at the lad. 'Don't worry. You'll soon get used to it. Are you afraid of heights?'

'Don't think so. I've climbed plenty of ladders.'

'I'm talking ratlines and rigging, lad.'

'I don't see what's the difference. The ladders at the shipyard reach above the top of a ship's side. That's around thirty or forty feet high depending on how many decks she's got. If you're standing on the slipway beside a ship-of-the-line even without her rigging, she looks almost as tall as an oak before it's felled. Besides, them ladders aren't always fastened at the top like the ship's rigging is.' He laughed. 'I reckon it'd be no harder climbing the rigging on a ship at sea than climbing up the side of a ship's hull in a strong wind.'

'You ain't seen a sea when it's really rolling.'

'Them yard ladders sway and bend when you go up them especially when you're carrying a stack of timber on your shoulder.'

'Well, if you're keen, you're bound to get your chance afore long, but most landsmen I've known won't even try.'

Will smiled. He liked the carpenter.

'With all these ships being built in your village, didn't you ever want to go to sea?'

'Never thought about it. Never wanted to leave my family. And Buckler's Hard is a good yard.'

'There's word around that since the war ended there'll be scarce demand for line-of-battle ships. They say they'll be breaking the old ones up for timber to build merchant ships. Some folk say many of the dockyards in England will close and the shipwrights and carpenters will be out of a job.'

'There'll always be work on the Beaulieu River. In the old days they made plenty of merchant ships. Been building them there for a hundred years.'

'Well, there's plenty of work here, too.'

'Yes, sir.'

'From now on when you're down here you can call me Chips or Dickie Bird – that's the name I cop from them what knows me. My real name's Percy Sparrow and they say I chirp like a sparrow. It don't rightly bother me what they call me so long as they leave me alone in my workshop.' He blew a cloud of sawdust from the bench. 'But mind – you must give me my full handle when we're on deck cos I've got a warrant. That means I'm an officer of sorts. What did you say your name was?'

'It's Will. William Ethridge and thank you for letting me come down here.'

'Aye, well, you don't need to thank me cos I'm just looking after myself. I'd be a fool to say no to a good hand. It'll make my job a bit easier. As for yourself, don't count your chickens just yet. Bide your time and your tongue and you'll do all right.'

As the carpenter spoke he swung a length of solid timber up onto the bench. His right forearm was as thick as a leg of lamb and the

muscles twitched and flexed like those of a sheep that had just had its
throat cut.

'You don't often get what you ask for on His Majesty's ships. Not
unless it's for the good of the ship. Sometimes you've got to use your
noggin and ask in such a way the officers think it's their idea. Then
they pass it on and if all's well, they get the credit for it. Of course if
problems arise, then Billy Muggins here cops it – you hear what I'm
saying?'

Will nodded.

'But you'll be all right. Mr Parry's a reasonable man, though there's
a few tales about him being bandied round the ship – but best you
don't take much notice of those. Anyway, that's enough of my chit-
chat. Tell me more about that boat of yours.'

'It's the first one I've made on my own. Helped my grandfather
make a few. He made a boat every year out of chips.'

'The offcuts from the yard?'

'Yes. The shipwrights are allowed to take what they want. My
grandfather has enough timber in the garden to build a brig of his
own.' Will laughed. 'He jokes about it but the pile is twice as big as me.'

'So how come you found yourself floating round the Solent?'

'I wanted to swell the timbers but I never tied it up on the bank and
it slipped into the river. When I managed to get to it, I'd no oars, no
rudder and no shirt.'

'And no way of getting back to land?'

'If I hadn't drifted right up to the ship, I'd have been in the middle
of the English Channel by now.'

'And if you'd survived you'd have been washed up on the coast of
France and they might have eaten you for breakfast.'

'If only I'd taken more care.'

'No point crying over spilt milk. Tell me, can you hone a blade?'

'Yes, sir, I can put a razor-sharp edge on any tool. Too sharp
sometimes,' he said, thinking back to the blade on his grandfather's
adze.

'Right then. You go see Bungs, the cooper, and ask for a length of
hoop from an old barrel. He's got plenty of pieces cut down to size.
Grab one and come in here and grind it. Then you make yourself a nice
wooden hilt and bind it with cord and you'll have yourself a handy
knife. You'll need one before long. The stone's over there in the corner.
I don't mind if you come in here to use it – but only when I'm here,
mind.'

From the doorway came the muffled but unmistakable sound of eight bells being struck. Almost instantly, it was followed by the clatter of feet on the deck above.

'Best get up top, quick smart, lad. It don't pay to dilly-dally.'

'I'll tell Mr Parry I've spoken to you.'

The carpenter didn't look up. He was swaying back and forth to the rhythm of the plane as it hissed along the length of timber.

CHAPTER 8

Madeira

Sunrise saw the first of the fleet arriving off the island of Madeira but it would be early in the evening before the last of the convoy dropped anchor.

Even before the flagship and some of the merchant vessels anchored in Funchal Road, local vendors selling fruits and fish were attracted to the vessels like pins to a magnet. Anxious to sell their wares, craft of all shapes and sizes ferried between the ships, dipping beneath the cables and bumping against the hulls. Because of their number, they hindered the lowering of ships' boats and were a constant source of annoyance especially to the navy ships.

Elusive was moored to the south-west of the bay in the lee of a formidable cliff which rose vertically from the water to 200 feet. From the clifftop, the ground rose under a covering of lush green forest to the bare summit. The peak of the worn volcanic was crowned in a halo-like ring of cloud.

From every ship, empty barrels were being lowered into waiting transports and though only a nominal quantity of water had been used during the voyage from Portsmouth, the captains opted to take on fresh water while it was available.

'Mr Parry, have a boat ready, if you please. And arrange for this letter to be delivered to the flagship. I pray the commodore will oblige me and allow us to sail before the rest of the fleet. I have no desire to idle our time away waiting for seventy ships to be watered. In the meantime, I intend to spend a little time in the town. Please send a boat for me at four o'clock in the afternoon.'

'Aye aye, sir. Beg pardon, sir, but the men asked if they were permitted to go ashore.'

To get drunk, thought Oliver. However, an opportunity for the men, particularly those from the *Constantine*, to work off a little pent-up emotion was not a bad idea. Rather they brawl on shore than on deck.

'Providing all the fresh supplies are received and stowed, you may allow those not on harbour watch to have a few hours ashore. I will leave the numbers to your discretion but make sure every man knows when he must return to the ship.'

The streets of Madeira were packed – not with the regular traffic of children, nuns, beggars, local hawkers carting their wares on scrawny donkeys, or carts clattering down the rocky tracks, but with a conflagration of hot-blooded, shabbily dressed, vile-smelling seamen of all nationalities who filled the taverns or obstructed the narrow alleys.

With no carriages available from the shore, Oliver resorted to the local mode of conveyance – a mule. It was a large animal, tall as a horse, bony and with a rough coat dusted with lice. It was the only mode of transport capable of carrying him to the top of the steep hillside.

The route was circuitous. In some places the ravines and valleys cut by the heavy rains dropped almost vertically and the tracks, though well used, were wet and slippery. To a man who preferred to climb to the top of a lively swaying mast than venture up the steep sloping sides of a mountain, they appeared quite hazardous.

After almost an hour's uncomfortable ride he arrived at the house and as he had imagined, she was standing in the courtyard waiting for him. Draped over one shoulder, her long black hair shone like polished jet in the midday sun and was reflected in the colour of her eyes.

'I watched you winding up the hill,' she said, holding out her hands to greet him. 'Welcome.'

Quintrell took her hands and placed a kiss on her fingertips. 'I am relieved you received my letter. I feared it may not arrive before I reached here.'

'I received it two days ago. Oh, Oliver, what joy it brought me. I had thought I would never see you again.'

'Didn't I promise I would come back one day?'

'Come inside, out of the heat.'

Leading him by the hand through the portico, they stopped for a moment to allow a lizard to waddle across the marble paving. It sought shelter beneath the tangled roots of a pendulous creeper. The air was warm and moist, filled with a soft exotic fragrance.

Unbuckling his sword, he laid it quietly on the hall table and followed her inside. The room was cool, the open windows capturing the breezes blown off the sea.

'I watched for the ships all day yesterday but none arrived, then when I woke this morning the harbour was bursting with them. But there were so many and I did not know which you were on, and as the hours passed I feared that you would not come. And now you are here, I must ask when you will sail.'

'Tomorrow, possibly, or the following day.'

'And will you stay here this evening?'

'I cannot.'

'Oh, Oliver.'

The maid appeared with a tray carrying a jug of lemonade and two glasses.

'Thank you, Isabella.'

She waited until the girl had gone. 'You have aged,' she said, running her fingers gently across his temple.

'It has been a long time.'

'And I suppose you have changed over the years.'

'In some ways, perhaps. A little wiser, I hope. Older, certainly, and with the responsibilities which youth did not hinder me with.'

'Do you ever visit Cornwall these days?'

'Only occasionally from the sea. I doubt I have walked little further ashore than the wharfs in Plymouth since we said goodbye.'

'I trust your life is happy.'

'Content enough. Better now that I have a command. Better still that I am here with you.'

She looked at him quizzically.

'Do you want to talk?'

'Not really.'

'Then sit, relax and drink,' she said softly, helping him to remove his coat.

The sofa, upholstered in ivory brocade, was elegant and typically English in style though the other furnishings in the room had a distinct Iberian flavour. He sank back into the chair.

'Thank you,' he said.

'Are you hungry?'

'Hungry for you, Susanna. If only you knew.'

Standing before him, she lifted the remnant of his right hand, stroked it with her fingers and placed it against her lips.

He could see the tears glinting in her eyes and feel a fullness in his own.

'I am hungry also,' she said.

'Permission denied!' he repeated, waving the despatch just delivered by the launch from the flag admiral's ship. 'Permission denied to sail before this combined fleet is ready to depart! Good heavens, that could be days from now! Weeks even, the way these lubbers are conducting their business! It will take a veritable Pied Piper to clear the maritime rats from the streets of Funchal!'

'Then I suppose you've little option but to wait, Capt'n,' Casson said, flicking the invisible crumbs from the tablecloth with a napkin.

Oliver reflected. Of course, the commodore was correct in his decision and he had no right to such an outburst especially in front of his steward. He must bide his time and his temper and wait with the convoy. That was probably the safest course of action. But to be a naval nursemaid required patience and Oliver was running short of his share. After considering the options he consoled himself with the fact that a few days lost in Funchal would matter little to his mission. Beating out of the Channel could have taken a month, but it didn't. And the Lords in their wisdom had no doubt made allowances for those sorts of contingencies when formulating his orders.

So be it. If the frigate had to remain in Madeira for a week or more, then he would make the best of his time. In the morning he would return to the white house on the hill.

'Signal from the flagship, Captain. *Prepare to sail.*'

Quintrell gazed across the merchant fleet. It was a dismal sight. With no breeze to disperse it, smoke from almost one hundred galley chimneys hung at yardarm height around the ships. To the west, unassailable grey cliffs rose from the sea, while around the port, high walls and fortifications protected the old town. Morning mist shrouded the mountain tops extending damp fingers of cloud down the steep contours of the gorges and the tree-lined valleys. Behind the town the foothills rose sharply, the scattered rooftops appearing and disappearing in the swirling pockets of vapour which rose like columns of smoke from the verdant valleys.

From the deck, Oliver couldn't see her house but he knew where it was and he knew Susanna would be at the window. He remembered her as he had left her, standing alone in the courtyard; the red flower which he had plucked from the garden in her hair; a butterfly fluttering around her head before settling on the sundial; the sun glistening on the smooth mounds of her shoulders; the curve of her waist. He remembered the fragrance of the island. Her scent. He knew he would have to see her on his return – whenever that may be.

'The barometer is dropping rapidly, Captain.'

'That is quite evident without you having to inform me, Mr Parry,' he said, instantly regretting the sharpness in his tone. He was becoming impatient waiting for the sound of the signal gun, waiting for the puff of smoke prompting the ships to vacate the harbour and sail out like a swarm of faithful drones following the queen bee to a new location.

'The wind was ideal yesterday,' he said, 'yet look at it now.'

It was a long day, hotter and more humid than was usual in September even at that latitude, and it was not until the middle of the forenoon watch that the ominous grey clouds started forming, replacing the mist which had veiled the island's peaks. As soon as the first wind was felt, the gun boomed from the flagship. It was accompanied by the shrilling of whistles, calls from the decks, the squeal of hemp and the crack of parchment-dry canvas as it was loosed from the yards.

'Take her out, Mr Parry.'

'With pleasure, Captain.'

It seemed as though he had hardly closed his eyes when a knock came at the door.

'Mr Nightingale sends his respects, Captain. Says the wind is dropping and requests your presence on deck.'

'Thank you, Mr Wood, I shall be on deck directly.'

As soon as he swung his legs from his cot, Oliver knew that the frigate was sailing well. The buffeting it had received through the night had finally settled.

For more than four hours the storm had raged out of control. It wasn't rain that had thundered down onto the decks, but an outpouring from above as if the bung on the bath waters of heaven had been removed. There were no single drops in the downpour, just solid sheets of water cutting visibility to no more than a few yards.

At the time, all hands had been summoned and the ship had maintained its blind bearing under double-reefed topsails, the captain unwilling to spill the air from his sail, tack or wear ship for fear of being rammed from the stern by another ship. His hope was that the rest of the fleet would take similar action. Later, with the storm easing slightly and twenty nautical miles of sea behind them, Oliver took to his bed confident that in the morning he would be able to relocate the scattered fleet. Ironically, since the storm had broken he had adopted a sense of responsibility towards the merchantmen.

It was 4.30 when he stepped up to the poop deck.

'Good morning, Mr Nightingale.'

'Morning, Captain. Mr Parry said I was to call you if the wind changed. She's dropped since I came on watch. And still easing.'

The wind was from the north-west – a freshening breeze. During the last hour the rain had stopped and the night clouds were breaking up. The barometer, like the sun, was showing signs of rising. In the western sky some stars were still visible while to the east the horizon was preparing to greet a new day.

'Any sign of the Indiamen, Mr Nightingale?'

'No, sir.'

'Then we shall go about and endeavour to locate them.'

'Aye aye, Capt'n. Prepare to wear ship!' The young midshipman's voice carried well. The starboard watch who had had little time to sleep were nevertheless quick to respond to the call.

In less than fifteen minutes the frigate encountered the first of the merchant vessels. She was a big three-masted East Indiaman, considerably larger than the frigate, and she was under full sail and heading south. Passing *Elusive* within hailing distance, the captain of the East Indiaman said he did not know the whereabouts of the other vessels and he intended to maintain his course due south. Captain Quintrell requested he hove to until the convoy was able to reassemble. At first it appeared his instruction was going unheeded, then, with little warning, the ship slowly began to wear around. To the north and north-west a trickle of ships maintaining a similar course lifted from the horizon and it was not long before the royals and topsails of the navy ships appeared. Hundreds of billowing sails resembling patches of morning cloud were suddenly scudding around the rim of the world, while in the east, great golden spokes fanned across the sky like the helm of an ethereal ship which had risen from the seabed.

*

'Deck there! Wreckage in the water, two points to larboard.'

'Luff up, helmsman!'

'One of the merchantmen, do you think, Captain?'

'More than likely.'

The sea was littered with floating debris: wooden plates, stools, buckets and barrels. Pieces of wreckage were scattered over half a mile of ocean.

'Longboat, sir. Dead ahead. Six men aboard.'

'I bet they're pleased to see us,' Mr Mundy said, with a degree of jubilation.

Oliver, however, wasn't sure he wanted the added encumbrance of shipwrecked sailors, especially merchant mariners and more especially if they were of foreign origin. 'Bring her about and hove to, if you please.'

'Shall we lower a boat, sir?'

'Those men look quite capable of rowing to us. Mr Nightingale, attend to them when they come aboard. Food, drink and dry clothes for every man, and add their names to the log. I will speak with them later.'

Half an hour later, the master's mate rescued from the stricken ship related the events of the previous night.

'The rain was so bad you couldn't see your hand in front of your face and the first we knew we were in strife was when this sloop came up behind us and hit us. Must have been doing close to ten knots. Snapped our rudder clean off and stove a gaping hole in our stern. Fortunately the damage was above the water line and we were not taking water. Then within minutes another one hit us broadside on. You would think he was trying to board us. Trouble is he hooked his anchor deep in our fo'c'sle. For a while it was sheer madness on deck. We turned round and round like a sycamore seed in the wind. The captain tried everything he could but we couldn't break free. We were all locked together and certain of a watery grave till the men on the sloop cut their forestay. The sloop lost its mast but at least it got off.

'The brig, however, which was near as big as this frigate, was still hooked on and tried to haul her anchor out of our bow. I yelled for them to cut their cable but the captain thought he knew better. He gave the cable some slack and let his ship fall off, then once it was free, instead of cutting the damned thing he had the men on the capstan hauling it in.' The man shook his head. 'Damn imbecile saved his pick but opened us up right down to the hawse hole. Peeled off the top strake like the skin off a lemon and splintered her down to the waterline. We were taking water as soon as she pulled free.'

'Did the brig heave to and give you assistance?' the captain asked.

The seaman shook his head. 'She didn't hang around but in that rain we wouldn't have been able to see her even if she'd been within hailing distance.'

'So when did your ship sink?'

'A couple of hours before the sun came up. The men manned the pumps all night till one got blocked, but when the water in the hold reached chest height, we knew we couldn't save her.'

'How many on board? And what of the rest of the crew?'

'Fifty fit men aboard.' He sighed. 'Three boats got off before she went down, but when she rolled she tore out one of her stays. It catapulted across the longboat and sliced through it like a wire through a chunk of cheese. Went down as quick as you please. A dozen men in it, if not more. We pulled two of them out, but not quick enough. They'd swallowed too much water. I don't know where the third boat is. She kept her distance. As for the other men. . . .'

'Hopefully they'll be picked up by another ship. In the meantime, Mr Hazzlewood will introduce you to the purser. You will be issued with hammocks and dry clothes. We are well supplied with slops – almost sufficient to outfit another crew.'

'More names in the muster book, Captain,' Mr Parry reported quietly, as the men shuffled from the deck.

'At this rate we may have our complement of two hundred and fifty souls before we reach the equator! Have the men keep a lookout for that other boat. It could still be afloat. I shall go below and write up this incident in the log. The deck is yours, Mr Parry.'

The first lieutenant touched his hat. 'Aye aye, Captain.'

In the mess, the rescued sailors huddled around the mess tables anxious to eat their fill but unwilling to be interrogated about their experiences. Despite an uncomforatble mood developing, Smithers was not to be deterred and took a strange delight in persisting with his questioning.

'Where were you heading?' he urged. 'And what were you carrying?'

'West Indies,' one replied reluctantly. 'With a cargo of oak and elm.'

Smithers laughed. 'You should have floated with all that timber on board.'

The sailors found nothing amusing in his remark and, ignoring

Smithers, one of the bedraggled seamen enquired if *Elusive* was bound for the Caribbean.'

'Don't rightly know,' Froyle replied. 'The captain's not letting on. One thing's for sure, we've got ample stores – enough for a long voyage – and plenty of space in the hold. And because we've got lots of extra slops, I reckon we're heading for Africa to pick up a load of slaves. Take them to Jamaica or maybe Rio. That's what I think.'

Smithers continued perstering. 'What's your name then?' he said, peering at the man in the corner whose head was shrouded under a blanket.

He got no reply.

'Too much trouble to open your gob, is it? Perhaps we should chuck you back into the ocean. The fish know how to open their mouths.'

'Stow it, Smithers!' Froyle growled, while some of the men sidled away.

'His name's Guthrie,' the old tar said. 'And he's Bigalow and us three are all Kent men from Deal.'

'You'd have been lightermen in past times?' said Froyle.

'Until the press took us in '94,' Guthrie growled. 'Blast their eyes!'

'Hey! There's no swearing on a Navy ship. Not very grateful, is he?'

'You shut your face before I shut it for you! I didn't ask to be brought on board. I'd rather drown than serve in His Majesty's Navy.'

'Well, if you don't mind your tongue, you'll find yourself hanging from the end of a yardarm,' added Smithers.

Guthrie lunged forward grabbing for Smithers' throat across the table.

'Enough!' Froyle shouted, turning to see if any of the midshipmen had heard the conversation. 'Let the man alone. He's just lost his ship.'

'Don't bother me,' Guthrie mumbled, as he sat back. 'It's not the first wreck I've witnessed and it won't be the last, you mark my words.'

'Aye, I bet you saw your share of wrecks in the Downs,' said Jo Foss.

Smithers couldn't resist another quip. 'And scavenged from a few that ran foul of the Goodwin Sands?'

'Maybe I have,' Guthrie replied sharply. 'But there's many a sailor been glad to see my boat and thanked me for saving him from a watery grave. But there's them ungrateful dogs who never said a word.'

'Don't take no heed of him,' the old man said. 'I know what it's like when a ship goes down. Fear does strange things to a man's brain. I've seen a sailor drown his best mate by hanging off his head like it was a barrel. And I've known men drown because they had to dive back into the ship to retrieve a trinket or a bottle of brandy or some such trivia, but they never come up again. I've seen men so frozen with fear you had to chop their fingers off the mast to get them free of the ship before she goes under.' A shiver ran down his spine. 'Few men survive a night clinging to a mast, but them as do, I've seen them let go just as a rescue boat got near. Seems when the spirit runs out so does life with it.'

Smithers laughed. 'Sailors on merchant ships are weak as piss. Navy men is different.'

'Don't talk daft, you old fool.'

'Your mate's right,' the Kent man said. 'The currents have no respect for a uniform. I remember a ship that ran aground on the Goodwins about a year ago. Blown on, she was, as the tide was dropping. Found herself stuck solid, men clinging to her masts poking up from the sea. Hanging like scarecrows in a cornfield, they were. Grown men crying like babies. Not a trace of the vessel to be seen the following day. Every last inch of her sucked into the sand. Navy ship, she was. I heard later her captain was court-martialled for losing her.'

'What was his name?' Froyle asked.

'I don't remember.'

CHAPTER 9

Tittle-tattle

'Deck there!'

'What do you see?'

'Sail off the starboard beam. Looks like a frigate.'

Oliver Quintrell glanced around the fleet. He knew the position of the convoy's two other escort frigates. They were some distance off to the west.'

'Is she alone?'

'Yes, sir.'

'What bearing?'

'Due south, Capt'n.'

'I wonder what she's up to? Keep an eye on her, Mr Parry.'

'Aye aye, Capt'n.'

As the lookouts continued scanning the sea for merchant ships or flotsam, another call came. 'Frigate heading towards us, larboard beam!'

All eyes turned to the approaching ship.

'Is that not the same ship we saw two days ago?'

'Indeed. What do you make of her?'

'Corvette or frigate. Nice lines and obviously very fast. God damn her for not showing her colours!'

'She's opening her gun ports.'

'All hands, Mr Parry. Beat to quarters.'

The roll of drums brought every man to his station. Sailors spilled onto the deck from all parts of the ship and in less than ten minutes the deck was transformed. Every unnecessary item was hurried below, portable obstacles and the bulkheads quickly and efficiently removed.

With the order to run out the guns, the ports were heaved open, heavy breeching ropes unlashed and the guns were trucked into position. The deck was abuzz with half-naked men armed with rammers, sponges, wad-hooks and hand-spikes. The fireman hurried along the deck weighed down with heavy sand scuttles while young boys, whose voices twanged with the chords of a virgin's throat, skittered about distributing bags of powder. The smell of the slow match, burning in the match-tub, incensed the air.

'Shall I give the order to fire, sir?'

'No. Hold your fire! Surely this ship did not intend to take on the whole fleet single-handed! I wish I knew what she was up to!'

Oliver scanned the sea. A least a dozen merchant vessels were within two miles' distance, including one of the larger Indiamen. Unfortunately there was no sign of the other naval vessels. Since leaving St Helens Road it had been an impossible task to keep the fleet closed up, despite regular signals from the flagship ordering them to do so. The fleet was now scattered far and wide, which was a major frustration to the naval escort.

Nothing would have given Oliver greater pleasure than to take on this anonymous frigate. Their broadside poundage was approximately equal but he knew his English gun crew's timing would be faster than that of a foreign crew. He could easily outsmart the enemy, of that he was certain. But if he committed himself to stand and fight he would be countermanding his orders from the Admiralty. On the other hand, he could not afford to be ill prepared if an attack was launched against his ship.

'Masthead!' he called. 'Can you see the flagship?'

'Just coming over the horizon, sir.'

'Mr Nightingale, run up a signal: *unidentified ship approaching*. Get the helm over and bring us close up with those other vessels. Helmsman, bring us into the lee of that big four-master. I'm sure that mongrel will think twice about being peppered by our combined guns.'

'Perhaps if we put a round over her bow, sir.'

'When I want your advice, Mr Parry, I will ask for it.'

The midshipmen on the poop deck looked at each other.

'Aren't we meant to protect the squadron instead of hiding behind its skirts?'

Fortunately Mr Mollard's whispered remark coincided with the rumble of the carronade's wooden wheels and neither the captain nor the first lieutenant heard the subversive comment. But the young midshipman's question was overheard by the man on the helm and a seaman standing by the mizzen sheet.

'Enemy frigate, closing. Do we fire, sir?'

'Not until I give the order! I want to see what she has in mind.'

With a group of ten merchant ships in close proximity, and with brigs and cutters having at least a dozen guns each, Oliver thought it unlikely that a lone frigate would challenge their combined cannon fire. With the sight of the flagship on the horizon, his assumption was soon confirmed. The unknown frigate immediately altered her course and headed away.

Cheers echoed from the gun ports.

'She's changing tack. Do we go after her?'

'No.'

'Do you think she will be back, Captain?' Mr Mundy asked.

'Your guess is as good as mine, but I wager if she does come back, she won't be alone. Get two men in the maintop throughout the night. They must be extra vigilant. My orders are to get this vessel to its destination in one piece and I intend to comply.'

'Did you see the way the captain had the ship sneaking in behind that big fellow? Like he was hiding or scared to fight.'

'Watch your tongue, Smithers! Plenty of men been hung for calling their captain a coward.'

It didn't worry the sailor leaning against the gunnel. After coercing three of the topmastmen to hand over their grog ration, he was buoyed for an argument whatever the subject matter. 'Do you think when his hand was blown off, it took away his taste for battle?'

'Stow it, Smithers!' said Foss, knocking the ash from his pipe into his palm.

'I reckon he was scared. Instead of turning tail he could have chased that ship off and raked his stern with a couple of broadsides. Captain Bransfield wouldn't have hid like a girl. He'd have given him what for. Wouldn't have mattered what flag he was flying. I don't give much credit to a captain who won't fight.'

'You should take care what you're insinuating.'

'Ain't insinuating nothing. I'm just saying I'm wondering if we've got a coward for a captain.'

'Your tongue will be the death of you. That kind of talk will guarantee you a place on the yardarm,' added Wotton, the captain's coxswain.

'And I'll find a nice piece of rope to go with it!' said Foss.

'What would you know? You can't even read, can you? You listen to what I'm saying. I know them Articles of War better than any high and mighty lords at the Admiralty. And I bet none of them ever served before the mast. Peace treaty or no peace treaty, I say it's a sign of weakness if a captain don't stand to and fight.' He smirked. 'Typical of his sort. I know a bit about our Captain Quintrell. Comes from Cornish stock, he does. I'm always suspicious of them who come from there. Devious sorts, they are, with their false lights and thieving ways.'

'Shut your mouth, Smithers. There's more than a score of men on board who come from Plymouth way and I'm sure they'll be happy to cut your throat if you call them smugglers.'

The sailor shrugged his shoulders, leaned back and yawned.

'What else you heard about the capt'n then?' Foss asked.

'I heard he lost his mind. Blithering idiot he was, they say, fit only for an asylum. They sent him up to Greenwich expecting he'd spend the rest of his days there. That's why he had no command for over a year. Don't know how he got out but I bet he bribed the Admiralty to give him this ship. How lucky are we?'

'I ain't listening to more of this talk,' said Wotton. 'What you trying to do, stir up the men? Inciting mutiny – that's what it's called in those Articles you say you know so well. Well, I have no problems with the captain. In fact, I think we are pretty lucky. I've served under a darn sight worse. I suggest you keep your mutinous thoughts to yourself and stop blabbing your mouth off. There's only one imbecile on this ship, Smithers, and that's you!'

Smithers' arm swung at the coxswain's chin but the sudden heel of the ship sent the punch wide. With his weight following his fist, Smithers fell forward, to the amusement of the other sailors on deck.

'I'll get you, Wotton. And your stupid mate too.'

The officer of the watch approached. He hadn't seen the fight but had heard the raised voices by the pin-rail. 'What's going on here? You arguing again, Smithers?'

'I'm not arguing with you, Mr Tully, sir.'

'You're drunk then.'

'Not me, Mr Tully. Only drank me regular ration.'

'Then pick yourself up off the deck. One more peep out of you and your name'll be in the book.'

Smithers sneered, before replying: 'Aye aye, sir.'

Though not as tall as the sailor, Mr Tully stood his ground. He not only disliked Smithers but he was wary of him. Having served before the mast and learned his seamanship the hard way, midshipman Ben Tully had seen it all before. Seen scores of men bound up at the gratings. Been there himself a few times and bore the scars of the cat across his back to prove it. He'd seen traitors whipped around the fleet. Heard stories of the old days when pirates were hung and their corpses left to rot by the Thames' steps for all to see. He was prepared to give most men chance to vent their anger, but he also knew where to draw the line.

Men like Smithers had to be watched. They could never be trusted. Something about them set them apart. Something in their eyes. The toss of the head. The swagger. The tone of voice or turn of phrase. They were the sorts of men you never turned your back to on a dark night or climbed the main mast with if you were alone. Smithers fitted the bill.

'You tidy yourself up!'

'Aye aye, Mr Tully, sir.' Smithers raised his knuckles as he spoke, but as soon as the midshipman's back was turned, he dropped his hand, cursed quietly and spat on the deck.

Returning to the companionway, the midshipman overheard the mumbled profanity as clearly as he had heard the splat of saliva. Unlike many men who had served on a gun deck, his hearing was acute and the sailor hadn't realized he had been listening to his conversation for quite some time.

'So who said we was going to be carrying slaves? If that was the case, we should have been heading for the Guinea coast by now.'

Will looked across the mess table to Percy Sparrow. 'Is that right, Chips?'

The carpenter nodded. 'Glad we aren't going there. It's a killer coast.'

'Aye, it's breathing all that gold dust that kills you. Floats in the mist from the swamps,' said Bungs, the cooper. 'Yellow clouds of it. No man lives long once he's breathed that in.'

'Is that right?' said Will, looking to his mentor.

'Don't take any notice of him, lad. Kidding you, he is.'

'But is there gold in Guinea?' Will asked.

'Too true, there is. Both black and yellow,' said the cooper.

'I never heard of black gold.'

'Slaves, lad. That's what he's talking about.'

'Oh.'

'Aye,' said Bungs, 'just like some of them on this ship.'

'Don't talk daft!' the carpenter quipped.

'Slaves ain't no different to pressed men. They have their liberty taken from them.'

Wotton, the captain's coxswain, had been listening. 'I'll agree with you there, Bungs, though not many will. The press was evil. They treated a lubber no better than a black slave. I've seen poor devils herded round the streets of Portsmouth, beaten with rattans and whips like they were animals, while fancy folk stood by and watched and no one lifted a finger to stop them. And no one cared that those men were taken from their wives and families. At least the blacks can take their wives and bairns along with them.'

'That's true, Will. They take whole families on the slave ships.'

'Of course, when a sailor don't come home, his missus thinks he's been murdered or run off, and after a time she gives up on him and takes up with another man. If he ever manages to get back to land and go home then there's hell to pay.'

'Well, there ain't no pressed men on here,' Foss added.

'You speak for yourself,' Percy Sparrow said.

At the table, the seated men, swaying in unison with the pitch and roll of the ship, studied the carpenter's face.

'I was pressed into the service back in 1784. Young I was. Married with two little ones. A gullible fool I was in them days.'

Bungs laughed. 'A sparrow caught in a cage!'

Chips ignored him. 'A well-dressed fellow offered me a shilling to deliver a package to a ship in the harbour. Said I must be sure to hand it to the lieutenant in person. Fool that I was, I jumped at the chance of making the extra pennies. Of course, when I stepped on board, that was the last I saw of London for five years. I'll never forget the gent who set me up. I suppose he collected a nice bounty for his trouble.'

'So what made you stay?'

He shrugged. 'Don't rightly know. At first I hated it but after I was put to work in the carpenter's shop, I got to like it. Aye, and being young, I liked the excitement. Being a chippie, I was made carpenter's mate and eventually I got a warrant. Now I've got my own workshop with no watches, and down there no one to tell me what to do. I have a hammock to sleep in and plenty of rations and beside the wages there's always a chance of prize money.'

'In wartime maybe and providing the agents are honest!'

Ted Trickett was seated at the far end of the mess table, his shoulder leaning hard against the side of the ship. With his eyes shut, he appeared to be asleep.

'What about you?' said Bungs, flinging his empty plate along the table.

Trickett jerked his head up as the wooden plate struck him on the knuckles. Picking it up, he shoved it back. 'I ain't got nothing to complain about. I've made gunner's mate and one day I'll make gunner.'

'Aye, if you live long enough.'

'I've done all right so far, ain't I?'

Bungs laughed. 'I hear you were running a scuttle from Shields to Woolwich for seven years. I doubt there were many Frenchies scouring the coal run.'

'Well, there were a few didn't make it home thanks to me. And I don't mind admitting, I made my mark to get me hands on the five pound note they were offering.'

'I ain't never seen a five pound note,' said Will.

Chips laughed. 'Well, you're not alone. Bungs wouldn't know what to do with one if he found one. He'd probably use it for wiping his arse.'

'I've heard enough from you, Sparrow-brain. Let's see how loudly you chirp without any teeth in your mouth.'

The two men eyed each other while Trickett grinned.

'So, Mr Know-it-all,' said Bungs, 'where do you think we're heading?'

Chips stretched his neck. 'I got it from the master we're likely heading round the Horn.'

'And what, pray tell us, are we going to fill our empty hold with – gold from Eldorado? Chests filled with Dutch florins?'

'Maybe we'll take a Spanish ship loaded with emeralds and rubies. Imagine what that would be worth. We'd be rich men.'

'And it wouldn't sit in your pocket long before you spent it.'

Bungs shrugged his shoulders.

'Do you think we might sail to the Sandwich Islands and bring us back a ship full of natives?' Trickett asked.

'You'll not get me tangling with them women.'

'What? Scared of a good woman, are you, Chips?'

The mess table shook with the cooper's laughter but the carpenter's expression didn't change.

'It's said they can take you to heaven by just looking at you.'

'Well,' said Chips, 'they'll not take me anywhere cos I don't leave the ship when we go into foreign ports.'

'Maybe we'll go to Mexico,' said Bungs. 'I hear there are places where the natives paint themselves like skeletons and dance on the graves to wake the dead. In the mornings the spirits rise and float down to the sea in the mist. Don't it make you shudder?'

'Is that right, Chips?'

'Shut it, Bungs! Don't take no notice, Will.'

'So, if it weren't for the press, I wonder why men go to sea?' the young shipwright asked.

'I've known men. . . .'

'Listen to Sparrow,' Bungs said. 'Chirping again. From the way he talks, he must know more folk than live in the whole of London.'

'Well, perhaps I do. And perhaps I wash my ears out regular, not like some folk who wouldn't know a piece of soap if he slipped on one.'

'What you trying to say?'

'Not trying to say nothing. Just answering the lad's question.'

'Aye and what were that?'

Percy Sparrow's eyes glinted. 'Why do men go to sea? Why don't you tell him, Bungs? Could it be the governor of Newgate Prison didn't give you much choice in the matter?'

The handle of the cooper's knife reverberated as he stabbed it into the mess table. 'Volunteer, I was!'

'That's not what's written in the muster book.'

'Tweet, tweet. You like to sing, Mr Dickie Bird, don't you? Well, you'll not sing so sweetly with your throat wrung!'

'Stow that talk, you stupid blighter!' Chips replied, quite unconcerned. 'His bark's worse than his bite, Will, and everyone knows it.'

'Just you wait!' Bungs said, pulling his knife from the deal and pointing it threateningly towards the carpenter. 'I'll get you one of these days!'

Froyle was tired of listening to Bungs. The cooper was forever hogging the conversation. 'Well, I'll admit to being taken by the press but I didn't complain. Glad to sail off and see the back of my missus, I was. Bad sort, she was. I heard later she was sentenced to swing, and good riddance, says I. Then I heard she was put on a prison ship – like them slave ships only worse. Ha! Perhaps the hangman's noose might have been kinder after all.'

'Hey! Muffin man. What about you?' said Bungs, pointing his knife at the sailor's face. 'You don't say much either, do you?'

91

'Me? I got picked up in an alley when I was eight or nine years old. I was fitted up with a set of clothes and put on board my first ship. Kissed the gunner's daughter the first week. Thought I was going to die.'

'What you do? Piss on the poop deck?'

'No. Some evil bastard, like you Bungs, thought he'd have a bit of fun. Sent me down to the magazine with a lighted lantern in my hand. Told me to sweep the place up. I was lucky the powder hadn't come aboard. But I learned quick after that. And I waited my time and eventually got my own back.'

'What you do? Blow his head off?'

'Never you mind.'

The sound of feet dancing to the tune of a hornpipe brought a lull to the conversation.

'I once seen a man . . .' Chips continued.

'Here he goes again.'

'I once seen a man eat a foreign crab and his tongue swelled up so much it killed him. At first he couldn't talk and we thought the shell was stuck in his throat. Then his face went bright red like the colour of the crab itself. Then he went white as a sheet and couldn't breathe. Stone dead within a few minutes, he was. Surgeon said it was the crabmeat that killed him. I ain't never eaten a crab since then and if I were you Will, I wouldn't chance it.'

'And when were you last served a crab for supper on one of His Majesty's ships?'

'Oh, shut your face, Bungs. I'm trying to give the lad good advice.'

The cooper laughed and threw his arm around Will's shoulder. 'Don't have to worry your head about things like crabs. But step ashore on the Ganges River and you'll get snapped up by crocodiles. And there are lions on the beaches of the Barbary Coast.'

'Aye,' added Muffin, trying hard to keep a straight face, 'and the Barbary pirates take Christians and eat them alive.'

'And if you fall overboard in the Amazon the fish will pick your bones clean in a trice,' Foss added.

'Don't worry about the wild beasts, Will. You don't even have to step off the ship in Panama to be cursed by the Yellow Jack.'

Though tears rolled down the faces of two of the men, Will's face never flickered as the mess mates' banter continued.

'Ignore them, Will. You'll hear no pearls of wisdom here. Take it from me, lad, you'll be all right if you keeps your nose clean.'

As usual, Bungs made sure he had the last word. 'I'll give you something to think about when you're in your hammock wishing you were back sucking on your mother's tit. But, just mark my words, as sure as there's water under this ship, the devil will get you one of these days and believe me he wears lots of different disguises.'

The following morning Will limped into the carpenter's workshop carrying one of his shoes. The skin on the back of his heel was a weeping mess.

'Happens all the time to lubbers. Barefoot for you, lad, for a while. Keep your feet dry, if you can, though a splash of seawater when they're swabbing the decks won't do them no harm. Best medicine is a dose of hot sun. Do as I say and they'll heal up a treat in no time.'

Will watched the spiralled shavings curling from the hole the auger was drilling.

'Can you write, lad?' Percy Sparrow said.

'Yes, I can.'

'Then why don't you write and tell your mother where you are? I'll hand your letter to the purser when we go into port and I'll ask him to send it for you. At least you can put her out of her misery as she probably thinks you've drowned by now.'

'I'd like to do that.'

'You'll find a pencil in that box yonder and I'll get you a piece of paper. Tell your ma that Chips will keep an eye on you.'

Will smiled.

'And don't take too much notice of the men in the mess. There's two hundred crew on board and most will mind their own business and not trouble you. But be careful who you choose to confide in. There's always one or two rotten apples in a wooden tub like this one, them that bears a grudge against everyone and everything. Them sorts are born with a nasty streak in their blood and a temper strung tighter than a forestay in a roaring gale. I don't mind a man who goes off like a vent full of powder. No,' said Chips, 'it's the ones that smoulder like a yard of slow match you've got to be wary of.'

CHAPTER 10

Neptune's Wrath

Captain Quintrell donned his hat as he stepped on deck. It provided some relief from the equatorial sun, which was almost directly overhead, but none from the glare mirrored from the sea and from every metal plate and eye on the frigate that blinked constantly with the pitch and roll of the ship. On the quarter-deck, the officer of the watch touched his hat.

Oliver glanced at the latest entries on the log-board. 'Maintaining nine knots. That is good. The winds are in our favour, are they not, Mr Mundy?'

The sailing master sniffed the air. 'Aye, Captain. Let's hope they stay that way.'

Scudding along under full sail, *Elusive* encountered the smooth Atlantic's rollers beam-on and with more than a ship's length between each trough, the ship dipped and swayed like a drunken man navigating an alley.

Nothing marked the clear tropical sky save a single speck of black and white. This silent blue world, far from any continental land, was the domain of the great sea birds, the petrels, fulmars and shearwaters. But occasionally the broad Atlantic heaven became a highway for huge flocks of land birds moving as one, sailing and wheeling in a kaleidoscopic feathered cloud; each bird as independent as a single raindrop, yet from the ship the flock appearing as a dusky smudge on the watercolour backcloth of sky.

Aloft, the man in the foretop relaxed against the creaking mast, which swayed lazily with the rhythmic swing of an inverted pendulum. From the sea's surface, flying fish, glistening like silver arrows, darted from one wave to another, at times shooting across fifty yards of sea.

'Where is Mr Parry? Is he on deck?'

'Aye, Capt'n. He's gone for'ard. Said he was going to speak with the bosun.' Mr Smith turned the half-hour glass and nodded to the marine whose job it was to strike the time. It was two bells.

Both watches had eaten and under the present idyllic sailing condition there was little for the seamen to do. Some dozed on deck. Some read. The bosun's mate was aloft with a tar brush and rag while on deck the sail-maker and his mates were seated cross-legged against the starboard gunnel sewing a long patch into a torn staysail.

Under the canvas awning in the ship's waist, the bosun instructed the young midshipmen in the art of tying knots, teaching them not only how to form them but where on the ship to use them. In the shade beneath the longboat, two of the seasoned old salts sat cross-legged, picking fibres from pieces of old rope. Though it was a chore often given as a mild punishment, the men were happily stuffing the loose fibres into hand-sewn linen bags. While feathers were not available, teased oakum made a comfortable pillow.

The laughter quietened as the captain stepped onto the quarter-deck and the men on the larboard side shuffled automatically across to the opposite side and out of his way.

Oliver leaned over the rail at the waist and listened to the voices coming from below. The tone was healthy. The men appeared content. But the lull of the ocean and the idyllic azure surrounds could be a deceptive cradle which easily rocked a ship to sleep. It was something he wanted to avoid at all costs.

In the bow, a group of men were unaware of the captain's attention. They were laughing and pointing. Porpoises, no doubt, he thought.

'Pass the word to Mr Parry,' the captain said to the officer of the watch, as he climbed the steps to the poop deck.

Mr Smith, the youngest of the midshipmen, acknowledged the order and hurried to the bow.

Oliver watched as his first lieutenant immediately came aft, walking as smartly as if the ship were not rolling at all.

'Well, Mr Parry?'

'Checking the hawse holes, sir.'

'Indeed. And those men who you were examining the hawse hole with seemed to find some amusement in your company.'

'Not at all, sir. Merely distracted for a moment by a group of porpoises.'

'And have you never seen a porpoise frolicking in a bow wave before?'

'Indeed I have, sir. Many times.'

'And no doubt the men have seen them also.'

'Indeed, Captain.' The lieutenant was somewhat puzzled at the line of questioning.

'Let me put this to you, Mr Parry. From my brief observation, those seamen appeared to be exuding a considerable degree of over-familiarity with a senior officer. Furthermore that senior officer appeared to be condoning and, might I add, encouraging that over-familiarity.'

'I'm sorry, sir. I did not mean that to be the case but they are—'

'They are what, Mr Parry? In my eyes they are common seamen, nothing more or less. Or am I missing something? Should I use a glass to examine them more closely?' He glared straight ahead, as if his view of the men standing near the heads was not obliterated by the sweeping canvases of the fore and main courses. 'No! I should not! But perhaps you will give me your educated opinion of those men who were wasting time in the fo'c'sle, sir.'

Simon Parry looked uncomfortable. 'They are men who served with me on my previous ship, Captain.' He paused for a moment before continuing. 'Men who, like me, at one time thought there was no hope of rescue and yet were miraculously plucked to safety. It is my belief that when men face certain death and share a similar fate, they carry a bond of allegiance.'

'Interesting philosophy, Mr Parry. However, you are neither dead nor maimed, nor are any of those men. And pray tell me this, how many times have you been under fire from an enemy's broadside, or on a deck raining masts and spars; or on a ship when it is boarded?'

'Many times, Captain.'

'And in such instances is not every man in imminent danger of meeting his maker? In such instances, doesn't every man on the ship share the same fate?'

'Yes, Captain, undoubtedly they do.'

'And wouldn't you agree that almost every seaman with more than ten years' service has suffered at least one shipwreck in his career? And has not every man aboard this ship, excluding the young gentlemen, fought in a sea battle?'

'I believe so.'

'Then according to your argument, every man aboard must feel this *certain allegiance,* as you put it?'

'Indeed, Captain.'

Quintrell sniffed. 'When the occasion arises that you have command of a ship, Mr Parry, then it will be up to you what behaviour you condone between the ship's officers and her men. As my first lieutenant, I remind you that there are Articles which dictate what behaviour is acceptable and what is regarded as insubordinate. You would do well to refresh yourself with all the Articles of War. They apply to everyone serving on one of His Majesty's vessels, including you and me.'

'I shall do that,' Simon Parry said obediently.

'Let me further remind you that this ship is under my command and I advise you against encouraging any form of familiarity with any man of inferior rank irrespective of whether he is your brother or son. It is too easy to bend the spectrum of strict discipline, but should it be broken not only does the officer put himself at risk, but he places the rest of the crew and indeed the ship itself in jeopardy.

'Unlike a uniformed officer, these seamen may look motley in their potted garb, but do not be deceived by their appearance. Believe me, there are quick brains and even quicker tongues amongst them. One taste of vulnerability and they will suck on it like honey from a spoon. Do I make myself clear, Mr Parry?'

'Indeed, Captain. It will not happen again.'

'I am pleased to hear that.'

Mr Nightingale entered the ship's position on the log-board.

The fifteenth degree of latitude was the parting of the waves for the fleet. The day the convoy of merchant ships and its escort divided into two parts; the day *Elusive* excused herself from any further obligations to the flagship.

From the deck, the officers witnessed the series of signals exchanged between the navy ships culminating in a final gun salute. Of the fleet, more than half were bound for the West Indies and from the current latitude they were ideally positioned to catch the trade winds which would carry them to the islands in the Caribbean Sea. Sailing with them was the hundred-gun triple-decker flying the commodore's pennant, also one of the sixty-fours and a frigate.

Crossing the Atlantic through the idyllic latitudes of the tropics posed few problems but as the large, heavily laden Indiamen bound for the West Indies neared their destination, the dangers facing them would be twofold – from attack by pirates or rebels, and from the sudden vagaries of the weather. Late summer was renowned for hurricane-force winds and tropical lows which in the blink of an eye could turn ideal sailing conditions into a recipe for a ship's graveyard. Although it was October, the seasonal danger was not over.

The remaining thirty ships were heading south west before bearing east around the Cape of Good Hope. Accompanying them was a frigate and the second sixty-four-gun third-rate with its supercargo of diplomats and chests of gold to refurbish the Ceylon station. For this group, danger lurked on all quarters. Apart from the possibility of pirate attack, the fickle winds and currents of the southern African coast could not be trusted. The consequences of being becalmed, compounded by the intolerable heat, was a lethal combination, yet making landfall to replenish water was fraught with two-fold dangers – attack by hostile natives or the legacy of a lingering death from the fevers contracted on the disease-ridden African coast. But despite the obvious hazards, the guarantee of reaping rich rewards from the spice trade was a temptation the greedy city merchants and trading companies could not resist.

For several hours knots of white sails dotted the distant sea as *Elusive* headed on her new course bearing west-south-west. One by one, as the day wore, the merchant ships disappeared, slipping beneath the hazy dome of the horizon to leave *Elusive* alone on an empty ocean.

For the next five days the winds blew favourably but on the following morning there was hardly a breath of breeze. As dawn broke, the first rays of sunlight bathed her sails in gold and, as if weighed down under a layer of gilt, the canvas hung heavily.

'I trust this is not a foretaste of what is to come, Mr Mundy,' Oliver said.

Every seaman on board who had previously sailed for South America was familiar with the problems of being becalmed. Delays in the doldrums could last for days, even weeks. Yet Captain Quintrell was acutely aware of his instructions. He had been told he must suffer no delays. That fact had been reinforced in the sealed orders which he had opened when they crossed the fifteenth degree latitude, north of the equator.

The contents of the vellum pouch marked with the word *secret* had provided him with details of his final destination – but with little else. The information which he had read and re-read several times raised more questions than it answered, and for that reason he had no intention of sharing the new orders with his officers, not even his first lieutenant. At this stage, all he was prepared to reveal was the course – a south-westerly bearing which would carry them to the coast of South America.

Fortunately, with the light conditions, the crew were kept busy. In an attempt to catch every fleeting zephyr, the crew were forever adjusting sails. No sooner had the yards been braced around than the breeze would change again, as if intent on indulging them in some fickle game.

For a time, life on deck had been pleasant, but when the winds failed completely, the heat bore down oppressively. With every exertion the seamen dripped with sweat. Their hands slipped on ropes, lines and standing rigging. Melted pitch oozed from the cracks between the deck planks, blistering bare feet. Men cried out when their hands touched on the metal plates and fittings. Even the wooden deck lockers were too hot to sit on.

Two days of lazy sailing brought the frigate across the equator. It being Sunday, the crew was assembled and Captain Quintrell chose a psalm as a suitable reading before leading the men in the Lord's Prayer. The reading which followed was from the Admiralty's Articles of War.

Before the men were dismissed, Oliver gave permission for them to perform the maritime rituals which crossing the line demanded. Hopefully the morning's light-hearted ceremony would serve to improve the sailors' spirits. If nothing else, it would provide a break from the present boredom. With not a breath of air on the flaccid sails, it was unnecessary for the ship to come about. *Elusive* was sitting perfectly still on the glassy sea.

There were few candidates on this cruise to be presented to King Neptune. Three midshipmen (which should have been four, but Mr Mollard was conveniently confined to the sick bay), a couple of lads who had fought at the Nile but never sailed south of the Tropic of Cancer and young William Ethridge, acting carpenter's mate. Every man who had sailed round the Cape of Good Hope on the *Constantine* automatically qualified for an exemption.

With preparations duly completed and a canopy erected over the deck, the court of King Neptune was called and acknowledged by the cheers and jeers of the whole crew gathered on the deck.

One by one the reluctant victims were obliged to pay homage to the maritime ruler and to his decidedly unfeminine wife – Smithers – draped in a sack-cloth skirt and decked in a wig of dried seaweed. In turn, each novice was force-fed a foul-smelling concoction created in the galley; the resulting retching and facial contortions from the recipients produced howls of raucous laughter from the crew.

Finally, daubed with a mixture of tar and paint and dusted with flour and feathers, the subjects were prodded and shoved through an invasive corridor of hands to emerge in an unrecognizable state at the gunnel. From there they were unceremoniously tossed overboard to be cleansed by the sea.

Will Ethridge was the fourth to hit the water but being a strong swimmer, he surfaced quickly and paddled back to the rope ladder, smiling. The Right Honourable Mr Smith came next while Mr Wood was last in line.

In trying to resist the inevitable dunking, Wood slipped on the wet deck but there was no escape. Grabbed by the wrists and ankles, he was dragged to the rail. Below, in the shimmering water, a pod of porpoises serpentined along the surface, passing within a few yards of the ship. Their timely attendance was hailed with approval by the members of King Neptune's court.

'I can't swim!' Pud Wood yelled, as he was flung over the side. But his cry only encouraged the enthusiastic crowd.

'You'll soon learn,' a lone voice shouted.

The midshipman, being the heaviest candidate, created the greatest splash. For a while he bobbed on the surface, coughed and spluttered, flailed his arms, then sank. The sailors watched and waited. The jeering continued. Someone reached for a rope but before the line could be tossed to him, the water bloomed red.

Silence. Then the chubby painted face appeared again but only for a second. The alarmed eyes were wide open. Shock was written on his gaping lips. Then he disappeared.

In the final moments of revelry, no one had noticed the single dorsal fin slicing straight through the surface as if drawn to the ship on the end of an invisible line.

How insidious the movement of the shark, so different to the gaily frolicking mammals it had been chasing.

'Back to your stations. Now!' the master yelled. 'Clean up this mess!'

The hour of fun and games was over. *Elusive* had lost a midshipman, and the incident would hang heavily on everyone's conscience. The event, which Oliver had hoped would raise the sailors' spirits, had done just the opposite and the men's disquiet was magnified by the oppression of the equatorial climate.

Six bells in the forenoon sounded.

'All hands on deck,' Mr Parry called.

The men shuffled around. Few had gone below after completing the work of cleaning and holy-stoning the deck. The heat below deck was too oppressive.

Without being ordered to silence, the low hum of voices hushed when the captain approached. Those wearing hats removed them; even knotted neckerchiefs covering sunburned scalps were pulled off.

For Oliver, the responsibility of saying words for Midshipman Wood did not come easily. His death has been totally unnecessary – the waste of a life and waste of a promising career. Men were cut down in battle serving their king and country. Some died of scurvy or fever. Others died when they fell from the rigging. But to die the way this young naval officer had perished was tragic. No one deserved that fate and every man-jack of them aboard knew it.

As the deepening shadow of gloom settled across the ship, the heavens took on a similar garb. By evening, banks of dark clouds were gathering in the western sky.

'The barometer's falling, Captain,' Mr Mundy commented. 'If we're in luck we'll see rain before nightfall.'

But Oliver was not so convinced of their luck. He had skirted a hurricane before and was wary of the formations the clouds were adopting.

'Keep an eye on that sky,' he said. 'It looks ominous.'

The storm struck in the middle of the second dogwatch. Some members of the starboard crew had just snatched a little sleep but the larboard watch had had none when all hands were called. Stormclouds had gathered on three sides, heavy black clouds which appeared to hover just above the horizon – curtains of steel-grey rain. As if suspended on invisible rails, the wet drapes moved, at times closing with each other or overlapping before finally coalescing. As the crew watched, smaller storms were spawned – independent storms with minds of their own. From the deck the officers observed the major front approaching. As the line of bouncing rain advanced, the sea's surface boiled and bubbled, churning and spitting wildly as if a ghostly regiment of cavalry was galloping across it.

Having previously been chasing the fleeting wind, *Elusive* must now try to outwit it. But the new wind had an argumentative will, first blowing violently from one direction, then turning a full circle and blowing back upon itself with a vengeance.

Before the storm hit, the topsails were triple-reefed and all but one of the headsails had been struck. With no hope of sailing into the wind, the frigate tacked and with the wind astern, sailed out of the storm.

At midnight, the starboard watch went below while the remainder of the crew, who had had no sleep since the previous night, had another four hours' duty before they could take a break. It was exhausting work but at least it served to take the men's minds from the death of the young officer. Fortunately too, the winds were courteous, carrying the frigate closer to the coast of Brazil.

For several days the lookouts saw no other sail, not even a trace of weed, whale or turtle.

The log-board bore hardly a mention of activity save for the occasional exercises on the guns but even these were kept to a minimum as Oliver was conscious that the explosive sounds could attract unwanted attention.

That night, as he gazed at the blackness of the night sky sprinkled with a trillion stars, the luff in the sail alerted him.

'We are losing the wind, Captain.'

'Then we must make the best of what we have. Bring us up on the coast of Brazil, Mr Mundy.'

'Will we be making landfall?' the master enquired.

'Check with the cooper. Providing our water lasts, we will sail for Rio de Janeiro. If not, then we shall drop anchor at Recife.'

CHAPTER 11

Quicksand

With the evening meal over, Oliver dabbed his lips and returned the napkin to the table.

'I regard my departure from my last command as ignominious,' he said. 'I learned later I was carried from my ship in a hammock, rolled in canvas like a damaged chart, and transferred to another ship. I was then despatched to the wards of Greenwich Hospital, where it was considered I would possibly spend the rest of my days.

'It was there I learned that the men who die in battle or under the surgeon's knife make a more pleasant departure from this life than those subjected to months of anguish within the confines of that spartan establishment. I am of the opinion that the aim of a sojourn within its opulent buildings is to ensure maximum suffering for an extended period with a minimal rate of recovery.'

The captain leaned back in his chair. 'I trust you will not use those words against me, Mr Parry. Greenwich Seamen's Hospital offers sanctuary to almost three thousand old and injured seamen whose final years would otherwise be spent in abject misery. I am, in fact, extremely grateful to the surgeons and physicians of that institution for resolving more than one malady in my case. Unfortunately, however, that period of enforced rest afflicted me with a chronic dose of cynicism from which I am still trying to recover.'

'Are you ready for coffee, Capt'n?'

'Thank you, Casson.'

'A good man,' said Oliver, as his steward disappeared through the door. 'When the peace came and he returned to England, he sought permission to visit me at Greenwich. It was there I offered him a post as valet at my home. John Casson has served as my steward for five years and he probably knows, far better than I, what a miserable state I was in. He sat by my bed for many hours reading aloud the journals and gazettes which my wife delivered on a weekly basis. Sadly my somewhat addled brain was incapable of retaining his words and most of the events which took place during the period of my illness remain a mystery to me.'

'That is understandable.'

'No matter. When we first met at the Admiralty, I was at a loss for your background. It was not until you came aboard and I reviewed your papers that I realized you had had your own command; that you had subsequently lost your ship and faced a court-martial.'

'Which exonerated me.'

'Indeed. But you did not receive another command?'

'No. And, as I had been commissioned only to the rank of commander and never promoted to post captain, once the ship was gone, my rank naturally reverted to that of lieutenant.'

'And had those unfortunate circumstances not occurred you could well have been elevated to post rank by now. You may have even been given command of *Elusive*.'

'I doubt it, sir.'

'Do you wish to speak about those past events? I am not pressing you and I respect your right to remain silent. I don't doubt the matter was investigated very thoroughly by the Admiralty Board and imagine that must have been a particularly trying time for you.'

'It was indeed.'

The atmosphere was a little tense and the arrival of the coffee and the appearance of a box of fine cigars was a well-timed interruption.

'That smells delicious. Thank you, Casson.'

'My pleasure, Capt'n.'

After a moment's deliberation, the lieutenant continued the conversation: 'I lost my ship, sir. That is the top and bottom of it, and I still find it hard to believe.' He paused, breathed deeply and for a moment watched the steam curling from the spout of the pewter pot. 'I lost her to a sea as smooth as the linen cloth on this table and in doing so I sentenced seventy men to a diabolical death. Seventy men, goddamnit. Left seventy mothers mourning sons. How many children without fathers? And wives without husbands? I can only hazard a guess.'

'The sea has no conscience, Mr Parry, and that number, if you will excuse the pun, is but a drop in the ocean when compared to the casualties of sea battles. I am pleased, however, to see that you have not left the service.'

'How could I leave a life which I love? I wish for nothing else. I was taken to sea as a boy only eleven years old and like Nelson was a midshipman at the age of thirteen and lieutenant six years later. From there I was given the rank of commander on three occasions, and had hoped to be raised to post captain after my last voyage. Of course, after losing my ship, that never happened.'

'What was your ship?'

'A twenty-four-gun sixth-rate. A frigate. The *Gallant*. She was old but a well-constructed, fast ship. She was capable of fourteen knots in exceptional conditions.'

'Were you with the Mediterranean fleet?'

Simon nodded. 'For a while. I was patrolling the northern beaches of the Mediterranean when I was surprised by three French corvettes. With the fleet some distance away, I was outnumbered and outgunned. I fought back and dismasted one, but with the odds and the weather gauge in their favour, there was little hope. Had the fleet not returned and given assistance, *Gallant* would not have remained afloat. She lost her mizzen but fortunately the fore and main held and rather than refit in Gibraltar I was ordered back to Falmouth. When the new mast was stepped and she was rerigged, we joined the Channel fleet scouting the northern end.'

'No doubt you fell foul of a French ship-of-the-line.'

'No, sir. I fell foul of the Goodwin Sands.'

Captain Quintrell ground his teeth.

'There was a storm brewing and I was not far off the white cliffs. The barometer suddenly plummeted and I decided the safest option was to head for the Downs and wait until it had blown itself out. We crept in close-hauled and anchored off Deal but in the night came this enormous storm. Both cables parted and I was woken to learn *Gallant* was drifting towards the sands. The only solution, I thought, was to navigate the deep-water channel which runs between the northern and southern outcrops.

'I took all precautions and had men on the lead on either side but as we headed through a seemingly safe channel I suddenly discovered it was a stew of quicksand. The deep-water passage no longer existed and we were soon stuck as solid as a brick in mortar with a gale shredding our sails and the sea sucking on our hull.'

'And what state was the tide at the time?'

'Receding.'

'You were hoping she would lift on the next high?'

'That was my only hope and a faint hope it was. I had heard stories of ships which had succumbed but for me it was inconceivable to think that my ship would become one of them.'

He sucked in a deep breath and continued. 'Early the following morning the sea was calm with little or no wind and we were on a bar which encroached into Kellet Gut. *Gallant* had sunk in the sand almost to her gun ports and was sitting bolt upright with not the slightest inclination to heel over. I remember thinking it lucky that the tide was on the ebb.' He paused, shaking his head. 'Even before light, I had all hands down on the sand, digging with whatever tools they could muster, even their hands. Surprisingly the surface was hard and dry and they dug with the fervour of wild dogs unearthing a cadaver. But the constant digging served only to create a six-foot moat around the ship. The keel was another twelve feet below, held by suction which was tight as a barrel's stave.'

'An impossible task.'

'Impossible indeed.'

'But if your fate appeared fixed, surely you had no alternative but to abandon ship and get your men ashore?'

'Of course. But even with the predicament as it was, that was not a straightforward decision to take. So while the sand was hard and the men dug, I encouraged them. But there were Deal and Ramsgate men amongst the crew – men who related tales their fathers and grandfathers had passed down to them. They spoke of the ferocious storms of 1703 when fifty-three ships went down, of ghost ships and ghost crews appearing at night, and wrecks by the hundreds fixed to the chalky bottom. The men were bewitched by the tall tales and despite my attempts to bring them to order they were stirred to a point of near panic. When a local boat came out from Deal and the fisherman shouted to us to get off while we still could, the men went crazy with the idea of rescue.'

'So what fate befell your crew and what of the ship's boats?'

'The tide was on the make and we could see it sliding along the sands towards us. Its pace was such that the men who had gone out to hail the local boat had to run to outstrip it. But as the water drew closer, the sand around us changed. I felt it soften beneath my own feet. What appeared to be firm ground was an illusion. It was thinner than the skin on a bowl of custard and at times it quivered like jelly. I could do nothing. I watched helplessly as my men tried to make it to the ship but as they ran their feet sank, and within minutes they were up to their knees unable to pull one leg out and place it in front of the other. Fortunately I was near the ship and was able to climb aboard. From the deck I watched helplessly as those sailors sank deeper into the stew and were slowly sucked under. When I close my eyes I can still see their faces – hear their gurgling screams as the liquid sand ran into their throats and choked them.' He sighed. 'Quicksand provides an evil death.'

The captain stirred the sugar which had settled in the bottom of his cup. 'And you say the gale had died?'

'Completely. The morning brought bright sunshine, light winds and a flat, calm sea. I entered it in the log that morning.'

'But what of the other men? A frigate of that size would have at least one hundred and fifty men aboard.'

'One hundred and sixty.' He drained his cup and continued. 'As the tide rose we realized the ship had sunk lower and before long water was seeping in around the lids on the gun ports. I ordered the boats swung out and waited as long as I dared before having them launched. Eighty men crammed themselves into the three boats. That was all we had.'

'And you were in one of the boats.'

'No. I stayed with the ship with a handful of volunteers.'

'A brave decision.'

'Not so,' he sighed. 'I had little choice. The boats were already overloaded and would carry no more. Fortunately those men were in luck. The sea was calm. When they left I instructed my officers to send a boat back to collect those of us who had remained behind. At the time, I did not share my thoughts with the others but my concern was that when the tide reached its full and the sand returned to its fluid state, it would release its grip and the ship would heel over. I also held grave fears that the boats would not return quickly enough.

'We, who remained, watched the tide as it rose. We watched it running across the deck, sliding like spilt wine over a polished table; smooth as quicksilver, silent as the grave, slithering into every vacant nook and cranny.' He sighed. 'It was not the shipwreck you would imagine. No raging torrent crashing over the bow, just clear translucent water trickling across the quarter-deck and pouring almost delicately through the open hatches – the level growing visibly deeper with every passing minute.'

107

'Did she go over as the tide filled?'

Simon shook his head. 'No. The sand did not release its grip on the keel as I had expected. In fact, the suction increased, so with the remaining men I climbed the rigging. All we could do was cling to the yards and pray she would stay upright until the boats returned.'

'Obviously you eventually made it to shore.'

'A group of boats appeared. They were not the ship's boats but local men from Deal. They were familiar with the area. They knew the tides and winds and above all the moods and movements of the shifting sands. And their boats were almost flat-bottomed, which allowed them to skim the surface without danger of becoming stranded.'

'Were all your men saved?'

'Not so, unfortunately. In their panic, two of my men dived from the rigging, but being exhausted and unable to swim far did not make it to the boats. The fishermen did their best though I must admit some seemed more interested in what items of value could be salvaged from the flotsam.'

'But you were rescued and taken ashore?'

'I was, sir, along with several of my men.'

The lieutenant paused as the captain refilled the cups.

'I never saw *Gallant* slip under the water but by the next day there was not a sign of her to be seen.'

Oliver shook his head.

'As three merchant vessels also broke their moorings in that gale and were never seen again, the court-martial board deemed that the loss of the ship was not entirely of my doing and exonerated me. However, I was reprimanded for my ill-chosen decision of trying to sail through Kellet Gut rather than the Gull Stream to the north. Apart from the reprimand I was made to forfeit the prize money due to me from my service in the Mediterranean.'

'A bitter pill to swallow.'

'Indeed.'

'At the time, how did you receive the board's findings?'

Simon pondered for a moment. 'I respect the findings of the court-martial but let me say, if the same events occurred today, I doubt I could or would do anything differently. Had I tried to make it through the northern passage, with the wind blowing at gale force, I would have been pushed onto the North Goodwin bank. Unfortunately, I was unaware at the time that every seven years the Sands move from east to west and back again and that the channel which flows between the two banks has a habit of closing up.'

'I did not know that either.'

'But I am thankful that almost ninety of my crew survived and the officers and seamen who served with me bore no malice. However, the fact remains I lost one of His Majesty's frigates and sacrificed men's lives – not in the cause of battle but as a result of a woeful decision. I alone am responsible and every day when I look out at a flat calm sea I am reminded of it. As for my rank, I know full well I will never be raised to that of captain again.'

Carefully pouring two glasses of port wine, Oliver chose not to be drawn into conjecture on that score. 'The sea and the weather are as nebulous as the thoughts and desires of a woman. We are teased and tormented by both and yet cannot resist the temptation to return to them. He is a clever man who can predict how a woman will behave and a clever captain who can predict the changing moods of the sea. As far as the fair sex are concerned, knowing what is simmering beneath an innocent visage can sometimes be more challenging than setting forth on an uncharted ocean. I propose a toast,' Oliver said, raising his glass. 'May we gain wisdom from past experience of which every ounce is worth its weight in gold?'

'Wisdom from experience,' Simon Parry echoed. 'Worth its weight in gold.'

CHAPTER 12

Rio de Janeiro

Not long after the coast of South America was sighted, the hold became the centre of activity. Having inspected the vacant space in the bowels of the ship, the captain decided it could be put to good use until it was needed for more important cargo. Anticipating the inhospitable conditions facing the crew as they headed south, Oliver considered that a contribution of fresh meat to the men's diet would improve both their physical and mental wellbeing. When they anchored in Guanabara Bay, he planned to go ashore and order three beasts, which he would pay for out of his own pocket.

Percy Sparrow, Will Ethridge and the two other carpenter's mates were the team engaged in the construction of three wooden cattle pens. The work in itself was not heavy, but the air in the hold was thick and stagnant and the stench from the bilges was foul enough to turn a strong man's stomach. After working with the smell for a few days, however, the men appeared to become accustomed to it, or at least they complained less.

For Chips and Will, building the pens was an enjoyable job as they liked working together. Firstly they constructed a wooden platform above the shingle ballast and on it erected a row of three holding pens, each one strong enough and broad enough to take a full-grown beast. The sail-maker was charged with the responsibility of containing much of the excrement before it could seep into the ballast and foul the ship. After much deliberation he did this by lining the floor of each pen with canvas and venting it to allow the waste to be channelled into collecting troughs. As it would be necessary for the troughs to be emptied several times a day, one of the crew would be designated to undertake that unenviable task. Apart from the carpenters and sail-maker and his mates, the only other person involved was the cooper. Barrels had to be relocated to make way for the pens.

A veil of liquid air hung over Rio de Janeiro as *Elusive* sailed into the broad expanse of Guanabara Bay. White-lace beaches circled the bay, stretching into the distance as far as the eye could see. From the water's edge, giant near-vertical granite domes, skirted in verdant forests, sprouted from the steep slopes. Beyond them a backdrop of rugged angular mountain peaks zig-zagged the skyline. Nestled on the eastern shore was the town with its dirty wharfs and opulent white mansions. On the water, numerous small boats dotted the sheltered anchorage together with many large merchant vessels – cutters and packets, brigs and sloops bearing the flags of various nations. Some of the ships were ready to head home to Europe while others were preparing to face the most hazardous part of their journey – around Cape Horn.

Resting along the frigate's yard, the topmen furled the squares into harbour trim while on the bowsprit the staysails were neatly pleated and tied down. On deck Mr Smith was responsible for the ship's boats being swayed out while Bungs, the cooper, had come up from the hold to supervise the hoisting of the water barrels. As the containers appeared on deck they were lined up in readiness for being ferried ashore. *Elusive* would take on almost 200 tons of water.

Within less than half an hour of dropping anchor, a small convoy of local craft stood alongside. On board, colourfully clad vendors offered a bounty in exotic fruit, fish, tobacco and crabs for sale. However, as Percy Sparrow's stories about shellfish had circulated the mess, no one was prepared to chance eating seafood of any description.

'Get that damned monkey down from the rigging!' Mr Parry shouted, as it leapt for the ship and ran up the ratlines. Two topmen scampered up the rigging in pursuit but the animal was too agile and led the sailors a merry dance before scurrying to the top of the main mast. A chorus of cries imitating the animal's shrieking commenced, much to the amusement of the men below. Sitting on the plate atop the mast – the highest point on the ship – the monkey let out a frightening screech of defiance and bared its teeth. The topman who was only a yard beneath it shot out his arm in an attempt to grab the plaited twine fastened to a leather collar around its neck. But with no intention of being caught, the monkey leapt into the air, dropped to the standing rigging and slid down the stay, landing neatly on the narrow gunnel, to the applause of the crew and the mounting frustration of the first lieutenant.

'Silence, you men! You think it amusing having a disease-ridden fiend let loose on the ship? You'll not be laughing if it bites you.' When the monkey hissed, revealing its long pointed incisors, the men backed away.

'In future, Mr Smith, you'll make sure any local boats are fended off before they get within an oar's length of the ship.'

'Yes, sir,' the Right Honourable gentleman replied.

As he spoke, a bolt of half-chewed tobacco was lobbed across the deck, distracting the animal's attention sufficiently for the cooper to get a firm hold on its lead. With a quick tug, he jerked it down to the deck and slapped a vice-like grip on the back of its neck. Being held at arm's length, the monkey screamed, writhing and twisting itself around the man's arm. But despite its contortions and high-pitched screeching, it couldn't escape the cooper's hand.

'Well done, Bungs. Get it off the deck and over the side. I don't care which boat you drop it into.'

No sooner had he tossed it unceremoniously from the gunnel than it set up a cacophony of curses on the boats below and though the language was foreign it was not hard to decipher what was being said. The sailors revelled in the commotion.

'Get back to work!' Mr Smith ordered in an uncharacteristically commanding voice. 'We don't have all day! And Bungs, go below and find out how many more empties there are left to sway up.'

'Another dozen to my reckoning, but I'll make sure.'

Mr Parry, who had been checking the anchor cables, returned to the deck. 'A word in your ear, Mr Smith. It's half an hour since we dropped anchor and the cutter is still not in the water. If you or any of the men want to go ashore while we are in port, I suggest you get a move on.'

Whether it was the heat and humidity and lack of any sea breeze, or the fact that the men had grown a little lazy after the easy sailing which they had endured down the South American coast, the crew were lackadaisical in their duties and needed constant prompting. But despite their tardiness, their half-naked bodies glistened as if smoothed with whale oil, and as work proceeded the deck was decorated with a polka-dot pattern of salty sweat.

A loud thud reverberated through the ship as a barrel swung loose, smashing against the companionway ladder and crushing a man's fingers.

'Take more care down there!' the midshipman shouted, observing the blood dripping from the man's hand. 'You'd better be quick and see the surgeon. He's planning to go ashore and he'll not be too happy to attend to you right now.'

As the final containers were being swayed out to a waiting barge, the hemp netting split.

'Watch out below!'

But the warning did not prevent one of the local victuallers overbalancing and falling overboard. Fortunately none of the barrels hit him but they splintered the side of his boat before splashing into the bay.

'For goodness' sake, you men. Who checked the netting?' Mr Smith was conscious that Mr Parry was watching from the quarter-deck. 'Someone get those barrels out of the water and get another net rigged up.'

'And get the longboat out of the way!' Mr Parry ordered.

'It's this place,' Smithers mumbled from the deck. 'Bad vibrations. I can feel it in my bones.'

'Don't be daft! We ain't in the Caribbean.'

'You might scoff but just you wait and see. I'm telling you, this is just the start. You mark my words, no good will come of this place.'

'You two!' Mr Parry called. 'Stop chattering and smarten up. We do not have all day!'

But the job of watering took until four o'clock in the afternoon.

The sun was just setting over the mountains and the sky changing from mauve to gold when the barge carrying three surprisingly healthy-looking beasts and a quantity of green fodder drew up alongside. But swaying the cattle aboard was not an easy task and proved to be painstakingly slow. The last bullock was particularly boisterous and seemed intent on launching itself into the sea. With horns as sharp as any pike and each one the length of a man's arm, the job of securing the harness under each beast's belly, without someone being gored, was extremely hazardous. The fast-approaching darkness added to the danger.

Finally, by the light of lanterns, the cattle were lowered into the hold where it was discovered that the pens were too narrow to accommodate their sweeping excrescences. The only solution was to cut them off. After various attempts with knife, axe and saw, resulting in blood being spurted around the hull as if from a loose hose, a wire, which cook used for cutting cheese, proved most effective. It sliced through the growths quickly and efficiently and cauterized the blood flow in the process. Even the beasts seemed to feel no discomfort and that helped reduce the level of noise.

The smell of bilge water in the hold was now complemented by the assorted animal odours – the cud, the sweat, the urine and seemingly non-stop streams of green excrement, which were bucketed to the main deck and thence overboard. The constantly filling canvas troughs of urine also had to be emptied regularly. An unenviable task, but surprisingly one man volunteered to be responsible for the cattle until they were slaughtered. Tom Masterton announced his mother had a house cow back in Hungerford. He alone regarded the cattle smells as rich and wholesome and said it reminded him of home.

For the others who had to venture into the hold, lumps of teased oakum in the nostrils helped reduce the reek of offensive odour.

By the following day most of the fresh stores had been loaded and the captain gave permission for the crew to go ashore. There were strict orders that no women were to be brought back on board and any man disobeying those orders or returning late was guaranteed a flogging. Furthermore, any sailor failing to return till the following morning, when the ship was due to sail, would be treated as a deserter according to the Articles of War.

After breakfast, the ship's boats ran a fairly constant shuttle service to and from the wharf. Will Ethridge was on the first to go ashore along with three of the midshipmen and the sailing master. The chance to step foot on South American soil was an opportunity too good to miss.

'You going ashore, Chips?' he had asked his friend.

'I'll get a later boat,' the carpenter had said. 'I want to check on those cattle pens before I leave. You stay close by the middies and keep your nose clean.'

As the day wore on, the sailors drifted back to the ship, the excesses of alcohol evidenced by the raised voices and singing from some of the boats. Though Guanabara Bay was as flat as any millpond, a few men swayed on the deck before heading down to the mess. For those incapable of standing upright, a bucket of seawater soon dampened their spirits. For a handful of others the threat of a dozen at the grating went unheeded and the marines were called to escort them below.

The following morning the sailing master rechecked the muster book.

'What's the situation, Mr Mundy?'

'Four men missing, Mr Parry.'

'Names and rates?'

'Guthrie and Bigalow. Both from Deal. Emile Lazlo – gunner's mate off the *Constantine*. And Percy Sparrow – ship's carpenter!'

'Chips?'

'Yes, sir.'

'You sure?'

'Yes, I checked. He's not come aboard.'

'The captain won't be pleased to hear that.'

Mr Mundy agreed. 'I presume his absence will not delay us sailing.'

'Indeed, Mr Mundy.'

At the frigate's painted belfry, the marine struck four bells.

'Prepare to weigh anchor, Captain?' Mr Parry asked.

Oliver nodded then looked across the bay to the busy town nestled along the coast. It was not the first time he had visited Rio de Janeiro, nor was it the first time he had left the place with a strange feeling of unease. For what reason he was not fully aware, but his impressions of the place were always the same. The town was set on a sheltered natural harbour offering ample fresh provisions and succulent tropical fruits. It was populated with wealthy merchants, rich plantation owners and Portuguese businessmen who lived in splendid houses furnished with imported pictures, mirrors and marble statues. The vast gardens abounded with water fountains, trimmed privet hedges and lush beds of brightly coloured exotic blooms. The local women were dark, luscious and as exotic as the native fruits and flowers.

Yet the wharves, streets, fields and gardens of the fine houses were agog with slaves – hundreds of men and women, boys and girls whose ankles bore the scars of shackles, marks engraved on their black leather skin during the months confined below decks in the transport ships. Then there was the dusty open market where the slaves were penned, paraded and sold in a fashion not unlike that of the cattle he had bought. Rio de Janiero was a place of such contrasts. It troubled him.

As the sun rose, the temperature rose quickly with it. It would easily reach ninety degrees that day though for the moment the heat on deck was tempered by a fine veil of moisture which encapsulated *Elusive* in a pocket of perfumed air. Lulled by the fragrant scent and the harmony of the African voices drifting from the wharf, Rio de Janeiro was beautiful beyond description but for Oliver Quintrell it masked a face of greed and corruption.

From the taffrail the captain was gazing at the spectacular granite cone to the south when a flock of black frigate birds flew in from the open ocean. He watched them glide across the sky, swooping and curling in the air; their beaks, wings and tails sleek and pointed, their iridescent plumage shining like polished jet in the sun. As they displayed their six-foot wingspan over the ship, the brilliant bloom of the male birds' throats shone scarlet as fresh blood. Looking back towards the clear Atlantic sky, Oliver questioned what the birds' presence foreshadowed. He was aware that they flew ahead of the weather fronts and that their return to land heralded a change in the wind.

'Weigh anchor if you please, Mr Parry. The sooner we are away from this place the better.'

'Aye aye, Captain. Anchor aweigh!'

The call echoed to the men on the capstan and with the first harmonious creaks, *Elusive* shook off her lethargy.

'Make sail!' Mr Parry called. 'Up staysails. Loose topsails.'

Aloft, a flurry of activity began along the yards and at the pin-rails sailors, working in unison, hauled rhythmically. As the frigate's anchor freed itself from the harbour floor and broke the surface, Will galloped up the companionway ladder three steps at a time, calling to his mates on deck.

'Has anyone seen Chips? I can't find him.'

'He'll be around,' Bungs whispered. 'Back to your station, Will.'

'Not till I find Percy. He's not in his workshop and I never saw him at breakfast.'

'Did he go ashore yesterday?' Froyle asked quietly.

'I'm not sure.'

'Don't worry yourself,' Bungs said. 'He'll be around somewhere. Have you tried the sick bay?'

'Not yet.'

'Maybe he got a dose of what that monkey was carrying,' Smithers whispered, and laughed.

'Loose the courses! Man the braces!' the lieutenant called.

'The ship mustn't sail!' Will shouted, running along the quarter-deck. 'Mr Parry, stop! You must wait! Mr Sparrow's not on board.'

'Be quiet, lad,' Bungs growled after him.

'No. I must tell the captain Chips isn't aboard.'

'Shut up, Will, the captain already knows.' But the cooper's warning came too late.

'Who's that questioning my orders?' Mr Parry yelled.

'It's me, Will Ethridge. Chips ain't aboard. Something's wrong.'

'Silence!'

'You must send a boat back to find him.'

'Marines, restrain that man and get him below. I will not tolerate insubordination.'

Before Will could utter another word, his arms were grabbed and a wooden peg was thrust between his teeth and secured with spun yarn.

'Take him below this instant.'

Working on the yards, the topmen had a bird's eye view as Will was dragged away gurgling and struggling while on the poop deck the captain turned to Mr Smith and spoke quietly.

'Search the ship. Make sure Chips isn't lying injured somewhere.'

The midshipman nodded and headed below just as the staysails filled and were sheeted home. The frigate was making her turn for the open sea when the jib flapped free, trailing a length of its sheet out on the breeze.

'Belay that line before it rips holes in the other sails!'

'It's broke, Mr Parry,' Froyle shouted.

'Then run it down! And pass word for the bosun.'

Resting their chests on the main yard, Smithers and five other sailors waited for the call to put a reef in the main course.

'Didn't I tell you,' he said sanctimoniously, 'that place was just the start of our bad run? You wait and see if I'm not right.'

The following morning, with the coast of South America visible only as a hazy scrawl on the horizon, eight bells rang from the ship's belfry and the men on charges were brought to the gratings for punishment.

With the frigate close-hauled and making ten knots, and in the presence of the whole ship's company, the charges were read and the punishments administered by the bosun's mates.

The three Irish seamen, charged with drunkenness, received a dozen lashes each and bore their punishment stoically and with little noise, and from the furrows of keloid scarring, it was evident that it was not the first time their backs had been opened by the knotted thongs.

But for Will Ethridge, this was a new experience, and as he was bound up his body shook with a combination of anguish, fear and anger.

'Sorry, Will,' the bosun's mate whispered through tightly clenched teeth, before swinging the cat and flaying the boy's soft flesh. For the crime of insubordination, Will received a dozen lashes and every man, whether he was observing or not, silently counted each stroke as it was delivered. When the punishment was over, Will was helped below.

Emile Lazlo, gunner's mate, was the last man to be bound up. He had returned to the ship at first light, being ferried out on a local fishing boat. When he had come aboard, he had pleaded for leniency, swearing he was not a deserter, and arguing that he had been set upon and robbed. From the bruises he bore it was obvious he had been in a fight, but unfortunately no one could verify his story.

On this occasion Captain Quintrell was lenient and did not punish him according to the charge of desertion as set out in the Articles of War. Instead, for disobeying orders and failing to return to the ship when ordered, Lazlo was relieved to receive only two dozen lashes. His sentence and punishment were entered in the muster book, but against the names of Guthrie and Bigalow, the two other men who had deserted, and that of Percy Sparrow, the letter 'R' was recorded along with the date that the men had run.

When Tom Masterton stepped down into the hold later that day and felt water wash over his feet, he was aghast. 'What have you been doing down here?' he shouted, shining the lantern over the water swilling about in the hull. 'Have you had the hoses going all night?'

'I swear I haven't used them once.'

'Then where's all this water come from?'

'I've been emptying the pee troughs like you told me but I guess them beasts was peeing quicker than I could empty it out.'

'Don't be bloody daft, man. That's seawater sloshing around your ankles.'

'Don't smell like bloody seawater to me.'

Tom shook his head. 'You've no more sense than a deck beam. Listen to the din them beasts are making. They've got more sense than you. An animal knows when things ain't right. Get up on deck right now. Find Mr Parry or the officer on watch and tell them to come down here. And be quick about it. Tell him we need the pumps. Tell him, if I'm not mistaken, the ship's sprung a leak and we're in danger of sinking!'

CHAPTER 13

The Ship's Hold

'Will Ethridge to see you, Capt'n.'

'Thank you, Casson. Send him in.'

Will appeared to shrink as he bowed his shoulders to stand beneath the deck beams.

'You are the sailor from the Solent, are you not?'

'William Ethridge. Apprentice to Master Adams at Buckler's Hard, sir,' he said with subdued pride.

'And I understand that until you came aboard *Elusive*, you had never sailed on a ship such as this.'

'That's right.'

'Yet from what I heard from Mr Sparrow. . . .'

Will's gaze dropped to the floor.

'I understand you had a certain bond with the carpenter.'

'Too right, sir.'

'And do you know any reason why he should fail to sail with us from Rio?'

'No, sir. Something must have went wrong. . . .' He was about to add more but the sting of the cat's tails still smarted on every breath he took prompting him to keep his mouth shut.

'Perhaps. I agree it seems strange that such a man should desert. However, what drives a man to disobey orders is a matter for his conscience alone to deal with, although I don't doubt that in time he will come to regret it. Now to the reason why I sent for you. When I last spoke with the carpenter he told me that in the short time you were assigned to him, you proved yourself to be a trusted hand, showed considerable skill in your craft and demonstrated you had a brain in your head. I might add those were Mr Sparrow's words, not mine.'

Will remembered Chips saying the exact same words to him.

'I have two reasons for wishing to speak with you. Firstly, I am rating you as carpenter's mate. Secondly, you will act as ship's carpenter for the present.'

Will looked puzzled.

'I realize there are two other rated carpenter's mates aboard, both with several years' service. However, in the last few days these men have failed to attend to the most basic tasks required of them and neither appear capable of preparing monthly accounts. I am hoping you will be able to succeed where the others did not.'

Will nodded. 'I'll do my best.'

'I can ask for nothing more. Now, that brings me to my third and most important point. I have just learned that the ship has taken water. Mr Parry has men standing by with the pumps but before I give the order for them to commence, I want you to sound the ship. I need to know the rate of seepage and the effect of the pumps. I presume you know where the well is?'

'Yes, sir.'

'Once you have ascertained the current level, find out where the seepage is coming from. Unless it is absolutely necessary, I have no desire to return to Rio. However, I do not wish to sail into the Southern Ocean if the hull is riddled with borers. Let us hope the damage is minimal and can be repaired at sea. As soon as you have news, report directly to me.'

Half an hour later Oliver was advised that the acting carpenter begged to request his urgent attention below decks. Without hesitation, he left his cabin and passed word for the first lieutenant to join him below. As the captain climbed down into the dimly lit hold, despite the noise of the cattle he could hear water sloshing about beneath him. The light of the swinging lanterns reflected on the dark oily surface.

'This is not good,' he said, stepping down and feeling the cold water washing over his shoes.

The three beasts bellowed a response.

Oliver sniffed the stinking air and looked up to his lieutenant gazing down from the hatch. 'Speak with cook. Arrange for these cattle to be slaughtered immediately.'

'Aye, aye, Captain.'

Will and the two other carpenters knuckled their sweat-streaked foreheads and stepped back from the piles of stones and pebbles they had been digging through.

'Over here, Captain,' Will said, pointing to a strip cleared of ballast. Though the water slapped back and forth with each pitch and roll of the ship, the evidence he had uncovered was not hard to see.

'A light,' Oliver said, examining the hull and the four wooden plugs protruding from it. He was puzzled.

'I plugged them,' Will said. 'They look like shot holes but I can tell they've been bored right through to the copper plates from this side.'

'Is it possible the sheathing slowed the flow a little?'

'A bit, maybe. I think because they were buried below the ballast it wasn't obvious that water was pouring in from them.'

'Are these the only holes?' the captain asked.

'Yes, sir. I've checked right around and couldn't find any others.'

Squatting on his haunches, Oliver ran his finger around one of the wooden plugs. 'Did you make these?'

'No, sir. I found them hidden amongst the stones. I'd say whoever drilled the holes made the bungs to fit, plugged the holes and then, when the time was right, pulled them out and shovelled the shingles over them so no one would see the water spurting in.'

'And when would you think that was done?'

'From the amount of water we've taken in and the size of the holes, I'd guess them bungs were pulled before we sailed from Rio.'

'And can you repair the damage at sea?'

'No trouble, Captain. I'll plug them up good and proper and seal them so tight you'll never know there were any holes there.'

'Good man,' Quintrell said, ignoring the water staining his white stocking. 'Set to it and keep me informed about the level.'

'Aye, sir.'

'Mr Parry, you may proceed with the pumps. If nothing else, let's hope this flush of seawater will reduce some of the stench down here.'

'It must have been the carpenter,' Simon Parry said. 'Everything points squarely in Sparrow's direction.'

The captain combed his finger through his hair. 'But from what I've heard about the man, this premeditated act seems totally out of character. I am not totally convinced. . . .'

'But the fact that the holes were made with an auger, and the fact that the carpenters were working in that area for over a week before the ship anchored, plus the fact Sparrow deserted in Rio. . . . If a court-martial was convened to consider the charges, those facts would provide sufficient evidence to send him to the gallows.'

'Um. But what if we were to discount the ship's carpenter, who else might we consider?'

'Are you suggesting there may be someone else aboard trying to prevent us from sailing south?'

Oliver nodded. 'It is something which concerns me. If Percy Sparrow was not the culprit then I fear the situation we are confronted with is far more sinister. We must consider the possibility that there is someone aboard who does not want this voyage to succeed. It is possible someone secreted themselves on board with the sole aim of sinking the ship and preventing us from reaching our destination.'

'But if I may say, Captain, no one, apart from you, knows the purpose of this voyage or where we are heading.'

'This is something I had assumed until very recently. However, in light of the present happenings, I have to question that premise. As you will know, until we reached the tropics and I opened my secret orders, I was unaware of our destination and even as we speak I am no wiser than you as to the manner of cargo we are to collect. Though I have followed my instructions and revealed our destination to no one, I am convinced that fact is not entirely unknown.' Oliver's brow furrowed and for a moment, he gazed at the red wine washing from one side of the crystal glass to the other.

'On the day we met at the Admiralty, the details of this voyage were discussed at length by several senior admirals and respected ministers of the government. Besides the admirals and dignitaries, there was also a clerk present who transcribed a record of the proceedings.' He sipped his drink. 'I am not accusing that young man, merely pointing out that spies can lurk in the least expected places.'

'I find it hard to consider such a sad state of affairs exists.'

'Nevertheless, when I vacated that interview room, I had no knowledge of the purpose of this cruise or our destination; however, I believe every man in that room was privy to that information.' Quintrell leaned back in his chair. 'Even now as we approach the Horn, I can only speculate. Perhaps we are to locate a treasure ship or retrieve a cache of gold and silver plundered from the ancient cities. If it is a foreign treasure we are seeking then the French, Spanish, Dutch or Americans would be keen to prevent us locating it and any one of them would be eager to claim it for themselves.'

'Indeed they would.'

'Remember the ship we saw off the Canary Isles? Was that perhaps the same ship we saw off Recife and again near Rio? Was its presence there by coincidence or by intention? Remember the lookout was unable to detect a flag. Is it possible we are being followed?'

'Is it also possible we have a spy on board *Elusive* at this very moment?'

'I have pondered on that possibility long and hard,' Oliver said. 'No. I believe our bird has already flown. I believe the holes in the hull were drilled well before we reached Rio and the bungs were pulled before we weighed. The perpetrator was hoping to scuttle the ship and did not want the damage to take effect until we were far from land.'

'So whoever it was jumped ship in Rio rather than chance staying aboard and being apprehended.'

'Yes, Mr Parry. I believe even the most loyal spy may baulk at the idea of forfeiting his own life when there is still chance to secure freedom. That is why we must consider other possible culprits apart from Mr Sparrow.'

Simon thought for a moment. 'The sailors picked up off Madeira.'

'But those men were off a merchant ship.'

'So they said, but their sinking could have been engineered. A ploy to get them on board *Elusive*.'

'Unlikely, I think. What of the crew from *Constantine*?'

'No. Those men were ferried up from Falmouth and conveyed straight on board. There was no obvious dissension or dissatisfaction amongst them. In fact, from being fish bait off the Lizard, most men were grateful to be alive and to be transferring to *Elusive*.'

'Did they have opportunity to make contact with anyone in Portsmouth?'

'No,' said the lieutenant.

'Did you allow women onboard before I came aboard?'

'Definitely not, sir.'

'And you said there were only a handful of marines guarding the ship and a few dockyard shipwrights finishing work below decks?'

Simon Parry nodded.

'And those men were working on board for several days without constant supervision. Is that correct?'

'I had forgotten about them. I suppose they had the opportunity.'

'Indeed they did.'

'Did any of those men sail with us?'

'No, sir.'

'Then, as we have excluded the men from the *Constantine*, we should consider the carpenters from the navy yard and the group of men you signed from the Hard, the men who assisted with the early victualling. They all had access to the hold and access to the shore via the lighters and ship's boats.'

'Yes, they did.'

'How many men did you sign on that first day?'

'Twenty-one.'

As he was thinking, the captain traced the number twenty-one on the table.

'Simon,' Oliver said, shifting uncomfortably in his seat, 'not more than four weeks ago, I reprimanded you for appearing familiar with members of the crew. That was my duty. Now I am countermanding my own orders because I feel it is necessary. Without jeopardizing your authority or the respect which the men show you, I ask that you speak intimately with those seamen. Sound them out and if any one of them raises your suspicions even in the slightest, refer the matter directly to me.'

'Yes, sir.'

'I see you are a man of discretion, Simon, and I rely on you to uncover any unrest simmering below decks. But I must ask that this matter remains one of confidentiality between us. Believe me, I fear this recent incident may be just the tip of our troubles. Who knows what will happen when we sail into the higher latitudes of the Southern Ocean.'

The barren coast of Patagonia dragged slowly by, mile upon mile of boring treeless plains, inhospitable low white cliffs speckled with rows of black cormorants, and beaches littered with sleeping seals which through a telescope's lens appeared like brown seashells scattered on the sand. A swarm of thousands of tiny white moths floating on the breeze was one of the few distractions. Considering the ship was miles from the coast, it was a talking point amongst those seamen who took an interest in nature. But it was a source of annoyance to those who had to swab the dead insects from the deck during the afternoon watch.

As *Elusive* sailed south, the days began to lengthen while at night the temperature dropped noticeably. One month after leaving Rio, *Elusive* neared the Strait of Magellan. Few of the men from the *Constantine* had sailed that far south before but those who had rounded the Horn argued about the route the frigate would take. Some were adamant that the strait offered an easy passage. Others argued the route taken by the great explorer was near impossible to get through, and that the western exit to the Pacific Ocean, with its myriad of islands, was a maritime maze to navigate. A few old salts preferred the challenge of Cape Horn. But for Captain Quintrell the question was irrelevant. He had his orders.

With the entrance to the strait behind them, word quickly passed around that they would soon be rounding the notorious Horn and with the winds gathering force, *Elusive* pitched and rolled even though she was still in the lee of the Land of Fire – the island of Tierra del Fuego.

Aloft, the topmen scanned the horizon, monitoring the rocky outcrops, the fragments of broken land – the tail end of the Andes mountain chain as it buried itself into the sea. Below deck, the men off watch waited, anticipating the call for all hands to be called to change course. On deck, the helmsman continually looked to the master who had been studying his navigational charts. From the fo'c'sle Mr Parry studied the bow waves while at the gunnels the topmastmen sat waiting for the captain to give the order to go aloft.

But the day wore on and no orders were given. *Elusive* crossed the fifty-sixth degree of latitude and maintained its southerly course, leaving the rocky outcrop of Cape Horn in its wake. The weather was good. They were at the point on the charts where the Atlantic and Pacific Oceans came to blows; where sailors could toil for a month attempting to sail west but manage only a few short miles and eventually be forced to turn back and circumnavigate the globe in order to reach the west coast of South America.

But with a fresh wind blowing from the west and her squares filled, the frigate sailed due south across the notorious Drake Passage, making an easy nine knots. On this occasion neither the winds nor the petulant oceans lived up to their reputations.

'Maintain your course, Mr Parry. Double the lookouts.'

'We are entering uncharted waters, Captain,' the sailing master commented.

'Thank you, Mr Mundy.' But Oliver Quintrell did not need reminding. He was well aware of that fact.

CHAPTER 14

The Island

'Whale off the larboard bow!'

On deck, all heads turned towards the dark shape which appeared to make its own response, venting a column of misty spray high into the air. Two other whales breached close by, splashing playfully alongside the frigate at a distance of less than fifty yards. From the deck the crew watched for a while till, one after the other, the great mammals sounded, creating barely a ripple as they dived beneath the surface.

'Land ho!' came the call from the cross-trees.

'Where away?'

'Four points off the starboard bow.'

Heads turned in the opposite direction; eyes peered into the haze trying to differentiate sea from sky and make sense of the cloudy shapes hovering on the water. Slowly an outline emerged from the mist. Lying less than a mile off the starboard beam was a floating island of ice. It was twice the height of the ship and twenty times its length, with waves creaming around its feet. An hour later another massive float was sighted and as the ship sailed deeper into the southern waters, sightings of ice became a regular occurrence.

'It's not them that's the danger,' Smithers said, turning up his collar against the bite of the wind. 'It's them that's under the sea with only the fingers of ice poking up that's the worry. It's said they've got sharp claws like the captain's hand and they're hidden beneath the surface ready to rip a hole in the bottom of any passing ship. I tell you they can slice through a hull as easy as a boat hook can split open a man's belly. You listen tonight when you're laid in your hammock – you'll hear them claws scratching on the hull trying to tear it open.'

'Enough of that talk, Smithers!' said Mr Tully, looking anxiously over the side. 'You'd best spend your energy using your eyes instead of your tongue. Keep it flapping the way it is and if we're lucky it'll freeze solid inside your open gob.'

It was a strange eerie night for those on watch who had to remain on deck. The watery mid-summer sun melding in the swirling mists dipped only briefly beneath the earth. Extra men had been posted as lookouts and the lead had been cast non-stop throughout the long light night. The cry, 'no bottom' was the monotonous call. But the growling sound of the ice floats scoring the hull's copper plates provided an uneasy night for those in their hammocks. Few sailors slept soundly as ice threatened to invade their vulnerable wooden world.

At ten o'clock the following morning, five days after leaving the Horn, solid land was sighted. An island. It was an uninspiring colourless sight. Black on white. White on black. Rising almost vertically from the grey sea, the mountain peaks dissolved into the grey sky like an illusion. The land mass was visible for a while then, almost in a flash, thick cloud enveloped it, obliterating it from view.

On the yards the topmastmen worked to reduce sail.

'It's bleeding cold!' Adam Froyle murmured, his frozen fingers struggling with the fastenings.

He got no reply.

'You reckon the captain knows where we're going? If we get frozen in here the ship'll be crushed to splinters and we're all dead men.'

'Shut your mouth,' said Wotton. 'I heard Mr Parry say Captain Cook sailed further south than this and he survived.'

From the poop deck, Oliver studied the snow-covered peaks through his telescope.

'What do you make of it, Mr Mundy?'

'Judging from here I'd guess its six hundred feet high and perhaps ten miles wide. That's definitely black rock where the snow hasn't settled. I'd say it's an island all right but it looks inhospitable.'

'And you have double-checked my calculations?'

The sailing master nodded.

'Then I believe this is the place.'

'But where do we make landfall? I can't see any beaches, just sheer rock faces and vertical sheets of ice hanging down into the water.'

'We must sail to its southern end.' Oliver studied the sketch in his hand. 'If it is the place we are looking for then we should find a break in the cliffs. Pass word for the lookouts to search for a cove, an inlet or a fjord.'

'Aye aye, Capt'n.'

With double reefings on the mains and topsails, progress was slow but Oliver knew that making haste in visibility of such a fickle nature would be foolhardy. As they skirted the long, dead-straight stretch on the eastern edge of the island, cloud descended over the snow-covered peaks leaving only a long low strip of unhospitable coastline visible.

On deck, Smithers tightened the muffler around his neck. 'I tell you, it's a fiendish place and if the weather comes in bad, we're doomed.'

'One more word from you, Smithers, and you'll find yourself in irons. Do you hear?'

'Aye, Mr Tully.'

No one spoke as the ship approached a point near the south-east tip of the island. They were within a cable-length of it.

'No closer please, Mr Parry.'

'No bottom!' the man on the lead called out.

'This island must rise straight up from the seabed.'

Suddenly, as if a dozen guns loaded with grapeshot had been fired into the ocean, the steely sea around them erupted, churning and splashing like a bubbling pot.

'Look at all the ducks,' old Jeremiah cried, pointing to the thrashing of hundreds of flippers and immature wings as they scurried from the frigate in an unsuccessful attempt to fly.

'They're not ducks, you blind fool, they're penguins!' Mr Tully said.

The old man scratched his head. 'Well, I'll be. Ain't never seen nowt like that afore. Must be thousands of them.'

'There! See the sea elephant after them. That's what stirred them up, not the ship.'

For a while the seamen gazed at the bubbling water. The air was cold but with the extra layer of slops' clothes issued to every man, some argued that the summer temperature of the southern latitudes was preferable to the freezing cold of the Baltic ports in midwinter. The addition of a layer of baize sewn into their jackets also provided extra insulation from the wind and weather.

In the distance, off the larboard beam, another black and white peak became visible, but the captain showed no interest in it.

'Deck there!'

Eyes turned to the topmast and then in the direction the lookout was pointing.

'What do you see?'

'A break in the cliffs.'

'How far distant?'

'Just beyond that black crag.'

'Steady as she goes, quartermaster. Sail by. Handsomely now.' From the poop deck Oliver and his officers were unable to see beyond the cliffs, which rose perpendicular to several hundred feet. The jagged rock faces were black as jet and sharp as fractured glass. They appeared impenetrable and totally inhospitable. Not a word was uttered on deck, the only sound the creaking of cold timber and the occasional rattle of running rigging.

The master shook his head as they rounded the craggy outcrop then cries erupted as everyone saw it at the same time. There was a chink in the mountain's armour – a way in. Not a bay or estuary or regular inlet, but an unnatural opening. It was as if a hundred broadsides had bombarded the island, blowing a giant hole in the towering walls and creating a channel of water which led into the heart of the mountain itself.

'How wide would you say, Mr Parry?'

'One hundred and fifty yards, perhaps two.'

'Aloft there! What do you see?'

Every man on deck looked to the mainmast to hear the words of the lookout.

'The ocean goes right in, Captain. And there's a great lake inside.'

'How much floating ice?'

'None as I can see. Looks clear and calm.'

'Do we venture in, Captain?' Mr Mundy quizzed.

'Not until I'm certain we are not going to run aground. It may look safe but, like the island itself, it may be deceptive. We must first ensure there is no bar across the entrance and that if we sail in there is sufficient water for us to go about.

'Mr Tully, lower the longboat. I want a good man in the bow with the lead. And once the boat is away, stand the ship off. We don't know the tides or currents in these waters and I don't want to get too close to those cliffs.'

'Aye aye, Captain.'

From the ship's deck the ocean around them appeared relatively calm. There were no white caps, only occasional splashes from seals and penguins. But when lowered onto the water, the longboat bounced like a cork. Aboard, the boat crew struggled with the oars. The water splashing on their faces stung like daggers of ice.

'No bottom!' was the cry from the first cast.

'Ease your oars,' Mr Tully called, as they glided between the cliffs.

'Five fathoms!'

'And a half four!' The man on the line looked to the lieutenant.

'Cast again!'

'Three.'

'What's below us?'

'Nothing on the lead. Must be rock.'

'Steady men! Keep casting.'

'Five fathoms.'

By now the boat was gliding easily over water which was noticeably calmer.

'No bottom.'

'Strange,' murmured the midshipman.

Once through the channel, the soundings continued. The longboat swam forward, entering the sheltered waters of a huge inland lagoon similar in shape though smaller than Guanabara Bay. On the starboard side was a naturally curved bay with a slate-grey beach. It was surrounded by black rocky cliffs and backed by steep dry rivers of shale. The silent crew gazed wide-eyed at their eerie surroundings.

'No further, coxswain,' Mr Tully advised. 'Take us back across that bar at the entrance and cast the lead again.'

'Aye aye, sir.'

The lonely call echoed in the still air as the boat returned through the break in the black cliffs. Astern, everything was calm. Ahead, waves and wind awaited them while *Elusive* rolled on the water, its sails luffing as it hove to.

'Five fathoms! Four fathoms! No bottom on this line!'

The coxswain shuddered.

Despite the mittens the men's hands were almost frozen when they came back on deck but the boat had to be swayed up and secured. Meanwhile the captain had the final decision to make before giving the order for the frigate to sail through the gap in the island's fortress-like walls.

'According to the lead, we have three fathoms at the shallowest point. We will sail in slowly and see what is waiting for us. Steady now.'

Mr Parry called the order, to wear the ship around on the open sea till the bowsprit was pointing directly towards the gap in the island's wall. But as *Elusive* approached the channel, an icy blast suddenly gusted from the south.

'Hold her steady as she goes.'

Mr Mundy looked worried. 'A storm blowing up?'

'We'll be safe once we are inside,' Oliver said.

'An ominous looking place.'

'Indeed.'

For a few seconds, as they sailed through the channel, it seemed as if the sand in the hourglass had stopped flowing. There was not a sound and on deck every man suddenly became conscious of his own heartbeat.

'It's like going through the gates of hell!' Smithers murmured. 'It's the devil's own lair in there, I'm telling you.'

No sooner had he spoken than the wind died completely. The sails luffed, flapped and fell, though the frigate continued drifting into the island's lagoon.

'No bottom,' was the last cry from the man on the lead-line.

Suddenly a grinding scrape sent a shudder vibrating along every inch of the ship's rigging. *Elusive* lurched forward and the men on deck automatically reached for the nearest handhold.

'The lead! What have you?' the captain called.

The seaman cast again. 'Eight fathoms,' the hand replied, shaking his head.

After checking from the gunnels on both sides, Oliver turned to his officers. 'Whatever we hit, I believe we have passed over it. Mr Tully, get the carpenter to sound the ship. Mr Parry, find some wind from somewhere and get us into shallow water if there is any. Helmsman, that bay to starboard looks a likely anchorage. Let us pray we make it.'

The deck burst into life. Men scrambled up the ratlines. Leather shoes clattered along the teak boards. Yards creaked as the braces hauled them around the masts. Orders were shouted. Repeated. Voices murmured. Oliver watched and waited. Then a light breeze blew across the sails. But it did not come through the break in the rocks as expected. It had blown down from the craggy peaks to the north.

'She's not badly damaged,' Will shouted from the hold to Mr Tully, who transferred the message to the captain. 'There's a leak but I can't quite get to it. I need Bungs to move some barrels before I can check it properly.'

The message was quickly relayed.

'Get some men below. As many as necessary. I want to know how much water we have taken and how quickly it's rising. And get men on the pumps. Smartly now.' Oliver turned to the quartermaster on the helm. 'Is the rudder answering?'

'Aye capt'n, it is.'

He nodded. 'Let's hope the keel is intact also.'

As the frigate neared the slate-grey beach, the man on the lead announced the consistency of the seabed: 'Shale and cinders, Capt'n.'

'Prepare to drop anchor, Mr Parry.'

The order was relayed along the ship and as they sailed into the semi-circular bay, Oliver gazed in awe across the immense lagoon beyond, completely enclosed within a circle of mountain peaks. 'This place is like a giant teacup with a crack down one side. And we have just sailed into it.'

'An interesting allusion, if I may say, sir.'

'Well, Mr Parry, I am pleased to advise that we have successfully reached our destination. Now let us hope that when the time comes we are able to leave it in one piece.'

As he spoke Will Ethridge's head appeared from the waist and Oliver beckoned him onto the quarter-deck. He wanted the acting carpenter to deliver his findings personally.

'I think the damage is minimal, Captain.'

'That is truly remarkable, considering the effect it had.'

'If we're lucky, sir. Probably just scratched the copper but I'll have to go over the side to check it properly.'

'That may not be possible. This water will freeze your blood in a matter of minutes.'

The frigate was closing on the beach.

'Strike all sails!'

'Five fathoms. Ash and cinder,' called the man on the line.

Silence reigned.

'And a half four.'

'We are almost on the beach, sir,' the sailing master prompted.

'Thank you, Mr Mundy. I can see that.'

As the anchor splashed from the bow, the ship's forward momentum was slowed, not by the iron pick but by the sand and cinders beneath its hull.

'That's it. We're done for,' said Smithers. 'Stuck like a severed head on a stake.'

'Mr Smith. Take that man below and clap him in irons. And one word from any other man and he will be left to freeze at the gratings.' Oliver turned to his sailing master. 'I do not think we will sink while we are resting on a bed of cinders.'

The duty marine struck eight bells and the men who had been on watch hurried below. After the second dog watch, only a handful of men were required for harbour duty. Before night fell, stoves were lit on the decks and in the waist of the ship in an effort to combat the cold but the radiated heat was insufficient to prevent the water in the drinking butt from turning to a solid block of ice.

CHAPTER 15

Secret Orders

With the hearty meal warming their stomachs and a flush of wine glowing in their cheeks, the officers seated round the captain's table relaxed. Excusing himself for a moment, the captain retrieved a vellum pouch from his desk drawer, and returned to his seat. Taking out the four folded sheets of paper, he read through them. The conversation died as the company waited for him to speak.

'Gentlemen, it is time for me to share some information with you. When we sailed from Portsmouth I never expected to be arriving in a place such as this. Only when I opened these orders was I provided with our current bearing along with this rough sketch.' He laid a pen-and-ink drawing on the table. Its simple lines traced the outline of a horseshoe-shaped island, its arms almost pinched together. One by one the officers examined it. 'I think you will all agree we have arrived at the correct location.'

A patter of applause ran around the table.

'I now understand why I was instructed to proceed without delay. It was essential for us to arrive here in the middle of the southern summer as this mild weather' – he smiled – 'will not last very long.'

The party responded in good spirits.

'You will be interested to learn that this particular island is not charted on any modern map yet ironically its location has probably been known for many years. It is likely it was sighted by Portuguese explorers back in the 1500s and by a convoy of Chinese traders at an even earlier date. And it is believed the island was rediscovered more recently by whalers navigating Drake Passage. For various reasons, however, no one has made an attempt to chart it or claim it. Needless to say, we have arrived here almost intact and no doubt you are all wondering what is in store for us. I cannot answer that question categorically. I can state, however, that we are here to pick up a cargo, but the nature of the cargo has not been divulged to me in these papers and from the wording of my orders I am not sure that even the sea lords have that information.'

'Intriguing,' said Mr Mundy. 'May I ask what they do know?'

'They believe the French are aware of a treasure trove hidden somewhere in the Southern Ocean, but not of its actual location. What the nature of this treasure is remains a mystery. It may be booty from a privateer's plunder or a frozen storehouse belonging to Dutch traders. Perhaps if I read the closing statement it may help answer your question.

'*Napoleon Bonaparte intends to extend his campaign in Europe. In consequence, the Spanish government is being pressured to meet its outstanding dues to France. In Britain, the burden of debt from the recent naval war is only partially being met by collection of the unpopular income tax. At this point in time any treasure which can be honourably plundered and returned safely will be fortuitous indeed. Your voyage is of vital importance. Succeed and England will be forever in your debt.*'

'The likelihood of a knighthood, sir?' the lieutenant added, with a grin.

'I think not, Simon. Our first goal is to find this elusive cargo. But if we fail to solve the mystery of this treasure hunt, I can guarantee on our return to England we will receive a welcome far chillier than the present outside temperature.'

Mr Mundy screwed his nose. 'Looking for treasure in a place like this could be like searching for a needle which has slipped into a hayrick.'

'And a frozen hayrick at that!'

The officers laughed and drained their glasses.

The captain did not share their hilarity. 'I know much of what I have told you is pure conjecture but what is certain is that this inhospitable place holds something of value and we have been sent here to find it. My thought is that we are searching for a ship, probably Spanish, blown off course as it rounded the Horn. Perchance the vessel found its way into this *harbour* but never got out again.'

The realization, that they too might be stuck in this isolated place wiped the smiles from the officer's faces.

The captain continued. 'However, when we sailed into this island, the lookouts saw no other ship or wreck.'

'Perhaps it sank,' said Mr Nightingale.

'But before it went down its cargo was off loaded and buried,' added Mr Tully.

'It is possible. Any other ideas?'

Mr Parry spoke tentatively. 'Perhaps these mountains contain veins of gold or pockets of gemstones. It is likely we would not see that from here.'

'A good suggestion. I will consider that when I explore.'

'Anything else, anyone?'

'A building maybe?' said Mr Hazzlewood. 'Perhaps there are men living here?'

The captain shook his head. 'This place is too inhospitable for anyone to survive for more than a few weeks. You are forgetting, Mr H, it is now mid-summer. In winter this lagoon will be locked solid with ice.' He looked to the other midshipmen at the table.

'There are seals and whales. Maybe there are walruses or polar bears. Perhaps this is a graveyard for horns and ivory. Perhaps there is a cache of skins.'

'Thank you, Mr Smith, but I think the Guinea coast supplies enough ivory from its trade in elephant tusks and I cannot imagine the Admiralty sending one of His Majesty's frigates to these regions to retrieve a boatload of fur skins.' He paused. 'Gentlemen, if there are no more suggestions, I am inclined to favour a ship. Hopefully tomorrow we will find one resting in a bay hidden from view. However, I must accept Mr Nightingale's suggestion. If a ship was anchored here and sprang a leak, it would have quickly disappeared into the depths.' He cast his eyes around the table at the concerned faces. 'Think hard, gentlemen. Our time is limited. Mr Mundy,' he said, turning to the sailing master, 'in the morning you will take one of the boats and re-check the bar across the entrance. It is possible that what the frigate grazed was neither reef nor sandbar but a single pinnacle of rock hidden beneath the surface.'

The sailing master nodded.

'If that is the case, I need its exact position and its distance from the cliffs. We cannot afford to make contact with it when we sail out.'

'Aye aye, sir.'

'Mr H, when you leave here you will organize a canopy to be rigged over the waist. Get the sail-maker and bosun to assist you.'

The oldest midshipman, recently rated as acting third lieutenant, acknowledged.

'In the morning I will first ascertain what repairs to the hull are necessary. Then I will take a boat and circle the lagoon. I estimate it to be about fifteen miles in circumference and it may take some time to explore. Mr Parry, I want you to personally monitor the tides. I must know the exact level of the high and low and the specific times. In the meantime, I rely on every man to keep his eyes and ears open. I fear our job will not be easy.'

The officers nodded.

'Gentlemen,' he said, lifting his glass. 'I trust you will sleep soundly tonight as tomorrow our work begins. But first a toast. To a treasure hunt extraordinaire!'

'A treasure hunt extraordinaire!'

The smell of fried kippers hung in the air as Oliver lavished the remains of the greengage jam on his toast.

'More coffee, Simon?'

'No, thank you, that was quite sufficient.'

Pushing his plate aside, Oliver drained his cup.

'What is the present mood of the men?'

'As unpredictable as the weather in these parts,' Mr Parry said.

'What concerns them?'

'I can speak only from what I observe. I have overheard some hands discussing the voyage but when their voices turn to whispers, I know their chatter is up to no good. A few of the crew are weighed down with the events which occurred at Rio; a handful fear the ship is harbouring a spy. However, since the ship hit the bar every man shares the same worries. Now they fear for their lives. The word is about that no one can survive in these latitudes and these worries reflect badly on their temperament.'

'One thing we cannot afford is dissent.'

'I agree.'

'Then you may tell the men that our latitude is close to sixty-two degrees south. That we have not crossed the Antarctic Circle. Tell them that James Cook's *Resolution* ventured to seventy-one degrees south in his search for the Great South Land and that the ship which carried Nelson to the Arctic as a midshipman crossed latitude eighty-one degrees north.'

The junior officers exchanged surprised glances.

'And you should remind the rumour-mongers that Cook lost no men to ice or frostbite or lack of provisions. In the meantime we must try to occupy their minds. That may help raise their spirits. Reassure the crew that they will not starve, nor will they go thirsty. There is water aplenty and the melted ice will be far fresher than the water in the casks. I suggest you set some men on melting some ice today.'

As Captain Quintrell and Lieutenant Parry stepped out onto the quarter-deck, the smell of their breakfast followed them. Eight bells sounded but the crew did not appear with their hammocks as was customary. It was thought the canvas would freeze hard in the deck netting and when taken below in the evening would carry the cold air into the body of the ship.

The longboat was already in the water and Mr Mundy's boat crew was pushing off to investigate the bar at the entrance. The cutter, which the captain planned to use, had also been swayed over the side and was resting almost motionless on the shallow water. With the sun in those southern latitudes above the horizon for almost twenty-four hours, it was unlikely to get dark but a lamp was fastened to the stern post as a precaution against sudden fog. The coxswain and boat crew were already aboard and Mr Nightingale was sitting in the stern sheets.

After the captain had taken his seat, a small chest containing his navigational equipment was lowered together with a lead-line. With no wind, the sail was not raised and the oars were manned.

As the boat made its way around the inland lake, the scenery changed dramatically. First, sheer cliffs sheeted in ice – once white, now grey, streaked and patterned with criss-cross lines like torn lace curtains layered with soot. Next came broad blackened beaches and slurries of ash running into the bay. High on the peaks, which encircled the inland sea, a white glacier gouged a giant path down the mountainside and where it stopped, translucent blue caverns glowed within the crumple of ice. On flat shelves of rock near the water's edge, elephant seals lazed unperturbed, the bulls grunting occasionally for the attention of a female. The only other sounds were the slap of the oars, the creak of the rowlocks, and the voice of the man on the line with his monotonous call, 'No bottom!'

'I hope you can swim,' Jo Foss said. 'It's bloody deep!'

'Then keep your mind to your oars unless you're eager for a cold wet grave,' said the coxswain. 'Beg pardon, Capt'n. Might I ask what are we looking for?'

'Anything unusual, Wotton. A habitation. A suitable harbour.

Another ship. Anything apart from this infernal rock and ice.'

'Whalers, perhaps. Plenty of seals and whales, I reckon,' Foss said.

'Any whaler would be crazy to come here, if you asked me,' said a whispered voice from amidships.

'No one asked you!' the coxswain growled. 'Keep a look out, men – flotsam, submerged wreckage or anything unusual.'

With more than a dozen pairs of eyes scanning the internal walls of the island, the boat swam around the inland sea in an anti-clockwise direction, maintaining approximately thirty yards distance from the shore.

'Who made that stink?' said Jeremiah to the man sitting next to him. 'Phew!'

'That stink,' said Oliver, halting the boat for a moment, 'is sulphur, and if you look to larboard you'll see where it is coming from. Over there!' He pointed with his mittened finger. 'See that patch of yellowish green on the dusty grey surface? If you watch, you will see a stream of air being puffed out of it.'

'It's like the blowhole of a whale,' Jo Foss commented.

'What you smell is coming from deep under the ground.'

'I've never seen a rock fart before!'

The men seated near him laughed.

'Silence, men,' the coxswain called. 'Concentrate!'

As the boat slid across the water, Mr Nightingale, who was handy with a pencil, sketched a pile of ugly angular black blocks which ran down from the peak like a solidified river, ending in a tumbled promontory which extended into the water from the cinder shore.

Oliver studied the formations made by once-molten lava but did not share his knowledge with the crew. 'Keep well clear of those rocks. I fear they will be quite sharp!'

'This is an evil place!'

No one answered Jeremiah's words, but most of the boat crew heard them and no one disagreed. The sailors rowed on. By now they were three-quarters of the way around the lagoon.

'Smoke, Captain!' the coxswain called. 'Dead ahead.'

Oliver had already noted the apparent mist rising from the water. 'Wotton, take us around those columns of vapour and run the boat up onto the beach behind it.'

'Aye aye, Capt'n,' he said, swinging the rudder hard over.

Once they were a little closer, Quintrell removed his mitten and ran the tip of his finger in the water. It was as he had thought – the water was warm.

Jo Foss, the first to jump ashore, was shocked. 'The water's hot, Captain.'

'Indeed it is.'

With the boat dragged up on the ashen shore, the men were happy to paddle in the shallows and warm their red, chapped hands.

Oliver scanned the beach. It was the longest they had encountered so far. It was soft yet crisp underfoot but not soggy. Nor did it appear to be underlaid with jagged rocks. It rose gently from the lagoon to a plateau of rock which from the water's edge looked like a ledge or long, flat wall. It extended for several hundred yards and was an ideal resting place for a colony of seals, but for the present, only a few were in residence. At the back of the ledge, large rounded boulders, the colour and outward appearance of pumice, lined the base of a vertical cliff. Their orderliness gave the impression they had been washed up or placed there as a makeshift sea wall or barricade. Yet the tide did not reach that height. The captain looked quizzically at them and instructed his midshipman to make a sketch of the area.

'Do you see something in particular, Captain?'

'I'm not sure what I see, Mr Nightingale.'

A reconnoitre of the area confirmed what Oliver had initially thought. This cove was far preferable to the one they were in. The shallow waters would make an ideal anchorage, the vapour in the air was heated and the warm water offered the opportunity for a volunteer to dive below and investigate the damage to the hull. It was also possible that the hot springs would heat the ship inside and make the southerly conditions more tolerable. He smiled to himself. After many weeks at sea, a warm bath would be most acceptable.

'We shall return to *Elusive* and when the wind comes up, sail her over here.'

No sooner had he spoken than a freezing wind, blasting in through the crack in the island, hit them.

'Coxswain, get the men aboard. We must return to the ship immediately.'

'Aye, Capt'n.'

Though the frigate soon came in sight as they rowed across the huge lake, progress was slow. The surface was stirred by the bitterly dry wind and there was no shelter for the men. With the boat beating almost directly into it and with the spume breaking over the bow, the return journey was wet and exceedingly cold. Stepping back on board *Elusive* was a relief to every man, including the captain.

That evening excited voices were raised in the mess. The sailors listened as the captain's boat crew told tales of sky-blue ice, smoking water, farting rocks and a cove warm enough to bathe in.

CHAPTER 16

Floating Gold

News of the hot springs at the other side of the crater-lake was enough to change the mood of the crew and, when all hands were piped up the following morning, the men were eager to work. With the tide at its highest point, the boats were lowered. Their purpose was to haul the ship stern-first from the grey cinder beach and out into deeper water. Oliver had hoped for a convenient draft of wind to back the sails but there was little breeze and the zephyrs which shifted constantly gave no assistance. He wondered what the force of the wind was outside the island's mountainous protective walls. That was something he would concern himself with later.

Though it was cold, the sun glowed from a hazy sky and the crews in the boats were soon sweating under their double and sometimes triple layer of slops' clothing. It was an arduous job man-hauling a vessel the size of a frigate, but once the bow was released from the cinder beach, *Elusive* slid smoothly back on the silky water to a round of huzzahs from the sailors huddled on deck.

'Would you compare this to the Arctic, Mr Parry?' Oliver asked.

'I'd say it is very similar though I have never encountered anything quite like this place. At first glance its features look the same, yet when you study the place, it has so many different facets. There is a stark beauty about this isolation.'

'An interesting comment.'

'Pardon me for asking, sir, but if this land is uncharted should it not be claimed for England as Cook did with the Pacific Islands?'

'That is a question I must ask when we return to England but for the present the island's location must remain a secret.'

'But the log. That will record our position.'

'It will indeed!'

Oliver wondered as he gazed to the peaks rising to the north of the bay, to ice-covered black cliffs criss-crossed with deep scratches and to ghostly patterns gouged across them like etchings on a giant lithograph. This place was too inhospitable for any country to bother laying claim to it, and it was certainly not worth fighting sea battles over. The only people who would venture here in future would be the whalers. He felt sure of that.

Once the men and the boats were back on deck, they made sail. The helm was put hard over, the yards braced around, the topsails fluttered and finally filled and *Elusive* headed out across the water, swimming as slowly and gracefully as a swan on an English canal and creating even less wake.

From the gunnels, the sailors gazed in awe at the rim of mountains which surrounded the lake and little was said. Partway across the lagoon, snow started falling. At first the large flakes reminded Oliver of the thousands of white-winged moths which had drifted across the frigate off the coast of Argentina. A strange phenomenon, he had thought. But as the snow continued and settled on the men's felt hats, it brought memories of Cornwall. How unexpected and fortuitous that snowstorm had been. Drifts a foot deep. Tracks unrecognizable. The house guests stranded – unable to leave. Brushing a snowflake from the end of his nose, he thought of Susanna. How gently she had dusted them from his hair. Without the snow he would never have met her.

Now England was far far away and that wintry weekend was a very long time ago.

'Anyone would think you'd never seen a bit of snow before!' he shouted. 'Sweep it up before it melts and turns to ice! And you there, get some sand for the deck. Jump to it!'

For a moment the topsails fluttered, like a bird bathing its wing, then the breeze freshened again, filling the canvas and carrying them towards the western shore. A murmur of excitement ran around the deck when the ship neared the cove and the columns of steam came into view.

'Take her in, Mr Parry. As close as you can. When the tide goes out I want her nose in the sand.'

'Aye aye, Captain. Strike the topsails! Make ready to drop anchor!'

Mid-afternoon all hands were piped on deck and Captain Quintrell addressed the ship's company.

'Men, I want to thank you for your efforts and despite the cold I believe we should all thank the Lord for our safe deliverance to this place.'

As he opened his Bible, the soles of several buckled shoes shuffled uncomfortably on the decking.

'I shall read from Psalm 107:

They that go down to the sea in ships, that do business in great waters;
These see the works of the Lord, and his wonders in the deep, For he commandeth and raiseth the storm wind, which lifteth up the waves thereof.
They reel to and fro, and struggle like a drunken man, and are at their wit's end. Then they cry unto the Lord in their trouble, and he bringeth them out of their distress.
He maketh the storm a calm, so that the waves thereof are still. Then are they glad because they are quiet; so he bringeth them to their desired haven.

Oliver closed the Bible, looked at his shivering crew and repeated the final words. '. . . so he bringeth them to their desired haven.' He paused and looked around. 'I am sure you will all be pleased to learn that we have been brought safely to our desired haven and we will be going no further south. As you are probably aware, Captain James Cook sailed into higher latitudes than this, but he chose to sail in a Whitby cat – a coal carrier – not in one of His Majesty's frigates. Cook was indeed a discerning man and I admire his prudence. If only we were in a vessel which would sit upright on the sand without heeling over! Be that as it may, *Elusive* is not a flat-bottomed collier but she is now in a suitable situation where we will be able to inspect and repair any damage which the hull has sustained. I can assure you all, when we leave this place we will have a sound ship which will carry us home to England.'

Voices mumbled in recognition. A few cheered.

'I can assure you that our stay in this location will be brief – no longer than is necessary to make the repairs. In the meantime, I advise you to stay active and keep warm. When you are not working you have permission to go ashore and walk the beaches at will. A game of cricket, perhaps? Our enemy here is not the French or Spanish, pirates or privateers. Our enemy is the cold. Any man with fingers or toes which tingle should report to the surgeon. There is warm water aplenty to restore life to dead limbs and I will tolerate no cases of frostbite. This evening there will be a double serving of pork for every man. And I believe cook has managed to produce a considerable number of fruit puddings which I am sure you have been able to smell. In case you are not aware, today is Christmas Day and we are blessed with snow. Perhaps it will remind you of England.

'Let us pray that in due course we will return safely to our loved ones and that within a few months *Elusive* will be sailing into Portsmouth Harbour. I wish you all a merry Christmas.'

'Merry Christmas,' was echoed loudly in response.

'I had forgotten,' Simon said, as the men crowded around the main companionway to go below.

'I had not. If we had had a chaplain on board, I would have asked him to deliver the reading.'

Simon Parry nodded. 'I am sure there are those amongst the men whose spirits are raised by the Bible.'

'But would you not agree that for most the raised spirit will come from an extra tot of rum and not from the scriptures?'

'I am sure you are right.'

'Simon, would you join me for dinner later? And extend an invitation to Mr Mundy, Mr Hazzlewood and the other officers. An opportunity to raise our own spirits, do you not agree?'

Though his lips were dry and lacked their unusual rosy colour, the lieutenant smiled. 'This whole island is an active volcano, isn't it?'

'Indeed it is. In a way it reminds me of a trek I once made to the top of an old volcano in Italy. Though it was not as massive as this island, the crater resembled this place in shape and I can remember gazing down into the centre and seeing puffs of steam and smelling its offensive sulphurous fumes. However, that volcano was sitting on the land and this one is sitting on the sea bed. What we see here is only the tip of a gigantic cone which was blown apart many years ago.'

'I don't think the men are aware we are inside a volcano.'

'Then I suggest you do not tell them.'

Will Ethridge did not need to be ordered to examine the ship's hull. He had spent half his working life regarding ships from beneath the keel and was only too happy to volunteer. He'd helped lay the keelson in several ships, watched ribs rise and added the layers of planking which provided a ship with its protection for over forty years.

145

'You know what to look for?' the captain asked.

Will nodded.

'Be quick about it then. Don't dilly-dally below!'

The acting carpenter was eager to dive under despite the warnings about sea creatures, currents and temperature. Casting the blanket from his shoulders, he climbed nimbly down the ladder on the port side. As he descended, the rope secured around his waist was fed out by a sailor on the deck.

'It's mighty chilly,' he called, as he dipped his stockinged foot into the water.

'Take care,' old Jeremiah shouted.

When he first slid under the water his white shirt was visible but as soon as he dived down the brown water swallowed him up.

'Hold fast that line! Don't lose him!' the captain yelled.

After what seemed like an incredibly long time, Will emerged, gulped the cold air in short sharp gasps, then dived again.

The fifth time he came up was near the bow. 'It's here!' he gasped, knocking on the side of the ship.

'Mark that spot on the gunnel,' Mr Parry shouted. 'And come aboard before you freeze.'

Though he was in the water for only a matter of minutes, when Will surfaced his lips were blue and his heart was racing. As he struggled to climb back on board, his legs and arms shook and his teeth chattered involuntarily. One blanket was quickly thrown around his shoulders and another swung over his head.

'Get him below immediately,' Oliver ordered. 'When he is dressed and warm ask him to report to my cabin. Not before. Mr Parry, would you join me, please.'

'Come in, Will. Sit down and explain the situation.' The captain offered him a glass of burgundy but Will refused.

'We've shed a couple of copper plates, Capt'n, and one's hanging like an old farm gate. Apart from that there are only two planks which have suffered a minor mischief. Looks to me like whatever we hit was sharp cos it's gouged a single line along the side of the hull for about three yards.'

'Do the timbers need replacing?'

'No, I don't think so. There's some surface splintering but not enough to worry about. The reason the water's coming in is that a length of caulking has been completely scooped out. It's opened the joint and it's letting water seep through.'

'Can it be fixed under water?'

'I think so. It really needs planing and recaulking. But I can smooth it down with a chisel and then I'll caulk it up real tight though I'll not be able to get any hot pitch over it. Once that's done, I'll fix that copper plate in place and she'll be as good as new.'

'Are you sure that will seal it?'

'When I'm finished, Captain, it'll get us back to England with no problems.'

'But can you do the job under water?'

Will nodded. 'Apart from the pitch.'

'What about the temperature?'

'It's strange down there. Like jumping from a hot tub into one of ice. There's streams of hot water running through the cold.'

'Then what if we move the ship a little closer to the steaming pools?'

'Best test it first – it could prove a mite too hot.'

'What do you think, Mr Parry?'

'Sounds reasonable and I wish I could help but I admit I do not swim. But I'm sure amongst the *Constantine*'s crew there are a few swimmers – otherwise they would not be with us today.'

'Are you sure that is the only damage, Will?'

'Yes, Captain. I checked the hull from bow to stern and right down to the keel. That's all I could find and the starboard side is untouched.'

'Excellent!' Oliver said. 'Mr Parry, select half a dozen men to take turns to go down with the carpenter. I insist you do not go down alone, Will. And the bosun will rig a cradle of netting for you to work on. The cooper will heat up a pitch kettle for what it is worth. And pass word to the purser to make sure there are plenty of dry clothes and blankets for the hands who are working below. And an extra tot of rum for each of them when they are finished.' Satisfied that he had considered everything, Oliver leaned back in his chair. 'Then I believe that is settled and the work can begin tomorrow. Mr Parry will be in charge.'

Will thanked the captain and made his obedience to the officers as he left.

Waiting until the door had closed, Oliver spoke. 'I want lookouts posted port and starboard and a good man in the rigging. We don't want another man falling prey to a shark or a hungry elephant seal!'

On deck the smell of the pitch kettle was preferable to the sulphurous odours which at times drifted across the bay.

'Did you find anything, sir?' the lieutenant asked, as the captain climbed aboard from the longboat.

'Nothing, Mr Parry. That is the fourth consecutive morning I have circled the whole lagoon and I am beginning to fear that we shall be leaving this island without achieving our objective.' He sighed. 'Whatever cargo was supposedly here has been hidden, buried in the ash or removed before our arrival.'

'Or it is sitting at the bottom of these moody waters.'

Oliver sighed and rubbed his hands together. 'We have been lucky, the weather has been kind, but the days are ticking by and we cannot stay much longer without risking both the ship and the health of the men.'

'Morale has improved these last few days,' Mr Parry said. 'I think the men are getting used to it.'

'And how go the repairs?'

'The work is finished and the hold is dry. There is a stagnant smell in the ballast which will create an unhealthy atmosphere but there will be no means of airing it until we are in warmer latitudes.'

'The carpenter and his team are to be congratulated.'

'I will pass that message on.' Simon paused before putting his next question. 'As no treasure trove has been discovered, will we sail without it?'

Oliver sucked in a long breath of cold air. 'Today is Saturday, and it is the first day of a new year. Tomorrow the crew will be allowed time to relax a little, then if the weather is fair we will sail on Monday, but we must have the full of the tide and a favourable wind to take us out.'

'Aye aye, Captain.'

Oliver watched his lieutenant as he strode along the deck. He was satisfied. The Admiralty had selected well. Then he turned and looked across the body of water which he was beginning to know intimately. The surface of the enclosed lake shone like quicksilver with the sun reflecting on it.

Standing for a moment, he recollected his first officer's words: 'There is a stark beauty in this isolated place.' Oliver agreed. In his opinion there was no other place on earth quite like it.

Suddenly the ship shuddered as if it was about the keel over. But *Elusive* was not alone. The island had felt it too and for a moment the whole surface of the inland sea shivered.

'What have you got in the bag, Jeremiah?'

'Whale's teeth that's all.'

'Let me look,' the midshipman said, turning his nose up at the smell.

'Capt'n said we was to keep active, so I took myself on a walk and found a dead whale. I prized some of the teeth from the jaw bone. It's just for my scrimshaw. Folks back home will pay a shilling or two for my carvings.'

'All right, so long as you wash them before you take them below. And keep quiet about them. I don't want every man on your watch carting a sackful of rotten teeth into the mess.'

Overnight the beach turned white. It was Sunday, the second morning of 1803 and the crew arose to find half an inch of snow covering everything. Since breakfast, however, the fall had stopped and the sun was shining from a clear blue sky. With more leisure time than usual and fresh snow to amuse themselves with, several of the young foremast-jacks were having a snowball fight on the shore. From their laughter and antics they might well have been on a village common, not stuck in the crater of a volcano on the bottom of the world.

Wandering through the snow, the captain was pleased to hear the merry voices. It rekindled childhood memories. Leaning down, he picked up what appeared to be a ready-made snowball. Roughly rounded, it fitted snugly in the palm of his left hand. He examined it and scratched it with his claw-like finger. It released a strong musky smell. He recognized it. There was nothing else on earth quite like it!

Spinning around, he stared at the shelf of rock at the base of the cliff.

'My God! Why didn't I see it before? Mr Parry! Mr Parry!' he shouted.

The games stopped and the seamen looked at their captain, wondering what was amiss.

Simon raced across the beach towards him. 'What is it, sir?'

Oliver pointed towards the cliff. 'It's been sitting there all this time, right in front of our eyes. See over there! Those boulders!'

The lieutenant looked, as did the other men nearby. 'What am I looking at?'

'Those snow-covered lumps of rock, the rounded ones lined up along the ledge.'

'What of them, sir.'

'It's ambergris, Mr Parry! Floating gold! Call it what you will. If I am not mistaken every one of those boulders is a solid lump of ambergris and, if that is the case, they are worth more than a king's ransom!'

CHAPTER 17

Ambergris

First mention of the word ambergris attracted the attention of the sailors like bees to a honey pot, and from the beach the message was quickly relayed to the frigate. The seamen on board who had served on East Indiamen were familiar with its fragrance and its uses in making fine perfumes and pomades. But no one had previously seen it or held the valuable product and all were anxious for a closer look. Two seamen who had worked on whaling ships boasted their knowledge, but even for them the reeking cheesy content they had raked from the stomach of a harpooned whale was a far cry from the crusty grey object the captain was cradling.

Oliver regarded the small sample, turning it in his hand and assessing its weight, the same surprised expression still fixed on his face. 'I thought it was a ball of snow coloured with ash. Then I thought perhaps a piece of pumice.' He turned to his first lieutenant. 'What a damn fool I was! How could I not recognize it for what it really is?'

Simon followed him as he clambered up onto the ledge and walked eagerly along the line of boulders, touching some, shaking his head at others and gazing in awe at the sheer quantity of the cache.

'So much of it,' he said.

'But how did it accumulate here, Captain? Could it have floated into this inland lake?'

'Highly unlikely. There are very few beaches in the world where clusters of ambergris have been found. Usually it is in tropical waters and most often only a solitary lump is washed up. Unless it is broken apart to reveal its aroma, it may never be recognized. Single pieces are sometimes seen floating in the sea and often they are no bigger than this.'

'But we haven't seen a whale in the lagoon itself. Do you think this collection of ambergris just floated in? But if so, how is it the pieces are neatly aligned along this ledge? Were they washed up on a flood tide, perhaps?'

'I think not. I believe this precious commodity has been collected over many years and stored here. For what reason I would not hazard a guess. This is an uncharted island which no ship would choose to visit unless blown badly off course but someone obviously knows of it and has visited here many times. I think this location has purposely been kept secret, as indeed I have been instructed to keep its exact location a secret.'

'Then who holds the key to this treasure trove? Whalers? Privateers? The Dutch East India Company?'

Oliver thought of the trading ships, of the wealthy merchants and of the value they put on their exotic spices. But ambergris was different. 'It is an unprocurable product,' he said. 'It cannot be grown in the ground, picked from a branch or squeezed from a flower stem or pod. It comes from the foul-smelling excrement vomited from the stomach of a sickly whale. Once in the sea it changes in consistency and appearance. Rolled by the waves and currents, it is moulded into roughly rounded balls. Slowly its outer crust hardens while its soap-like centre becomes soft and waxy, concentrating its unmistakable aromatic perfume.'

The lieutenant sniffed a sample. 'And in that state it wanders the oceans until it is washed ashore or plucked from the water?'

'Correct,' said Oliver, his mind leaping ahead. He had heard that an ounce of ambergris would fetch a golden guinea. Yet here, before their eyes, were scores of great boulders, some weighing almost one hundred pounds. This quantity would fill the frigate's hold and if it could be worth about £1 million.

'My guess is that the Spanish are the bankers and the last thing they want is for this valuable treasure to fall into the hands of the French. You must realize, Simon, to the Turks and the French, ambergris is prized more highly than common gold.'

'Then it has a very apt name – floating gold!'

'Indeed.'

As they strode back along the ledge, the captain broke a piece from one of the blocks. Immediately the distinctive smell pervaded the cold air. It brought back a flood of long-forgotten memories. A privateer. A battle. A prize. Then the satisfaction of acknowledgement. That action had earned him promotion to post captain not to mention a full column in the *Gazette*. Was it the success of that cruise which had prompted the Admiralty to select him to command this voyage?

But what stuck in his mind from that past event was not the sea battle, the boarding, the condition of the ship or the handsome prize money he received, but the overpowering perfume which the ship emitted. It was unmistakable.

On the voyage home the loose pieces of ambergris, which he had transferred to his ship, had rubbed together, releasing the distinctive odour, and over the weeks at sea the smell had permeated every plank and joint of the ship. The muskiness had even invaded his skin sufficient for his wife to comment on it when he returned to the Isle of Wight. Yet the amount of ambergris in that cargo was miniscule compared to the vast hoard lined up on this rocky ledge.

Oliver wondered how he could carry this quantity back to England without the smell being detected by every passing ship.

By now a crowd of inquisitive sailors was gathered at a polite distance.

'Mr Parry, it will be impossible to post a guard on the beach overnight. Any man would freeze standing out here. I suggest you get the crew back on board and tell the marines to make sure that no one leaves the ship without my permission. Once word of the ambergris is passed around it will be no time before the men start helping themselves, breaking it up and secreting lumps in their pockets or under their hats. After two hundred pairs of hands have sampled it, we will find ourselves left with nothing but sweepings.'

By the time the captain and Mr Parry climbed back on board, news of the find was being talked about round every table in the mess. Those men who knew little about its properties learned quickly, but what most excited the seamen's attention were the tales of its inestimable value.

That night, despite the posting of marine guards, the precautions, and the direct orders, two sailors slipped overboard and braved the freezing waters to swim ashore. After loading their pockets and canvas bags, the pair set off swimming back to the ship.

As they neared the hull and were almost within reach of the rope dangling from the side, one of the men let out a blood-curdling scream. It broke the silence of the night.

Seamen muffled in blankets and scarves crept up from the mess. Mr

Tully, who was officer of the watch, leaned over the gunnels. 'Get him out of the water before he freezes!'

As they hauled the sailor from the water and dragged him onto the deck, his body appeared red and mottled. Someone commented that the water dripping from him was still warm.'

'It's the devil's own cauldron,' he gasped. 'I was near boiled alive!'

'Were you alone?' the midshipman asked.

The seaman's teeth started chattering but he didn't answer.

'You'll be in for it when Captain Quintrell hears.'

'What you got there?' Mr Tully said, wrenching the handmade bag from the man's hand.

'That's mine. I made it.'

'And what you got in it?'

'Nothing.'

The midshipman reached his hand inside and was surprised. The man was right. The bag contained nothing but a distinctive smell.

'Didn't get what you went for, eh?'

The sailor looked confused. 'Give it here,' he said, pulling himself free from the man holding him. 'Where is it?'

'You idiot! Don't you know ambergris melts in boiling water?'

The sailors huddled nearby laughed.

'Get him below! Get him some dry clothes, and then put him in irons.'

The following morning six men set out in the small boat to retrieve the body of the other seaman. It had been spotted bobbing in the shallows beneath the columns of steam.

When they reached the floating corpse, the coxswain tested the temperature of the water before reaching in and grabbing the man's wrist to drag him aboard. But the hand parted from the arm like a bone slipping from a lump of meat in a well-cooked mutton stew.

'He's been boiled alive!' he cried.

The starboard oarsman in the bow leaned over the side and returned his breakfast to the tepid sea.

'Fools!' shouted Oliver. 'I fail to understand why some sailors are such fools. They are brave beyond measure, they withstand the extremes of temperature, heat and cold, and they accept the discipline meted out at the gratings without complaint, but one whiff of ambergris and two of them go crazy.' Oliver shook his head. 'It's as potent to these foremast-jacks as the smell of a woman's purse and God knows, after weeks at sea, every man amongst them is festering to have a woman's legs wrapped around him.'

Mr Parry looked concerned. 'I'll double the guard at the gunnels tonight, sir, but even after this, it's not going to be easy keeping the men's hands off the stuff and returning home without some being pilfered.'

'I agree and I have been giving that matter considerable thought. The sooner it is loaded the better. Pass the work for the carpenter and cooper, if you please. Tomorrow you will take a party around the lake. You will need some good workers on board. Supply them with cutlasses, dirks, galley knives, anything sharp. And you will need sacks or bags or sheets of sailcloth. I want you to cut some grass.'

'Grass?' Simon laughed.

The captain's expression was serious. 'It will prevent the blocks from chaffing.'

'But where do we find grass here?'

'There is grass. Tussock grass. I have seen it. You will find it growing in a cove across the island. I will draw you a rough map. Take the longboat and tow the small handmade dingy behind it. When you locate the vegetation, cut as much as you can. Fill the bags and boat and return with it as soon as possible. I intend to pack it around the ambergris. We must handle it like the finest Waterford crystal. I don't want the French or Spanish or even English pirates getting wind of what we are carrying.'

The next day, Monday, came and went and *Elusive* did not sail as had been planned. Nor did Mr Parry and the longboat venture across the lagoon in search of vegetation. It was the same on Tuesday and Wednesday as the howling blizzard kept everyone confined below decks. There was not even a marine guard posted but neither was one necessary, no one was foolish enough even to stick his nose out into the wind. Blowing from the south, the wind channelled directly through the chink in the mountain's armour and swept across the water, whipping the erstwhile lifeless lake into a smouldering maelstrom. Wind and waves lashed across the lagoon, rocking the ship and threatening to lay it over on its side. Oliver held grave fears that if the ship was forced up on the cinder beach and heeled over, it would be impossible to either right it or float it off.

With the wind came sleet, shooting icy darts at anyone in its path.

After ripping the canopy which protected the waist of the ship to shreds, the tattered remnants were pulled down and all attempts to replace it were aborted. Below decks the mood was black and as the truth about their volatile location became known, the men grew increasingly unsettled. Some argued that the worsening weather was aggravating the volcano itself. Fear was that if the island seethed, its submarine activity would increase. The officers remained positive, reassuring the hands that the wind had blown the ship around on its anchor and set it closer to the steaming springs, providing some form of heat. The men were sceptical. Initially the warmth felt through the hull was welcomed until a rumour spread that the hull could easily catch fire.

This poppycock was the least of the captain's worries but, in turn, he did not want to lay the ship directly over the hot currents. He was not sure what effect the heat and poisonous gases would have on the copper sheaths and the fact that the paint was beginning to peel from the hull below the gun ports worried him considerably. But any attempt to move the ship until the blizzard passed would have been foolhardy, if not entirely impossible. Oliver knew there was little he could do. Like the crew, he must bide his time and be patient.

Thursday morning brought calm and the crew emerged from below to walk the deck and see what effect the bad weather had had. It was now almost two weeks since they entered the lagoon and everyone was becoming anxious to get away. The sight of the sun lifted the men's spirits. Although low on the horizon, it shone clearly from an azure sky. The colour reflected on the lagoon, which was as placid as a tropical atoll. It was as though the previous three days had never happened. Only the snow-capped mountainous walls surrounding them reminded *Elusive*'s crew where they were. Those remained unchanged – layer upon layer of dense white ice plastered haphazardly over angular and precipitous black rocks. Black and white. Completely colourless.

'Mr Mundy. Now it is fine, I want you to take a couple of fit men. I need you to reconnoitre the ridge near the entrance. Be very wary of the jagged rocks and keep well clear of the scree. I do not wish to lose any more good men.'

'Begging your pardon, Captain, but we could row to the entrance and glimpse the ocean beyond.'

'I realize that, but I need to know what the conditions are outside this unnatural enclave. Beside the sea, the wind, the weather, I want to know what else is visible – ice islands, solid islands, whales, seals? I need to be aware of any moving currents or partly submerged rocks – anything that might prove a potential danger to the ship.' He rubbed the whiskery stubble on his chin. 'While we are here we are cocooned in a false cloak of security. We are like prisoners in the Round Tower whose only world exists within the confines of its stout circular walls – like condemned men who have no idea of what is happening in the outside world.'

CHAPTER 18

Grass

It was a busy day, as noisy and industrious as an average workday at any dock or shipyard on the coast of England. *Elusive*'s deck took on the appearance of a carpenter's workshop, as every spare plank, box, empty barrel, butt and cask was hoisted to the quarter-deck to be converted into a container to hold the ambergris. Will, the carpenters' mates and any man who could handle a hammer were busy constructing wooden crates while the gunner and his mates scrubbed out the empty barrels which had contained salted pork or beef.

The crew were aware of the captain's instructions that the cargo had to be handled carefully and packed correctly. 'If the ambergris chafes it will crumble and fall to pieces. Each piece must be packed individually,' he had said.

On board there were no regular watches and everyone worked the same hours as the idlers.

The sail-maker, who had been up since early, was sitting with a team of men in the waist, finishing a batch of sailcloth sacks. Nearby a brazier burned fiercely, fanned by the prevailing steely wind. The blacksmith's hammer resounded in rhythmic bursts on the anvil as he bent or straightened hoops according to requirements. Nails, latches and hinges were all carefully forged.

From the fo'c'sle came the buzz of a dozen saws, as lengths of deal were cut to construct crates of various sizes. The beehive of activity extended to the bowels of the ship where the cooper and his mates were busy rearranging the stores to make space for the additional cargo; making sure that the cargo's bulk and weight was evenly distributed throughout the frigate's hold.

While work proceeded on deck, the longboat ferried men back and forth to the shore. The task of removing the boulders of ambergris from the ledge had commenced early, the sailors wearing shoes and extra stockings to protect their feet from the sharp cinders and hot vents on the beach through which the earth belched its sulphurous breath. The purser and bosun were made responsible for the ferry transport while the captain observed all aspects of the work from the quarter-deck.

As the ambergris was collected, the smaller lumps were placed in baskets like ostrich eggs. These were then delivered onboard and presented with the solemnity of chapel offerings at harvest festival. From the rock ledge, the larger lumps were lowered down and rolled to the water's edge avoiding the hazardous holes. From there they were placed into hemp netting and lifted manually into the boat. Meanwhile, two of the ship's boys ran back and forth like rabbits, picking up any broken pieces and tossing them into bags to ensure none of the fragments were left in the path of the rising tide for fear they might float away.

The objective was to maintain the integrity of the largest blocks wherever possible but such was the size of some they had to be sawn with a pitsaw before being transported to the ship. The strong musky fragrance of the floating gold hung heavily over the beach. It would certainly announce to any passing ship the nature of the cargo they were carrying.

Despite the fact he could see the shore activity from the deck, Oliver made two trips to the beach to satisfy himself that the loading was proceeding as he had specified.

'It is not only important for us to stay afloat on our return journey, but it is essential that we are not apprehended. This scent can be recognized far quicker than a farmer can sniff a dog-fox sneaking into his yard.'

The largest pieces of ambergris were hoisted on *Elusive*'s deck with considerable care and laid out along the quarter-deck in rows, like casualties of battle awaiting committal to the deep. Each consignment was treated with the reverence one would afford a corpse, and the work was conducted in silence.

From the rigging the bosun's mates watched Mr Mundy and his boat crew heading back to the bay where *Elusive* had first anchored. After a while they were but a blot on the water and once the boat had turned into the broad bay they were completely lost from view. Everyone knew that their climb to the top of the cliffs would be both difficult and dangerous and all prayed that the weather remained favourable.

As the job of loading the ambergris progressed, the cutter, carrying Mr Parry and his party, set sail towing in its wake the wooden boat which Will had constructed on Buckler's Hard. In it was an assortment of canvas sacks, knives and cutlasses. The distance across the lagoon was several miles.

With the rough map to refer to, Simon Parry identified some of the obvious landmarks as he searched for the patch of grass the captain had identified on his previous exploration. But as the cutter drew closer to the inhospitable shore, what he found was a broad river of solidified lava decked with the overnight sprinkle of snow. Ahead on the mountain's wall a glacier hung in ominous stillness but from its base the only streams emerging were flows of rocky grey moraine. Forlorn eyes gazed at the formidable landscape, wondering if the captain's eyes had deceived him. There was not a single blade of grass or bush, in fact no life at all. It truly was a godforsaken place.

While Mr Parry studied the scenery his thoughts drifted along a similar vein, though he was loathe to admit it, even to himself. Perhaps Captain Quintrell had seen a patch of moss or lichen. Perhaps the combination of sun and cold misty air had refracted the light, swathing the earth in a coat of dappled green, creating an illusion.

'Over there, coxswain. Take us into that sheltered bay in the lee of the mountains!'

As the cutter rounded the next headland, the wind dropped and the boat glided forward.

'It's there, dead ahead!' the lieutenant shouted gleefully. Almost unbelieving, the men stared at the patches of grass. It was not the soft sappy variety which is welcomed each spring in the English meadows, but a coarse, short, grey-green tussock variety, strong enough to cut a man's hands if he attempted to break it. They were prepared. The cutlasses and knives would make satisfactory sickles and scythes.

Once ashore, everyone worked, cutting, hacking and packing – stuffing the short tufts into the sacks the sail-maker had manufactured. It proved a fine way to counteract the chill. As each sack was filled, it was loaded into the boat till the small craft was packed to the gunnels. The remaining sacks were squeezed into the cutter till there was barely room for the men's legs. But when they sailed out from the lee of the headland and were caught by the icy wind, no one complained about the bundles which acted as insulation. Crouching low, with arms wrapped around themselves, the crew closed their eyes and prayed the journey back across the lagoon would be over quickly.

As soon as the boat returned from the harvesting expedition, the job of lining the containers with a protective layer of matting began.

'Looks like a bleeding manger,' one of the sailors jeered. 'All we need now is the sheep!'

'And frankincense and myrrh.'

'And what about the wise men?'

'Not many of them around here. In fact, anyone would say we're all damned potty being in this place!'

'Quiet there, Smithers. Keep your mind on the task!'

The work progressed methodically. The largest lumps of ambergris were laid carefully in the crates with fistfuls of grass stuffed around them. A valuable lamp or clock or heirloom could not have been more painstakingly packed were it to be transported by wagon across the potholed roads of Portsmouth.

After satisfying a final inspection by one of the officers, the lid of each crate was nailed down, the barrels sealed by the cooper, and the containers lowered into their rightful positions in the hold.

All hands worked feverishly throughout the day and no man shirked his duties. Perhaps it was the thought of the valuable cargo which excited them. But whether the crew realized it or not, this was no prize of war and not a single man aboard, including the captain, would see a penny of profit for their labour. A few men toyed with the idea of secreting pieces into their sea chests, or layering it in their shoes, hats and pockets, but if they were caught with any ambergris in their possession they would be charged with stealing, a crime punishable by hanging. Nevertheless the men worked with no complaint, their only reward an extra tot of rum at the end of each working day.

While the deck fires continued to burn and the hourglass announced it was night-time, daylight remained as the men gathered in the mess. With the sound of laughter and music it was hard to imagine *Elusive* was anchored in the most unforgiving corner of the globe.

It was just after midnight when a freezing squall hit the ship, heeling it over and forcing it up on the shore.

Despite previously checking the shallows for submerged rocks, no one knew what dangers were hidden beneath the cinder beach. The consequences of being holed again would be devastating but there was little anyone could do. Men were sent aloft to lower the yards in an attempt to prevent the frigate being driven any further, and for the next two days *Elusive* sat out the subsequent blizzards, laying at a perilous angle hard against the shore, shrouded in several inches of fresh snow. From the rigging, icicles up to a foot long pointed like daggers at anyone brave enough to walk the deck below. The only signs of life on board were from smoke coiling up from the galley chimney and from the larboard gun ports which were opened occasionally for the sailors to relieve themselves as best they could.

But the cloud which covered the ship was not from the sickening atmosphere. By now, the thrill of finding the floating gold had dissolved and any positive energy which had been generated while loading the cargo had melted as quickly as ambergris in boiling water.

Expressions were as dark as the scree on the cliffs, words as sharp as the jagged headlands, hearts as cold as the outside air. And as the days slipped by, hopes dwindled while apprehensions rose. The crew feared that the wooden ship would be their coffin. That if they got off the shore they would never make it across the lake. That if they reached the entrance the keel would be clawed apart by the unseen finger of rock lurking somewhere beneath its surface. That out on the ocean the patched hull would burst open and *Elusive* would sink. They feared crossing Drake Passage. It had been kind to them on the outward voyage, but they feared it would make them pay on their return to the Horn. Finally they feared that if they crossed the Atlantic without being becalmed or dying of thirst, there was still chance they would be set upon by pirates and sunk along with their cargo.

But the crew of His Majesty's frigate *Elusive* did not need to stretch their imagination any further. On the morning of the fourth day the sun shone. The icicles melted and the seamen resumed their watches, blissfully unaware that their worst fears were still to be realized.

CHAPTER 19

The Barrel

The southerly blizzard, which had blown for three days and turned the ship into a snow-castle, had died during the night and, as if in answer to the captain's prayers, a mild morning breeze was blowing from the north-east almost exactly as he would have wished. Providing it held, it would carry the ship from the island and back to a world of human habitation.

Stepping on deck, Oliver screwed his eyes to the glaring whiteness all around. His nose twitched like that of a hunting dog. 'Dear God, what is that smell?'

He sniffed again. The disgusting odour carried on the chilly air was not from the sulphurous fumes coughed up from the earth's crust. Nor was it from the volcanic dust which the wind occasionally whisked around the crater walls like flour in a pudding basin.

As he stepped up to the poop deck, he was greeted by the sailing master. 'Good morning, Capt'n.'

'Morning, Mr Mundy.' Oliver tried to sound agreeable but he felt mildly annoyed. Apart from the offensive smell, he had slept too long and he had pondered over his coffee unnecessarily and should have been on deck at least half an hour earlier. Already the ship was alive. The decks had been swabbed of snow. The rows of stalactite-like icicles had been fractured from the yards and tossed overboard – save for those which had slipped from the sailors' wet fingers. From his cabin he had heard the cries 'Deck there!' delivered simultaneously as the ice daggers struck the deck, shattering into hundreds of glassy pieces. He had not been amused.

With the crew back to their regular watches, the junior officers were busy with their own divisions. They acknowledged the captain as he paced the deck before returning to the con.

'Morning, Captain. A beautiful day.'

Oliver reluctantly agreed with his lieutenant. The sight of the sun in a clear sky was welcome in more ways than one. The barometer had risen dramatically. The air was already several degrees above freezing point. And the temperature was still rising.

Along with the temperature, the men's spirits had soared noticeably. For the first time in days the sailors were emerging from below deck like rabbits on the common venturing from a frozen warren. Aloft, the topmast men scurried through the rigging, bare hands happy to renew contact with the ratlines. The occasional burst of song and the sound of laughter was music to the officers' ears.

High overhead a solitary albatross glided by, its colours reflecting those of the island, black on white.

'The sun surely does make a difference,' he admitted. 'Apart from that diabolical smell.' Scanning the ashen beach, he noticed the line of human excrement which had blown from the ship and been washed up with each succeeding tide.

Mr Parry distracted his attention. 'Yonder beyond the point is a dead whale. Been there some time, I gather. Probably the sun is causing it to rot.'

Oliver thought for a moment. 'Speak with old Jeremiah. Mr Tully told me he collected some whale's teeth. Ask him if the seals and skuas have left any fat on the carcass. If so, I want Bible-sized pieces of blubber – any whaler on board will know what I mean.'

The lieutenant raised his eyebrows. 'The flesh could be foul.'

'Well, it may be,' Oliver said, considering the smell. 'Strange, is it not, that a whale produces a substance used to create the finest perfumes, yet once beached, it smells worse than a dozen dead cats in an attic?'

'Indeed.'

'However, the decomposition of the fat is not a concern, though no doubt the men will baulk at the fetid odour. Hopefully the flesh will still be frozen, in which case it will be less offensive. I suggest you make ready a boat and take my crew. But first tell the cooper to find another dozen large barrels.'

Simon acknowledged the order without questioning, allowing only the slightest puzzled look to cross his face. 'Barrels of blubber,' he repeated. 'And if we find none, would the flesh from some seals do the trick?'

Oliver nodded. 'You will attend to that as soon as possible. If the wind holds, all that remains here is to extricate ourselves from this beach and proceed across the lagoon. I intend to drop anchor in the sheltered bay adjacent to the entrance. We will remain there overnight and if all is well, the following day we will bid this island farewell.'

'I pray the wind holds.'

'Amen to that.'

Within minutes a boat was swayed out and lowered onto the silver-grey inland sea. In the waist the cooper scratched his head when more containers were requested. Every spare barrel and hoop had already been used for packing the cargo.

'I can break open some stores,' Bungs explained, 'or take out some of the ambergris and re-use those butts.'

'Open new stores,' Mr Parry said. 'Speak with cook. Ask him what he can use but be quick about it. Tell him he must store the food in the galley or even in cauldrons on deck. There is little chance of the food rotting in the near-freezing temperature. Quick as you can, man. There is no time to lose.'

'Aye aye, sir.' the cooper mumbled, as he descended the ladder into the hold. He knew that neither the purser nor the cook would be happy.

For the frigate, it was the first time in several days that the topmastmen had been aloft. But they were eager to sail home and with a flat sea and no immediate urgency, their work was done carefully and to the satisfaction of the captain of the top. Water dripped like rain onto the deck below as the frozen sails finally thawed.

By the time Mr Parry and the boat crew returned, a line of empty barrels was awaiting them on the quarter-deck. The cooper grumbled as he returned once again to the hold in an effort to try to procure more containers. There were scowls too from the hands at the thought of manhandling the layers of part-decomposed, part-frozen blubber packed into the bottom of the longboat. It was a morbid prospect.

'Mr Tully, help get that stuff aboard and be quick smart about it.' The captain was anxious not to lose the wind. 'And you there, Mr Smith, stop shivering! When the blubber's on deck get the slime swabbed from the longboat while it's still on the water. I don't want this deck swimming in grease or water and turning into a frozen duck pond.'

'Aye, Capt'n.'

'Bungs! Where's Bungs?' Oliver called.

'Here, sir,' the cooper answered, poking his head from the companionway leading down to the waist.

'When those barrels are filled with blubber, top them up with seawater and seal them. Then I want space made on the fo'c'sle to store them. And make sure they are well secured. Have you got enough men?'

'Beg pardon, sir.'

'I asked if you had enough men.'

'Aye, sir but. . . .'

'What is it, Bungs? We don't have all day.'

'Permission to toss this one over the side, sir? Most of the brine must have seeped out.' He pointed to a barrel set aside. 'By the smell of it, the meat's gone rotten. Just as well it's part-frozen or the stink would have been worse than the whale's.'

'Belay that, Bungs. We can't afford to forfeit a barrel. If it's holed I'm sure you can use the spare staves. As to the foul smell, you should be used to it by now. Besides, we will be underway as soon as this job is done.' There was no time to attend to it now. 'Leave it aside for the moment and concentrate on the job in hand.'

Though the week's work transporting and packing the ambergris had been conducted in a spirit of reasonably good humour, the work on the blubber again brought out the worst in the men. They were all aware that the fatty substance smeared over their jumpers and jackets carried a fetid smell which would stay with them for weeks and months. On deck there was an unspoken feeling of disgust.

Eventually, when all the available barrels were filled and sealed, Captain Quintrell turned to the cooper. 'You can empty that barrel now, Bungs. If it is as rotten as you say then I suggest you dig out the rotten meat. Tell cook to help you. You have permission to throw the contents overboard then scrub the container quickly and douse it with vinegar.'

The cooper nodded while the sailors stood around waiting for it to be made available.

As the lid was lifted from cask *389 Pork*, the men pinched their noses.

'Phew! That pongs!' said Masterton, the man who had a fondness for the smell of cattle.

The cook appeared from the galley, disgruntled and inadequately dressed for the cold. He was armed with a large copper ladle and the fork which was last used on deck as the trident carried by King Neptune.

Handing the fork to the cooper, he moved closer to the burning brazier and held his apron over his mouth.

'Get back, you men, unless you want to get splashed!' the midshipman ordered.

Bungs' expression was none too happy. It was obvious from his face that he believed the barrel should have been forfeited, and disgorging the rotten contents should have been the responsibility of the cook. But there was no point in arguing about it.

'Come along, Bungs! Look lively or we will all freeze.'

Once the lid was off, the cooper dug the long fork deep inside. What he retrieved was the ragged remains of two part-decomposed rats. Holding them out at arm's length, like crumpets on a toasting fork, he screwed up his face.

'How did they get in there?' the coxswain asked.

'Is that what the Navy Board is feeding us now?'

'Stinks worse than the bleeding volcano!'

'A bad egg would be sweet as a rose in comparison!'

'Silence, you men!' shouted Mr Tully. 'Or it'll be served up for your supper!'

Keeping the rodents at arm's length, Bungs flicked them over the side and into the sea. Closing his eyes and nose to the barrel's contents, he plunged the fork in again. This time a piece of bone became lodged between the tines. Dripping with necrotic slime, it had strips of putrefied flesh dangling from it.

'Get that overboard, for God's sake!' Mr Parry ordered.

The next thrust stuck fast.

'Come on, Bungs!' Mr Tully was conscious the captain was watching. 'It can't be so difficult.'

With his hand covering his mouth, Bungs leaned over the barrel and stabbed the fork in yet again. As it came free, splashing his face with brown fluid, he noticed something strange hooked on one of the prongs.

Bending forward, he peered inside.

'Aagh!' he blubbered, the wind carrying a stream of vomit from his mouth.

Smithers jeered. 'Got a delicate belly, have you, Bungs?'

'What is it, Bungs?' Mr Parry called.

The cooper's legs had collapsed beneath him. He was down on the deck on his hands and knees, shaking his head, saliva dribbling from his mouth and tears dripping from his eyes.

'Speak, man! what is it?'
'If I'm not mistaken, I think I've found Mr Sparrow!'

CHAPTER 20

Burial at Sea

On deck the earthly remains of Percy Sparrow, still coffined in the ship's barrel, were draped with the union flag. When the longboat was thoroughly cleaned of blubber and when all the preparations were complete, the officers and crew of *Elusive* were piped on deck. As the company assembled, there was no noise save for the shuffle of feet and a few whispered words spoken between shipmates.

No one looked at the barrel when the burial service commenced; the seamen's eyes remained fixed on the deck. They did not even chance a glance at each other.

Oliver Quintrell's voice was soft but clear when he delivered the service. On this occasion every man was listening.

After speaking the words 'being turned into corruption', the captain paused. In his mind, he considered that the carpenter's remains were perhaps the foulest corruption he had ever seen. He did not linger over the remainder of the ritual and once the verbal formalities were completed, the flag was slipped from the barrel and it was swayed out in a sling of hemp netting and lowered to the bow of the longboat.

As the boat glided over the shimmering pocked-pewter surface of the lagoon, the whole crew lined *Elusive*'s deck and watched in silence. Three hundred yards from the ship, the boat crew shipped their oars and the cooper carefully loosened the barrel's lid. Sliding the oak cask gently along the thwart, Bungs, Will Ethridge and Tom Masterton tilted it towards the water and with a gentle push cast it from the boat. A plume of water shot five feet in the air when it hit the surface and the boat's bow reared in response, almost tipping two of the unprepared oarsmen off their balance.

Mr Sparrow's curved oak coffin bobbed once then went straight down. With a loosened lid and the addition of eight twelve-pound cannon balls, it was guaranteed to sink to the bottom of the volcano's vent – however deep that might be.

An ear-splitting shot from one of *Elusive's* twenty-four-pound carronades shattered the silence and few men on deck were able to hold back their tears.

Mr Parry was distraught. 'What fiend did this? This is murder most foul. Why was such an inoffensive man as Mr Sparrow subjected to such an horrendous act?'

'I thought we had left this problem behind us,' Oliver said. 'But now it raises its ugly head again and this time uglier than ever.'

The lieutenant shook his head in disbelief.

'Now we know it was not the carpenter who drilled the holes in the hull. But who?'

'Someone with access to his tools?' Mr Parry added. 'Perhaps the same person who killed him tried to scuttle the ship.'

'I think Chips was killed because he was in the way.'

'Or perhaps he saw something he was not supposed to see.'

'Or sadly, was just in the wrong place at the wrong time.'

'Will Ethridge was certain Mr Sparrow had stayed on board in Rio to finish the pens when the others had gone ashore.'

'A high price to pay for duty!' Oliver concluded, leaning forward in his chair. 'How are the men taking this?'

'Very hard indeed, sir. Percy Sparrow was a very popular man. He would happily have a yarn with anyone. No one disliked him and as far as I know he had no enemies.'

'But I understand that he and the cooper used to argue, and that on more than one occasion Bungs had threatened him.'

'His mess mates assure me it was just playful banter with not a grain of malice in it. They say the two warrant officers were the best of mates. It seems they had served together for several years.'

'But Bungs, being cooper, was responsible for moving the barrels. He was handy with an auger. He could put a plug in anything. And he could seal a barrel as tight as a drum.'

'After adding half a dozen live rats?' The captain stated, as he raked his hair. 'Good God, who would do such an unspeakable thing, and why?'

'Perhaps he thought the rats would consume the carcass.'

'And they partially succeeded though I'm surprised the putrefaction didn't kill them first.'

'I only hope Sparrow was dead when he was put in.'

'The alternative is too awful to consider.'

For a moment there was silence as, without wishing to, the pair visualized the scene.

'So, Simon, we have arrived at the conclusion that the cooper had the skill, the strength and the motive, if you class the mess threats as serious.'

'But if Bungs had known that his mate had been stuffed in a barrel, he would not have been prepared to open it on deck.'

'But he didn't want to open it. He wanted to toss it over the side.'

'A good way of getting rid of the evidence.'

'But you saw the way the man wept on deck.'

'I did indeed.' Parry nodded with a sigh. 'Those were not the tears of a guilty man. They were tears a man sheds for a lost brother.'

'I will speak with our cooper, but somehow I don't think he is our culprit.'

Casson interrupted the conversation to clear the plates from the table while the captain and Mr Parry mulled over the question.

'But who else do we have as a suspect?' asked Simon.

'What about Will Ethridge, the young shipwright?'

'I don't consider him to have any reason.'

Oliver shrugged. 'With Sparrow out of the way, I rated him as acting carpenter. That is a rapid rise in ranking for a man with less than a few weeks' service on board ship, would you not agree?'

'Indeed,' said Simon, 'but Will does not strike me as having an ounce of evil in him. He is neither ambitious nor jealous and I cannot see that he would, or could, do such a dastardly deed. Besides, if he related well to anyone aboard, it was to the carpenter. From the day we plucked him from the Solent, Mr Sparrow took the lad under his wing and looked after him. To watch the pair together and listen to them talk, you would have taken them for father and son. Murder is no way to repay a friend and mentor. And the lad was so inconsolable when Sparrow's remains were found, the surgeon had to administer a draft of laudanum to calm him down.'

'Where does that leave us, then?'

The lieutenant thought for a moment. 'When we sailed from Brazil, three men were marked absent in the muster book. There was Guthrie, an ungrateful fellow who we rescued from the wreck in the Atlantic.'

'Such are the thanks we receive.'

'The second was Thomas Bigalow. The pair were mates and were often seen on deck together, but I thought nothing of it. I think they were both Deal men.'

'Interesting.'

'And the third was Mr Sparrow, who we assumed had run.'

'In retrospect, a regrettable assumption on my part.'

'But it was the only conclusion anyone could possibly arrive at,' Parry said. 'Those who knew him presumed he had gone ashore yet no one could confirm that fact and no one saw him return.'

'But Will Ethridge sensed there was something amiss and I felt it too, that was why I had the ship searched. Naturally no one considered looking in the barrels. A thousand curses! Now we shall never know. If it wasn't for my orders and the ambergris, I would head back to Rio and search every bar and bordello in that town until I found the man who did this. For a crime such as this, I would have him flogged around the fleet then hung from the yardarm and left to rot till every inch of flesh was pecked from his bones!'

Captain Quintrell glanced out of the window and poured himself a second cup of tea. He was satisfied with what had been achieved in the last week and was looking forward to the day ahead.

'Begging your pardon, Capt'n, one of the men is asking to see you. He says it's important and won't speak with no one else but yourself.'

'Thank you, Casson. Send him in and pass word to Mr Parry that I shall join him on deck directly.'

Pushing his cup aside, he watched the seaman shuffle in, his eyes down, head bowed and a black woollen cap screwed up in his hand.

'Speak, man. I do not have all day to listen to your problems.'

'Lazlo, Capt'n, sir,' he said, rotating the woollen hat in his fingers.

'Well, out with it. What is of such concern that you cannot discuss it with the officer of the watch?'

'It's about what happened at Rio, Capt'n,' the seaman murmured, his eyes fixed on the Indian carpet beneath his feet.

'Look at me, man! What about Rio?' the captain snapped.

'It's about that fight I was in. The one that made be late back on board.'

'Two dozen lashes, if I remember rightly. I can assure you that you were dealt with very leniently.'

'Aye, Capt'n. I ain't got no complaint about me punishment.'

'Then, for goodness' sake man, get to the point.'

'Capt'n, I came to tell you who I fought with. It was Guthrie and Bigalow.'

The two names still rung fresh in Oliver's mind. 'Continue.'

'When we dropped anchor in Rio harbour, I was in the last boat to go ashore. Them two jumped aboard just as we were about to pull away.'

'Was Mr Sparrow with them?'

Lazlo shook his head.

'So what can you tell me about the two men who ran?'

'Not much. I'd never had anything to do with the pair before that day. Usually kept themselves to themselves, they did. But when we reached the beach, Guthrie said he knew a bar where the ale was cold and the women were easy . . . if you know what I mean. Well, I'd never been to Rio afore and after all them weeks at sea, I fancied a good time.'

Oliver sighed. 'So you accompanied them?'

'Aye, I did, but after a few drinks they told me they'd no mind to go back to the ship. Said they'd spied a merchantman in the harbour and word was that she was bound for London and sailing the next day. They planned to sign on and asked me if I wanted to go with them.'

'And you declined, of course?'

Lazlo hesitated. 'I have to say in all honesty, I'd had a few drinks and I thought about my wife and bairns for a bit, but then I told them straight, "If we get caught, we'll hang for running", but Bigalow just laughed. "Better than going down on a sinking ship", he said. Guthrie thought that was funny.'

'But why didn't you report this when we left Rio?'

The gunner's mate shrugged his shoulders. 'I guess I didn't think about it.'

Leaning back in his chair, Oliver looked directly into the seaman's eyes. 'So why now?'

'There was more said than just that, but it didn't make no sense until they found what was left of Mr Sparrow.' Lazlo looked dolefully at the captain and continued. 'Guthrie said that if I was fool enough to go back, I'd not be needing any money. That's when he grabbed my purse and we got into a scrap. I could have taken them on one at a time, but the pair was too much for me. They dragged me out into the alley, gave me a beating and left me for dead. I felt like I was near dead. I couldn't move, but I could still hear their voices and I remember Guthrie's words as they walked away. "Shame we haven't got a barrel for him too!" he said.'

The colour drained from Oliver's knuckles while the air whistled as he sucked it through his clenched teeth. Extending a clawed finger and thumb on the table, he asked, 'Is anyone else aware of these conversations?'

'No, Capt'n. I thought it best to keep quiet about it.'

'Wise,' Oliver said, quickly assessing the information. 'I think it best you remain silent. Should word leak out, it could play havoc with the morale of the men and that is something I cannot afford to happen. Today we sail for England and for the present nothing can be done to change the events which took place on the South American coast. Do you agree?'

'Aye, Capt'n.'

'Then return to your station but be assured that your version of these matters will be recorded in the ship's log. And I give you my personal assurance that one day Guthrie and Bigalow will pay for the evil crimes they committed.'

Emile Lazlo knuckled his forehead and turned to go.

'Casson!' Oliver shouted. 'A tot of rum for Mr Lazlo, if you please.'

At eleven o'clock the capstan creaked and turned and *Elusive*'s anchor was raised from the cinder bed. The topsails were encouraged to back and as the crew anxiously held their breath, the frigate slowly slid noisily from the ashen shore. With the helm across, the staysails caught the wind and brought the head around in an arc of 180 degrees.

The distance to the entrance was only a few miles and after the short slow sail across the lagoon they stood into the bay where they had first anchored almost three weeks earlier.

By one o'clock there was not a cloud in the sky, the wind had veered more to the east and providing it did not blow from the south-east, preventing them from sailing out of the island, all would be well.

Pacing the quarter-deck, Oliver willed the hourglass to empty and willed the ebb tide to flow again. He needed to see how high the sea would reach up the rocky pillars, which rose vertically from the bottom of this fathomless pond. Waiting impatiently, his thoughts drifted back to his youth and recollections of saling close to the Giant's Causeway. But even those stark rocks were not as sombre as this ominous place. And nowhere else on earth had sights revolted him as the things he had witnessed here.

Quintrell knew he was not alone in his thinking. In his estimation

173

there was not a single man on board sorry to be leaving the volcanic island, though no one admitted it.

At two in the afternoon the sailors wandered about the deck. No longer were they huddled under layers of blankets for the day was no colder than an English winter's day. A few men went barefoot, such was the toughness of their leathered feet, such was the power of sunlight and such was the relief at the thought of returning home.

From the mess the lilting notes of a flute trilled the tune of a Charles Wesley hymn. It was accompanied by a choir of disorganized voices singing quietly. Others hummed the Sunday anthem.

'Deck there!' the cry came from aloft. 'Ship ho!'

Eyes turned. Blinked.

Sailors stared in disbelief, as the bow of a majestic triple-decked man-of-war came into view. The ship was sailing between the cliffs, passing through the crack in the rim of the caldera.

Every man on deck watched as it reached mid-passage. Suddenly its staysails luffed and the square sails collapsed noisily, spilling every breath of wind from them. It was the same sequence of events as had happened on the frigate.

In his cabin, Oliver had heard the deck call and before a message could be relayed to him, he bounded out to the deck.

'Spanish colours, Captain. Should we beat to quarters?'

'We are not at war with Spain, or we weren't when we left England. All hands on deck, Mr Parry – but quietly, if you please. We do not wish to alarm our foreign visitor.'

'I don't think they've seen us, sir.'

'Not yet, maybe.'

Streaming up from below, *Elusive*'s crew of 200 men gazed at the fighting ship as she reached mid-channel.

'I trust she is not planning to drop anchor there otherwise we will never get out!'

But as he spoke, a commotion broke out on the Spanish deck. Sailors ran hither and thither. Had orders been given for them to prepare to fire? Oliver wondered. Were they about to open their gun ports and run out their guns? He listened intently, hoping to make sense of the unintelligible voices. He was about to order his men to quarters but what he heard made him belay the order. The sounds coming from the stricken ship were not the wailings of an ill-disciplined rabble. They were frantic calls. Desperate cries for help. It was the combined chorus of fear. It was a sound he knew well. He had heard it many times before.

'What is happening?'

'If I'm not mistaken, Mr Parry, our visitors have fallen foul of the same underwater obstacle which we collided with. But on this occasion the water is still slack, the tide has only just turned, and that ship is far heavier than *Elusive*. If I am right, I'm afraid her damage will be far greater than ours.'

Still swimming forward with the speed with which she had left the open ocean, the Spanish man-of-war cleared the entrance and continued drifting, but listing heavily to larboard. From the frigate's deck, the crew could almost smell the malignant panic sweeping through the sinking ship.

'I fear that rock has gouged a hole in her hull.'

'What are your orders, sir?'

'Make ready to lower the boats!'

But any assistance to be offered by the frigate was already too late. *Esmeralda de Cadiz*'s heart had been rent open. Sailors jumped or were cast into the freezing sea even before their own boats could be swung out. Drifting helplessly on the incoming tide, the great ship pitched forward, her bowsprit slicing the lake like a hot knife through butter. And as the royals and skyscrapers leaned further and further till the tip of the main's yardarm touched the water, a figure dropped vertically from the mizzen-top as fast and straight as a sea bird diving for a fish.

It took less than two minutes for the Spanish ship to slide into the lagoon, leaving nothing but assorted flotsam and roiling bodies on the surface. After three more minutes every cry and movement had been stilled. The ice-cold water washed in from the southern latitudes had been kind and claimed its victims quickly.

'My God, there would have been eight hundred men on board her!'

The frigate's crew was silent.

The three-year-old Spanish ship-of-the-line, *Esmeralda de Cadiz*, had battled the southern storm for the past three days and finally found shelter only to sink, with all hands, like a lump of lead to the bottom of the inland lagoon. But unlike the lump of metal on the end of a lead-line, this wooden weight would never be retrieved.

'Do we scour the water for survivors, Captain?'

Quintrell shook his head. 'There will be none,' he said sadly.

'Did she follow us here or arrive just by chance?'

'Or was she here to collect the ambergris?' Oliver added. 'Those are questions we will never know the answer to. Only one thing is certain, she will not be returning to Spain or to the Spanish main and I doubt anyone will come here looking for her.' He paused and shivered. 'Tidy those boats away, Mr Parry. We sail with the outgoing tide. I do not wish to remain in this place any longer than necessary.'

Fifteen minutes before the tide reached its full, the order was given. The bosun's whistle piped and cries to make sail were carried along the deck. All that remained now was to exit the inland sea.

It was no time for the faint-hearted. *Elusive* made her way through the chink in the island's armour, sailing so close to the rock-face that the larboard yardarms almost scraped along it. From the deck the sailors stared awestruck at the jagged cliff-face towering three times higher than the main mast, and at the moment when the wind died and the sails luffed, every man held his breath.

On deck, Mr Mundy was confident. According to his calculations there was no bar crossing the full width of the entrance; the only obstacle was a stout rocky erection mid-channel with deep water on either side. It was this single outcrop which had clawed the caulking from the frigate's coppered bottom and gouged a hole in the Spaniard's hull, sending it down. If his estimations were correct, by sailing out on high water and keeping close to the cliffs, the frigate would avoid the submarine hazard completely. But only time would tell if his measurements were accurate!

Seconds ticked by. A minute passed. With not a breath of wind, *Elusive* swam forward on the minimal momentum she had managed to make on the crater-lake. Suddenly, when they were almost clear of the cliffs, the bowsprit jerked, sending a frisson of fear flashing through the heart of every man on deck. It lasted but a second though it seemed longer. Was the frigate about to suffer the same fate as the Spanish man-of-war?

But the jolt had not come from below. It was delivered from the outside world. Having poked its nose from the lee of the cliffs, the wind from the south had struck the frigate's jib like a blast from Neptune's bellows. The topsails clapped in thunderous applause before filling; the squares followed suit, while on the water thousands of tiny flippers flapped as if signifying their approval, churning up the surface of the already choppy sea.

'Clear the island, Mr Parry. Then north-east. And let us pray Drake's Passage is kind to us once again.'

With a favourable wind and a full head of sail, *Elusive* skirted several snow-swept islands to the north and by ten o'clock that evening the log-board recorded a distance of almost forty nautical miles. Throughout the short night, when the sun seemed unsure of whether to rise or fall, *Elusive* sailed under single-reefed topsails. The dim light made it harder to see the floating ice islands and Captain Quintrell had no desire to lose his ship in the Southern Ocean.

That evening he ate alone, his mind permeated with pictures of the living, breathing island which they had dared to enter and thankfully been delivered from. The fact the island had never been claimed or charted intrigued him. It was obviously known by English and Spanish sailors and probably by French and Dutch ships also. Was it so inhospitable that no one wanted to claim it? Or was its location a poorly kept secret guarded by the world's great cartographers?

He knew his orders. He was not to reveal the island's exact bearing to anyone and before the ship reached Portsmouth, he must ensure all his officers were sworn to secrecy. But what of the unequivocal evidence of the island and its location in the ship's log? When he returned, would the details of their time spent in the Southern Ocean be surreptitiously removed? But even if the location was revealed, he doubted few men would be willing to volunteer to return and once again challenge the hostile Antarctic conditions.

Gazing from his stern window at the weak sun suspended against a strangely illuminated glowing horizon, he pondered about the future. Was it possible that when *Elusive* returned to England he would receive no recognition for the voyage or the treasure he had retrieved? He also wondered how long it would be, despite the secrecy, before word of the frigate's expedition was bandied about on the docks. Not long, he thought.

Perhaps as a result of this cruise an official British expedition would be sent to chart the icy islands of the Southern Ocean. Would he be chosen to lead the venture? He thought not. Such an exploration would be offered to the likes of Joseph Banks or some younger Fellow of the Royal Society. But it was quite possible that before that happened the Spanish would announce the island's location and lay claim to it themselves.

Oliver pondered on the hundreds who had drowned in the lagoon: the high-ranking officers, lieutenants, diplomats, merchants, their wives and children, as well as ordinary seamen. Then he considered the alternative outcome. What if the *Esmeralda de Cadiz* had succeeded in entering the bay? What if war had been declared in Europe? What if the Spanish ship had not sunk but had opened fire? His lowly frigate carried far less firepower and it was doubtful he could have survived a full broadside from the man-of-war.

Later that evening, as he laid in his cot, his mind flicked over the recent events like the pages of a book on a windy day. He thought about his wife and how little she knew of his voyages – how little interest she had shown in any of his cruises. He closed his eyes and without intention, the mental pages turned to Susanna. Oh, how warmly her shoulders had glistened in the candlelight. How the sweep of her back had moved with the ease of a porpoise. How her skin tasted sweeter than the finest wine Madeira could produce.

If only.

CHAPTER 21

Sailing Home

Oliver gazed up at the heavens swaying back and forth above the mastheads. Never had he seen so many stars. Never did they appear so bright as in the high latitudes. On a backcloth of deep indigo, millions of silver sparks dotted the sky; even the dense clusters which Magellan had mistaken for clouds bloomed in bright profusion.

'That wind is strengthening,' he noted to the helmsman. 'Make your course east by north-east.'

Overnight the wind howled but was no stronger than earlier in the evening, but beneath the ship the sea rose dramatically, forming deep troughs which the ship rolled into. Waves advanced on each other in a display of unrelenting malice, viciously punching and slapping, stirring the surface to a whipped-cream consistency, and from an otherwise cloudless sky, spray and spindrift lashed the sails drenching the deck with foam and water. Though they were east of Drake Passage, they could still feel its anger.

'Make sure those barrels are secured, Bungs,' Oliver yelled.

The cooper, who had emerged from the waist, was clinging tightly to any hand-hold. But even with lifelines rigged from stem to stern, it was impossible to traverse the deck in a straight line. The ship was heeling at an ominous angle, the gunnels skimming the sea as it sank in every trough, sending water rushing along the scuppers.

'Hold her steady!' the captain cried.

The two men on the helm braced themselves as the bow buried itself into a cliff of water. *Elusive* shuddered from bowsprit to mizzen boom, the latter taking the full force of the blow and snapping its hemp sheet. Like a weathercock in a whirlwind, the massive mizzen boom thrashed uncontrollably.

179

'Secure the boom. Get that sail down. Watch your heads!'

The wind was enormous and the sail had a mind of its own. Dropping the wind-gripped canvas onto the poop deck was no easy task but it had to be done quickly to prevent it ripping the mizzen mast from the keep.

'Get the carpenter to check the step,' the captain ordered. 'If it works lose, we'll lose it!'

After an hour toiling on the pitching deck, the seamen secured the mizzen boom, and the bosun and his mates set about rigging a new sheet to it. With word from the carpenter that no damage had been done below decks, a shortened mizzen sail was hauled up. It was a long night.

By morning the sea had calmed to a manageable level and the frigate had logged sufficient sea miles to be clear of the confluence of the two great oceans. Heading along the outer rim of the Southern Ocean, the wind was favourable as was expected in that latitude.

'Begging your pardon, Captain, but will we be making landfall in Cape Town?' Mr Mundy asked.

'No. We drop anchor at Spithead. Not before.' As he spoke, the thoughts of a spell in Madeira flashed through his mind. How welcome the fresh fruit, the fresh water, the warm air would be. How welcome a pair of warm hands in his, warm arms around him. Warm legs. He must clear his head.

'The purser says we may not have enough water or stores to carry us home. And the wind up the west coast of Africa. . . .'

'I am fully aware of the winds, Mr Mundy. If it becomes necessary we shall ration the stores. Spithead, I said. You will navigate a course accordingly.'

The heat of the tropics was tiring. The March winds, reputed in England to bring snow, offered little relief from the burning sun and when they did blow it was often from an undesirable direction. The men joked about the cold they had left behind, wishing they had packaged some ice and brought it with them.

'It would have served us better than a hold full of ambergris,' one said.

Sailing north, parallel to the west coast of Africa, they joked limply about pirates.

'Not like your regular privateers,' said Smithers, trying to stir fear into the minds of the less experienced hands. 'No, these are the real mean buggers who'll chop out your tongue and liver before killing you proper.'

'Smithers!' Mr Tully warned.

Weeks passed and not a sail was sighted – till one morning a series of them appeared on the horizon almost dead ahead.

'Looks like a convoy. Heading west,' Mr Mundy announced.

'I agree,' Oliver said. 'A distance of about twelve miles perhaps.'

'Slave ships, do you think, Captain?' Mr Mundy asked.

'Quite likely. With a cargo of black gold to line some already rich trader's pocket. Take us about, Mr Parry. It will give the men something to do.'

'Helm a lee! Staysails haul!'

'When we are sure they are not interested in us, we will resume our course.'

From the deck the officers waited as the frigate completed its manoeuvre, but no sooner did the helmsman have *Elusive* back on its previous bearing than a cry came from the mast.

'Ship ho!'

'Where away?'

'Four points off the starboard bow. Bearing west.'

'She's following the slavers!' Mr Mundy stated.

'Or chasing them?'

'Ship off the starboard beam. Heading north.'

'Aloft there! Can you tell what she is?'

'Dutch East Indiaman. Big four-master.'

Quintrell put the telescope to his eyes but it only confirmed the information the lookout had provided.

'What a damned confounded stretch of ocean. Apart from the Spanish man-of-war we have not seen a ship in three months! Now we fall upon a dozen in less than ten minutes.'

'It would appear they are not sailing together,' said Mr Parry quietly.

'I agree.'

'Deck there!' was the cry from above. 'There are two ships, not one, off the starboard bow. They're changing course and turning south.'

'Describe!'

'Three masters. Brig and barquentine. Still turning.'

'What colours?'

'None.'

'All hands on deck. Beat to quarters, Mr Parry. Prepare for action.'

The sound of the drum and the peep of the whistles was almost lost to the thunder of feet on dry decking, the creak of port lids opening and the trundle of guns as their breechings were released.

'Damn their eyes. If I did not have this cargo, I would blow them both to kingdom come! Mr Smith, don't you have a station to go to? Get the idlers to light a brazier in the waist and tell the cooper to open a barrel of blubber and burn a few blocks.'

The midshipman looked puzzled. 'But the smell, sir. Won't they think we're whalers?'

'That is not the idea, Mr Smith. My intention is to foul the air with the stench of burning blubber to smother the scent of the ambergris. It's quite simple really. Get to it.'

The midshipman hurried off in search of the cooper.

Standing beside the binnacle, Oliver smiled to his first lieutenant. 'If luck is on our side, those pirates will attempt to take the rich Indiaman and ignore a stinking frigate. Aloft there!' he called. 'Lookout. Report!'

'They've completed their turn, Capt'n. I think they've spotted the Indiaman.'

From the starboard ports the gun crews watched. It was obvious the two smaller vessels were aiming to intercept the big trading ship heading for the North Atlantic and home.

'Shouldn't we go to her assistance?'

'No, Mr Mundy. I have my orders and that Dutch ship will have more guns than both those pirates ships put together.'

'Run up the colours, Mr H. let us show them who we are. Set a new course,' he said, turning to the man at the helm. 'North-west.'

As *Elusive* bore away from the busy shipping lane, the distant boom of cannon-fire could be heard but it was an hour before the order to stand down was given. Half choked on the smoke from rotting whale flesh, it was a weary crew who closed up the port lids and lashed down the guns.

Standing beside Mr Parry on the quarter-deck, Oliver smiled. 'If only those dogs had known what we are carrying!'

Within days of crossing the equator the captain decided it was necessary to reduce rations to three-quarters. It was not a popular order and had there been a barometer on board to log the temperament of the men, it would have shown how turbulent their moods were.

'Perhaps we should start eating ambergris. There's plenty of that on board.'

'Shut your face, Froyle. It ain't the captain's fault we've lost the wind. It's called the doldrums. Ain't you strayed this far from home before? Worried, are you?'

'We'll be right,' said Will, across the table. 'The worst must be over. When we're clear of the tropics it's only a hop, step and jump to the English Channel.'

'And where did you get your master's ticket from? You couldn't even steer a jolly-boat across the Solent.'

'I learnt geography in school. Didn't you go to school, Bungs?'

'He never heard of school let alone walked through the door of one. Anyway, what you going to do when you get paid off? Build yourself another boat and try to drown yourself again?'

The men around the mess table enjoyed the joke.

'I'm going back to Buckler's Hard to finish my time.'

'And what then?'

'Who knows. I might sign on a king's ship. I might even be able to get a mate's warrant with a word from the captain.'

'You never know, if old Boney is still up to his tricks, that peace they brokered might be broken and when we sail back into Portsmouth we could find ourselves transferred to a man-of-war. You might not even get chance to go home if we're shipped straight out again.'

'Aye,' said Froyle. 'Now the Navy's got its grubby claws in you, you might not see home for five years.'

'I'll be home in a month,' Will said. 'You mark my words. I'm going to surprise my grandfather and tell him what happened.'

'He'll never believe you, I reckon.'

CHAPTER 22

Spithead, April 1803

What a sight greeted the frigate as it headed into the Solent. It was not the array of navy ships littering the freeways – those ships-of-the-line still in commission rocking on their anchor cables – or to the north, the battlements and fortifications of England's premier naval port. It was the low green hills of the Isle of Wight, the broad stretches of yellow sand, wet and glistening on the ebb, the friendly clutter of merchant ships gathered on the Mother Bank, and beyond those, the stately structure of the Haslar Hospital – so very English. To the left of it was the entrance to Portsmouth Harbour and beyond that the Royal Naval Dockyard. And home. How appealing the prospect of a safe harbour was after a voyage of many months.

Elusive's men cheered as the weary frigate sailed boldly into Spithead, hove to and sounded a salute. Anchored nearby in the roadstead were the fighting ships, a pair of seventy-fours, a ninety-eight-gun ship-of-the-line and two frigates. But with their decks almost bare and with only a handful of crew and a few marines on deck, it was obvious that England was still at peace.

For Captain Quintrell and his crew, returning home on this occasion was unlike returning victorious after battle. The thrill of triumph, the exhilaration of success was lacking. It was dulled by the secrecy of the mission. Oliver had become increasingly aware that there would be no recognizable acknowledgement for either him or his men and that their voyage may not even merit a few lines in the *Naval Chronicle*. There would be those amongst his crew who would be sorely disappointed.

Despite that he smiled and cast his eyes around. Little did the casual observer know that aboard his weather-worn frigate was a treasure trove which would help fund another war with Napoleon or provide a substantial contribution to pay the debt for the previous one. On board *Elusive* was sufficient wealth to build dozens of war ships and guarantee England a superior naval force capable of sending the French fleet to the bottom of the sea.

Captain Quintrell was glad to be home. He was tired. The voyage from the Southern Ocean had been tedious – boring, in fact, like the monotonous food served up daily, and insufficient of it. But he had insisted that if the men had to survive on three-quarter rations then he and his officers would do likewise. That order had not been popular but he had enforced it.

The previous night he had slept well, the first sleep of more than a two hours' constant duration for almost a month. But if he was weary then his crew were equally exhausted, if not more so. The voyage home had taken longer than planned. Drinking water had been in short supply and rationed, and though there were ports he could have put into, he had not dared venture onto the African coast or the Islands of Verde or the Canaries. He had toyed with the idea of stopping briefly in Madeira. Battled with himself over the decision. Fresh meat and fruit and water would have been most welcome. Such provisions would have refreshed and invigorated his men and made the final days more pleasant. But the close encounter with the two pirate brigs off the African coast had put paid to that idea. Pirates and privateers had perfected the game of playing maritime cat and mouse, hiding at a safe distance waiting to pounce on fat juicy merchant ships which were brave enough, or foolish enough, to travel alone. Oliver was grateful his frigate had not fallen victim to the pirates' clutches. One whiff of his cargo and he would have been a prime target. All in all, he was certain he had made the right decisions.

After her month in the icy seas, after weeks battling the Southern Ocean and days suffering the hot African winds, after spending what seemed like an eternity steaming in the tropics with the searing heat bleeding black pitch from her veins, *Elusive* was home at last. But she was a tired ship. Her cordage had stretched till it could stretch no more. Her sails had split, been patched and split again until the sail-maker's palm was punctured and raw. Her mizzen mast was loose and urgently needed re-stepping.

The extremes had taken their toll. From heat which could parch a man's skin as dry as an autumn leaf, to cold, unimaginable cold, which could blacken a man's fingers and sear them from his hand. From gales and storms to deadly calms which stretched the nerve and sinew of every man, strained every shroud, stay, sheet, spar and inch of canvas till it could take no more.

Spithead at last! Oliver breathed a long, hard sigh. Now the tension could be released. It was over. He had coaxed both men and ship home safely. Now they could rest easy.

As the anchor splashed into the grey water, he thought about his wife. Had she been watching from the window for his return? Had she seen the frigate from their house? Was she waiting for news of his return? With many questions running through his head, he knew he must write immediately and notify her of his safe return to England. He wondered if she would join him in Portsmouth as it would be two or three days before he would be leaving the ship. She had never come to greet him in the past. Perhaps this time she would. Perhaps not.

After reaching Spithead, there was much to attend to. First, the magazine must be emptied before they could enter the harbour. Then he must report to the port admiral and ascertain where his cargo was to be unloaded. That was a job he intended to supervise personally. Being of such an unusual nature, he wondered how it could possibly be kept secret. Not long, he thought. The wagging tongues of paid-off seamen would quickly spread word round the town – that was if the strong musky smell of the ambergris didn't announce its own presence before that.

He was quietly pleased with his method of packaging the whale product – crated, padded with tussock grass, and the barrels, casks and other containers covered in sailcloth. Certainly not a distinguishable cargo to the casual eye. But to the nose . . . that was a different matter. He hoped the residual fumes of burning blubber which had penetrated the decks when they entered the Channel was sufficient to mislead all but the most astute connoisseurs.

'Have my boat ready, Mr Hazzlewood, and when we arrive in Portsmouth wait for me at the jetty steps. Mr Parry, while I am ashore, allow no one aboard. And no one is to leave the ship. Is that understood?'

'Aye aye, sir.'

'Welcome home, Captain Quintrell. I am sorry we kept you waiting.' The port admiral turned to the marine stationed by the door. 'You may leave us. Please, sit, Captain.'

Flicking up the tails from his best dress uniform, Oliver settled himself on one of the silk embossed chairs.

'Do I detect a slight hint of a smile on your face, Captain? Do you carry good news?'

'Indeed, sir.'

The admiral leaned back in his chair and breathed deeply. 'Amazing.'

Quintrell looked at him quizzically.

'From what I have been told, which is very little I might add, it is amazing that you located this elusive treasure; amazing that it actually existed; amazing that it had not been removed, pilfered, relocated. Amazing that you withstood the voyage – and returned. Amazing that it is currently sitting safely in Spithead.'

'Are you aware of the nature of my cargo, my lord?'

'No, Captain, I am not privy to that information and I shall not ask.'

'Then may I ask if there was some question about its distant location?'

The admiral leaned forward. 'Many messages and tales filter through the walls of the Admiralty both in London and here in Portsmouth – some are true, while some are extensions of the truth based only on fanciful ideas and speculations. However, in certain circumstances, those in authority cannot chance to ignore what may be the truth. In a case such as this, the Admiralty had unsubstantiated information of a cache of treasure but because of the reputed value of this item, it could not ignore the information thereby allowing the cargo to fall into enemy hands.'

'Then the Admiralty was not sure the commodity existed or if the location was correct?'

'I understand that to be the case.'

'Then it would appear my ship and her men could have been sailing on a wild goose chase.' Though this situation had been intimated at when he had received his orders and it was an idea he had toyed with, to hear it confirmed made him feel angry. Resentful. Disappointed. The treasure had been but a rumour. His recovery mission a whim. The likelihood of success a pipe dream. Had he been selected for this voyage because he was considered dispensable – perhaps also *Elusive*?

'Captain Quintrell, you were chosen because of your record, your character and ability, and you were furnished with some specially selected officers, and a working crew who were fit for the task.'

He had hardly considered that before.

'Now, Captain, I have your orders.'

The words came as a shock. Surely this was the end of his mission? Surely he was not being shipped out again? There was much work to be done. A cargo to unload. The men deserved a break. Oliver frowned at the sealed envelope pushed across the polished table towards him. He regarded it with disdain.

'I am instructed not to accept your cargo,' the port admiral said. 'I am told it is too valuable to unload here and transport to London by road. I can assure you, there are more thieves and robbers on the lanes and highways of England than there are on the high seas. Your orders, Captain Quintrell, are to sail to the Thames. You will find the details here.'

'But, sir, I must protest. *Elusive* has few remaining stores. We are virtually out of drinking water. We have no fresh food and the men are weary and anxious to return to their homes. Besides, the French have spies who are always vigilant in the Channel. What a travesty it would be to lose our cargo within sight of Dover's cliffs when we have carried it halfway around the world.' It went against the grain to plead his case but he had to try.

'I understand your feelings, Captain, but I too am only obeying orders. Your cargo must go to London. With fair winds it is a matter of three or four days' sailing at the most. You and your ship have come this far, I am sure you are capable of commanding her for another couple of hundred nautical miles.'

There was little Oliver could say.

The port admiral cleared his throat. 'If it is of any consolation, arrangements have been made to safeguard your voyage. You will not travel alone. Three naval frigates will accompany you. They are preparing to leave on Thursday which gives you three days to take on water and fresh supplies. I will personally organize the victualling to commence this afternoon.'

The captain nodded.

'I realize that your home is but a short distance from here and no doubt you are anxious to return, as are the local sailors. However, it is recommended that you allow no females or visitors of any description on board your vessel. We want no word of your cargo being passed to shore. I hope your boat crew can be trusted to maintain silent tongues.'

'They are reliable men.'

'Good. I am pleased to hear it.'

'Now, sir. On behalf of the Lords Commissioners of the Admiralty, I congratulate you on the success of your voyage and wish you a safe onward passage. Unfortunately the details cannot be broadcast in the *Gazette* but I am to assure you that the success of this mission will not go unnoticed.'

There was nothing else Oliver could say. He must return to the ship with all haste before the barges came alongside to offload the powder that might yet be needed in their magazine.

He was not relishing the response he would receive from his officers and crew when he conveyed the news that they would be sailing for the Thames. A few would be pleased – those from London or Deal – but most sailors, particularly those off the *Constantine*, would be sorely disappointed. They had been absent from home for more than a year and it was possible when they arrived in London they might be transferred to another ship and expected to sail again. But such was life in the service. Most of them knew that when they signed on.

For the Portsmouth men it would be a bitter parting – seeing the harbour wharves and buildings of their home town being but a few hundred yards from their families but not being allowed to disembark.

If the men were not permitted to go ashore or receive visitors, then he would follow suit. His conscience would not allow him to take shore leave while his men were deprived of it. He would write to his wife that afternoon telling her of his safe return and despatch the letter on one of the lighters or victualling barges with instructions it be forwarded with all haste to the Isle of Wight. He also intended to write to Susanna to inform her of his safe return to England. Any ship bound for Madeira would convey it to her.

Loading stores, water and replenishing the supply of powder and shot was done in a lubberly fashion. Raised voices were required to keep the crew to their tasks. Gone was the enthusiasm and industry they had shown loading the floating gold on the cinder beach of the volcanic island.

Oliver's memory of the living and breathing lagoon was like the imaginings of a dream which drifted in and out of his consciousness. Now it seemed so distant in time and space. So unlikely. Impossible even. Yet he and his ship had been there and had returned with over five tons of ambergris. He tried to calculate what that might be worth. He remembered the rumour – a guinea an ounce. But his brain was tired. Sixteen ounces in a pound, a thousand pounds in a ton. Five thousand pounds . . . five thousand multiplied by sixteen. . . .

He questioned the Lords of the Admiralty's decision to sail to

189

London. He had even protested about their orders with the port admiral, but to no avail. He must follow his orders.

'We sail on Thursday,' he announced to his officers on return. 'The frigates *Windsor*, *Foxglove* and *Pembroke* will accompany us and I will receive the three captains on board on Wednesday at noon. I am assured, though it goes without saying, these officers are of the highest repute. The crew, including yourselves, will say nothing of what is in our hold particularly to the visiting boat crews. And I want every deck scrubbed with brimstone and vinegar before noon on Wednesday. Hopefully it will disguise some of our smell.'

'I don't believe the ambergris smells now,' Mr Mundy said.

'The fact we can't smell it is probably that we have got used to it. Do you smell the tar on the rigging or pitch in the caulking? Do you smell wet sails or salt in the sea air?'

'Hardly sir.'

'But when you come near land you can smell the forests and marshes and fires before they come over the horizon. I think we do not smell what we live with, only what we have not experienced for a long time. Vinegar and brimstone, Mr Mundy. Had we any blubber left in the barrels we would have been boiling that.'

Despite the chill of a morning on the open waters of Spithead and the men's initial disappointment at not being allowed ashore, the overall mood of the crew was much improved. With only a handful of the starboard watch on harbour duty, most men had slept longer and deeper than usual, being lulled by the somewhat sheltered waters of a safe roadstead. The meals of the two previous days had also helped. Fresh meat and vegetables in ample servings had warmed both their bellies and their hearts. The fact they were to be escorted by three naval frigates, freshly painted fine-looking ships with white sails, not patched dirty grey ones like those which *Elusive* had been sporting, provided the crew with an air of pride. And for some the thought that when they reached their destination there may be an opportunity to transfer to one of those frigates led to some lively discussion in the mess.

On Wednesday at noon, *Elusive*'s crew lined the deck as the three captains were piped aboard. The smell which greeted them caused at least one of the visitors to curl his nose as he stepped aboard.

'I like a white deck,' Oliver explained, when quizzed over dinner. 'Of course, sulphur fumes are excellent for removing lice but I am sure you are aware of that.'

He was fully aware of the flippancy of his conversation, particularly as two of the captains present bore two epaulettes on their shoulders, but it was the only way of avoiding awkward questions. In one regard he welcomed their visit. There was much he wanted news of: the state of the country, the fragility of the peace. He had been absent from England since August of the previous year without mail or newspapers and only limited information from other ships. It reminded him of the time he had spent in a hospital bed when the brain fever had robbed him of several weeks; when the world had continued rotating but had left him behind.

Now at his dining table he was confronted by three men whose main concern was the list of recent promotions – commanders and captains whose names he had never heard of before – and the names of familiar fighting ships which had been decommissioned as a result of the peace.

The intriguing events in the Americas and Indies were spoken of at length as was Boney's ambitious expansion through Europe. Napoleon's terrestrial invasions had taken his land forces much further than anyone ever envisaged. Then there was discussion of the British temptation to take vulnerable French ships. In a time of peace it made for interesting conversation.

'So what of this secret cargo you are carrying? It seems odd to me that it had been stored in a frigate. Surely it was a job for a sloop.'

The question was so forthright Oliver did not respond.

'Tell me,' the eldest of the three frigate captains asked in a confidential manner, 'did you take a Spanish treasure ship loaded with gold? Or is it prisoners of diplomatic significance you are transporting?'

'I am not at liberty to say, sir. Those are my strict orders.'

'But, sir, from one captain to another. A hint at least?'

The interruption was well timed. 'Begging your pardon, Captain.'

'What is it, Mr Tully?'

'Some more ordnance arriving, sir.'

Quintrell was grateful. 'Gentlemen,' he said, 'you will have to excuse me. We are due to sail tomorrow and I have final preparations to make.'

It was not the cordial conclusion Quintrell would have wished for, but he was grateful to avoid providing any opportunity for further questioning.

The shrill of the bosun's pipes accompanied the visiting officers' departure and Oliver was not sorry to see their heads disappearing over the side. He had enjoyed the converse with two of his guests though the captain of the *Foxglove*, who had been designated commodore of the escort vessels, was a pompous bore – the type of man he had little time for either on land or sea.

'A message arrived for you, sir,' said Mr Hazzlewood, handing it to him as the three boats were rowed back to their respective frigates. 'It was delivered by the port admiral's launch only a few minutes ago.'

The linen package bore the distinctive anchor seal of the Admiralty. A change of orders, Oliver thought, as he headed directly to his cabin to open it.

Breaking the seal, he peeled back the wrapping, expecting to find new instructions. But the packet held nothing but a private letter sealed in its own envelope. He examined the scrawled handwriting but did not recognize it.

Opening the correspondence, he read:

My dear Captain Quintrell,
I trust that this letter finds you in good health.

Mrs Quintrell, your dear wife, is in receipt of your letter saying that you have recently been delivered safe home to England but stating that you must forthwith attend at the Admiralty in London.

We thank the Lord for your safe homecoming; however it is regretful that you are unable to return to Bembridge, no matter how briefly.

As your good friend and your wife's physician, it is my unfortunate duty to inform you that your wife is gravely ill.

If it is within your power, I strongly recommend your urgent attendance at home.

I am however aware of the limitations which His Majesty's service places on you.

I remain,
Your friend and obedient servant,

Jonathon Wilberforce

'Damn! Damn! Damn!' Oliver gritted his teeth and screwed the letter in his hand. If only he had known his wife was ill. If only there had been a message waiting for him when he arrived. It was his own conscious decision which had stopped him from making a visit home and now it was too late. That annoyed him and thoughts of Susanna, of Madeira and of what he coveted there, inflamed his sense of guilt. He could have taken the launch from Portsmouth on the first day and been to Bembridge and back in a matter of six hours. Now such a visit was not possible. *Elusive* was due to sail at first light and the three frigate captains had their orders and were ready to sail with him. There was no way he could respond to the doctor's request.

But what had happened? When he left England his wife was well. Now there was a chance she might die before he reached her. The thought she was possibly already dead burned briefly in his mind. It was an eventuality he had sometimes considered as all men who go to sea must do, but for Oliver they were dangerous thoughts which he battled against. Now his mind was burning like a slow-fuse lit in a powder room; a fuse he had dared to kindle before but always managed to dash out. He admonished himself. He had loved Victoria sincerely and deeply as she had loved him, but somewhere on the great gulf of ocean which had flowed between their different lives, their love had sunk to the fathomless depths, leaving barely a few remnants of their past affection floating on the surface.

Struggling to pen a letter, tears rolled down his cheeks. He was unaware such intense emotion was rooted within him.

My dearest wife,

It pains me immensely to read of your illness and I am truly distraught that I cannot visit you while I am in Portsmouth. I have only just received revised orders which instruct me to deliver my ship to The Thames.

The Admiralty's strict orders prevented my men from disembarking in Portsmouth and because of this I refrained from allowing myself the opportunity to return home for a brief visit. Now I regret that decision.

Dearest Victoria, you have my word that as soon as my ship is delivered to Greenwich, I will return to you. Hopefully, that will be one week from this day.

I trust Mr Wilberforce will afford you the best of care and I pray for your speedy recovery.

Your affectionate husband,

OQ

CHAPTER 23

The English Channel

Will Ethridge leaned on the larboard rail and gazed dolefully across the water to the Hampshire coast as it faded further and further away. The ship's acting carpenter had come so close to his home; so close to his mother and grandfather; so close to the shipwrights he had known before that fateful voyage in his hand-built boat. The Beaulieu River and Buckler's Hard were just a few score miles from Portsmouth. It was so near and yet so far.

For more than eight months he had been waiting for the opportunity to go home and when *Elusive* had sailed into the Solent and anchored in Spithead he, like many others, had been filled with anticipation. How well he could imagine the expression on his mother's face, the surprise in his grandfather's eyes, and picture the tears of joy streaming down their cheeks when they saw him. Just the thought of them brought tears to his own eyes.

But as *Elusive* sailed south and the coastline disappeared in the haze, bitter disappointment tore at his belly. He had never wanted to go to sea and now being unable to get away from it angered him. He knew he was not alone. Amongst the crew, the Portsmouth men were of the same mind as were the men of Plymouth, Torbay and Falmouth. From the harbour they could find a berth on a coastal trader to carry them to their families. Other men had hopes of signing on a higher-rated ship, and Portsmouth was the place for that.

But now the port and the Royal Naval Dockyard were behind them and London loomed ahead. It was a city Will had heard of but knew nothing about. More than once during the last three days he had toyed with the idea of running. He was fit and strong and could swim to shore. It was not far away. But he had learned that distances at sea were deceptive and adrift in his hand-built craft he had felt the force of the Solent's current first-hand. Besides, if he jumped ship now, the marines on the battlements would spot him. If he was not shot, he would be caught when he came ashore at the jetty. The charge for desertion according to the Articles of War was death.

He was distraught, frustrated and confused.

For a time he had harboured fond thoughts of returning to Buckler's Hard, of selling his boat and giving the money to his grandfather. But as the months and miles had slid by, Will had realized that his wooden row-boat was no longer his property. It had been commandeered by the navy just as quickly as his name had been entered in the muster book. Now they both belonged to the service.

In the mess the men had other grievances. In return for the voyage they had undertaken, with all its horrors and hardships, the crew would receive only their regular pay. Not a penny more or less. For their part in returning the valuable cargo of ambergris there would be no prize money, no spoils of naval warfare. Every ounce, crumb and grain of the floating gold would go into the government's coffers with not so much as a thank you for their efforts.

The grumblings had grown louder when no wives were allowed on board ship. After months spent swaying in a cold hammock, packed tight as pilchards in a fishwife's basket, to be deprived of female company when they were within sniffing distance of the wharf was enough to drive a man crazy. No one was allowed onboard. No one was allowed off. That was the order. Except the captain and his boat crew, of course! It was unfair.

Will had tried to get a place on the captain's boat, but all seats were occupied by the regular boat crew.

Maybe he would run when the ship reached London. But he didn't know the town, the dockyards or the Thames and the rumours he had heard about the ugly happenings on the wharfs and jetties were enough to deter him.

Returning to England was not what he had expected. Then he thought about the men he had come to know like family; men he had shared his every waking hour with; their joys, their pain, their idiosyncrasies, their arguments, their fights, their everyday lives. He had laughed with them, cried with them and learned more from them in the few months than he had learned in his lifetime on Buckler's Hard. He had faced real dangers and experienced unimaginable horrors on the island, and stood shoulder to shoulder beside them. It made him feel proud.

He thought of his friend Percy Sparrow though he wanted to forget the recurring nightmares which had troubled him since the barrel had been opened. Chips had been kind to him, nurtured him in the early days, been like a father to him – and he had grieved his passing more than that of his own father, who he had hardly known.

He had grown up in the last eight months far quicker than he would have at home. Now he wasn't sure if he wanted to be a shipwright on the hard – laying keelsons, carting timber and hammering trunnels for hours and hours with never a break. Sailing on one of His Majesty's ships was far more exciting than building them.

'Signal from the commodore, sir,' Mr Smith said.

'Well?'

The midshipman read from his slate. 'Our number followed by, *Close up and proceed to the Downs.*'

Oliver rubbed his clawed hand across his brow.

'Set the main course,' he called, scanning the English Channel. The sky was leaden. The chalk cliffs of Dover were duller than he remembered; almost as grubby as the spread of the ship's canvas.

'I have a bad feeling about this, Mr Parry. Close up and keep pace with the three frigates. This wind will take us around the South Foreland. When we enter the roadstead, be prepared to make anchor.'

'Aye aye, sir,' Simon replied, remembering a similar order he had given the time he had attempted his fateful passage. A fair wind had been blowing and had carried him in, allowing him to anchor with several score vessels, all praying for a blow to carry them safely from the Downs, all anxious to avoid that illusive and often invisible barrier to the east – the Goodwin Sands.

It was not a place the lieutenant would voluntarily choose to revisit, and like the majority of the crew, Simon Parry had been disappointed at leaving Spithead.

Hadn't Oliver explained that his ship had a damaged hull? Wasn't it essential to remove the cargo as soon as possible? Surely by sending the frigate into the Channel there was a chance of losing it – to storm or shipwreck or an unprovoked attack by the French, the Dutch or some privateer. He wondered about the logic of the Admiralty's order.

He had experienced the Sands. He had learned to his cost of their insidious nature. He knew that when the Goodwin Sands swallowed a ship, they consumed it completely, regurgitating nothing.

'Could I make a suggestion, sir?' Simon said, over dinner.

'Go ahead, Simon.'

'With an escort and with these prevailing winds, would it not be preferable to sail to the east of the Sands?'

'Close to the French coast, is that what you are suggesting?'

'Yes.'

'Why so?'

'If the weather does not improve, a confrontation with the shifting sand and tides could prove costly.'

'I can understand your concern, and I am not happy being dragged along the Channel on a naval leash. But I have my orders, Simon, and for the present must abide by the commodore's decision. We must bide our time, but I too have an uneasy feeling.'

'The barometer has fallen dramatically, sir,' Mr Nightingale said.

'I can sense it.'

'Signal from the flagship, sir. Sail to starboard!'

'Mr Parry, speak to that man aloft. Either he is blind or fast asleep. If the frigates can see a ship, then the lookout should see it also. Goodness, I can almost see the French coast from here. Acknowledge the flagship and find out what colours it is flying.'

But before the flags could be run up there was a shout from the masthead. 'Deck there! Three ships. All Frenchies. A ship-of-the-line and two corvettes.'

'What bearing?' Oliver called. 'Let's hope they are heading for the Mediterranean!'

He reserved his own thoughts on the alternative. Had the ships appeared by accident or intention? Was it possible word had carried that a frigate carrying a fortune in ambergris was sailing up the Channel? Surely that could not be the case. Then he reminded himself of the ship which had shadowed them in the Atlantic. And the *Esmeralda de Cadiz*, which had foundered at the entrance to the horseshoe-shaped island. How many people knew about this so-called secret cargo? Had the wharfside mumblings already been passed around? Were the walls of the Admiralty offices made of papier-mâché? Could no one be trusted no matter what sphere they worked in?

'Bearing nor-east!' The words rained down from aloft. 'Same as us and closing.'

'Damn! Damn! Damn! Is this a coincidence or is she preparing to provoke another war.'

'Signal from the leading frigate confirming the French presence,' Mr Nightingale added.

'How far to the Downs?'

'A little over two hours if this south-westerly holds.'

'All hands on deck, Mr Parry. Beat to quarters.'

Within minutes the deck was swarming with men. With news of the ships off the starboard beam, any lingering thoughts of wives, sweethearts or of going ashore were quickly forgotten. Though they were not at war, the fear of attack and being blown to pieces by the broadside of a ninety-eight-gun ship-of-the-line was enough to remove any idle thoughts and occupy minds afresh.

The youngest midshipman, with his book and board, came running along the quarter-deck, his nose quite white after scratching it with chalky fingers.

'Our number, sir. *Proceed with all haste.*'

'Acknowledge, if you please, Mr Smith. Mr Parry, let's show these Frenchies what a tired frigate can do.'

As the three escort vessels bore to starboard with *Elusive* in their lee, she braced her yards around and closed on the English coast. If she could make it safely into the Downs it was unlikely the French would follow. The roadstead would be teeming with ships, albeit mostly merchant vessels but possibly some English men-of-war.

On deck, tensions were high but the barometer was low and thick cloud was forming. Once it engulfed the ship it prevented them seeing the approaching squall. Spawned on the coast of France, the gale arrived suddenly, the rain battering the Channel like grapeshot from a hundred guns as it thundered towards them. When the first mighty gust roared over her beam, *Elusive* heeled dramatically, the main yard almost dipping its arm in the boiling sea. On deck neither officers nor crew were dressed to greet it.

'Hold her steady!' Mr Parry shouted to the quartermaster. 'More hands to the helm!'

The sleet-cold rain was delivered in a tangible shroud and *Elusive* found herself floundering beneath the wet blanket. 'Hold your bearing! Get a double reef on the topsails and take up the courses. We'll not get into the Downs if we cannot see where we are heading.'

Oliver pricked his ears. It was difficult to hear above the wind, hard to distinguish which sheave was shrilling or which sail crackling, but the sound of a cannon being fired, even in the distance, carried on the wind. It was a single shot. He waited, poised for a response. Had the French ship opened fire on the frigates? Were the escort ships trying to establish their position? Was it a poorly timed salute or were the frigates drawing the attention of the French corvettes?

It sounded like a forward-mounted carronade. But why such a powerful shot? And was it fired in defence or attack? What would the ramifications be? The answers to those questions would have to wait until they were safely delivered into the Downs. For the present Oliver's only concern was to maintain course and get out of the fog and trust that the three frigates did the same.

By seven o'clock that evening, *Elusive* was anchored off Deal with fifty other assorted vessels. The south-westerly had carried them in. The squall, as if suddenly struck by the blade of Madame Guillotine, had died instantly the frigate entered the roadstead. Within minutes the cables rumbled through the hawse hole and the anchor settled itself into the shingle bottom.

Though the journey from Spithead had been neither long nor particularly arduous, the men looked tired. Mental rather than physical anguish was beginning to etch deep lines on the faces of both officers and men. Captain Quintrell was not immune to frustration and as a lugger sailed in to anchor within half a cable's length, he bellowed from the quarter-deck: 'Make sure they keep their boats clear. I want no one coming aboard.'

Mr Hazzlewood shouted from the fo'c'sle. 'Boat approaching, Captain. From the direction of Deal.'

'Find out what he wants,' Oliver said, gritting his teeth. 'And get rid of him as quickly as possible.'

The boat approached in the fast diminishing daylight and bumped alongside. There was an exchange of shouts and cries then questions about water and women, but with no business to conduct, it hastened away, heading for the lugger alongside.

With all hands furling sails and all eyes on the lights of other vessel, no one noticed two seamen slipping from one of the starboard gun ports and dropping onto the crest of a passing wave.

The midshipman had made an unfortunate choice picking two Deal men to guard the cargo in the hold. They were men who knew the local water, knew the currents, knew the tides and possibly even knew the men who were in the lugger. Another thing they certainly knew was the value of twenty pounds of ambergris. They also knew that unlike most heavy contraband, which would sink like a cannon ball, this jetsam, if tied up in their shirts, wouldn't drag them down – on the contrary, it would help them stay afloat. They could not have planned their escape better. Within only a few yards distance from the frigate, their bobbing heads were lost in the white caps of the turning waves.

Not a soul on *Elusive* saw them run.

'Are you certain only one crate has been opened?'

'Yes, Captain.'

'Get Bungs and the carpenter down here! Secure that crate and check the others. And double the guard. You, Mr Hazzlewood, go though the muster book. I want every Deal man on the ship taken below and held until we reach the Thames. Do you understand? And I want no lights or signals and no more men going over the side.' He shook his head and turned to his first lieutenant. 'You realize, Mr Parry, that within a few hours all this coast will know what we are carrying. And here we are stuck in the Foreland Passage waiting for a favourable wind to carry us out. Sitting ducks we are.'

Damn the Admiralty! he said, to himself. Damn! Damn! Pray the Lord we do not founder or we will be stripped as clean as a piranha peels meat from a man's bones – and twice as quickly.

CHAPTER 24

The Downs

Eight bells was struck, announcing the first watch of the night, and at the sound of the bosun's pipe the deck came alive, the entire ship's company scrambling to collect their hammocks and take them below. Lookouts were changed and the starboard crew took its positions. The well-practised sea-going ritual was performed without fuss or question. Only one change was made to the standard events. Instead of dousing all lanterns at this time, the marine on duty was ordered to light additional ones. The captain knew it was going to be a long night and he was uneasy.

Having remained on deck for the past two hours, he had taken Mr Nightingale's watch and encouraged Mr Parry to go below to get a little rest, though he doubted his lieutenant would sleep. Scouring the sea and the empty expanse of moonlit beach till his eyes had grown sore, Oliver had tried to convince himself that his concerns were unfounded. Perhaps the nine months at sea had warped his thinking. He had brought his ship to the safety of the Downs and was now anchored off an English port little more than two cables' length from shore. A short distance away, rising almost from the beach, was the turreted circular keep of Deal Castle which, surrounded by its six petal-shaped bastions, housed up to 200 guns. It was a fortification which had protected England since the days of Henry VIII.

Apart from the security offered by the fortress, anchored in the roadstead were scores of English ships with a collective armament of over a thousand guns. What situation could have been safer?

But Oliver's instinct told him his enemy would come from the land and not from the water and it would present as an insidious invasion, not heralded by a flash of light and complemented by the crashing of splintered timber. It was an unsettling feeling and as the sand slipped from the hourglass and he witnessed it being turned, and turned, and turned again, his feelings were magnified by the clouds forming over the Kent countryside, forecasting an approaching storm.

As night thickened, the stars disappeared. The moon followed shortly after, leaving only the meagre light from the swaying lanterns and casting curling shadows on the ship in the areas immediately beneath them. Like the frustrations of a newly blinded man, Oliver lashed out. He growled at a sailor sprawling on the deck even though it was night and they were at anchor. But anchor watch had never been called and according to the log-board the full starboard watch was still on duty.

As tiredness swept through him, he knew it was not the physical exhaustion of a day which had begun at four in the morning. His weariness was rooted in frustrations provided by the latter part of the journey. He had brought *Elusive* home, safe and fairly sound, but was now tied to the apron strings of a trio of naval nursemaids. But the subservice he was obliged to pay to the commodore of the escort fleet incensed him. This captain was younger than himself by several years – a post captain who had seen little action but had been elevated through the untrammelled path of aristocratic patronage.

He recollected the orders he had received: *Close up. Make haste. Bear away.* He had conformed to each one and followed his orders to the letter. The last signal he received was to proceed to the Downs. Now in his present state of vulnerability, at a time when he needed support, the Admiralty's escort was nowhere to be seen. This further exacerbated his frustrations. Having expected the three escort ships to follow him into the roadstead, he could only assume that the commodore had signalled the frigates to peel back and engage the French fleet. In his opinion, if such a course was taken, it was foolish in the extreme. To engage a ninety-eight-gun ship with a pair of corvettes in attendance and within shouting distance of the French coast was madness. And to instigate such an action could be seen as a provocation of war.

But his biggest source of aggravation was the incident with the two Deal men. That was something he had not foreseen and he reprimanded himself severely for not considering the possibility. The loss of a quantity of ambergris was a responsibility he must accept, but he had no intention of sending men ashore to search for the thieves or their booty. At least he had their names from the muster book.

'They will be found,' Oliver said to Mr Smith, the officer of the watch, who did not know what his captain was referring to. 'And they will face charges of theft, desertion and damaging a king's ship plus attempting to incite mutiny. I have not yet calculated how many Articles of War they have contravened. But they will hang.' He paused and added, 'It is a shame we can only hang them once for their crimes, don't you agree?'

Oliver knew that in no time word from the two deserters would spread like wildfire to the local ports. By now it was likely all Deal knew what the frigate was carrying. And if word had not already filtered along the Kent coast, by morning any onshore breezes would deliver the aromatic news as effectively as if it was shouted from the topsail yard. It had quite amazed him that neither he nor his officers had noticed the sweet scent which had been released in the hold when one of the great lumps of ambergris had been broken apart.

For the present nothing could be done save remaining alert. There was no wind to carry them out, no chance of escaping the Downs. The tide was low. It was dark as pitch and from the deck the steep beach was no longer visible, but the sound of water hissing as it was sucked through the shingles was relentless. The port town, half a mile away, was a haven for hovellers and luggers and the men who had grown up on this stretch of coast, which was as infamous as that of Cornwall.

From a ship anchored nearby came a plaintive string melody played remarkably well, the accompaniment of voices spoiling an otherwise tolerable performance. For a few moments the music occupied the captain's thoughts.

Not a great distance away was a large Indiaman. He had watched it sail into the road earlier, drop anchor, attend to its regular harbour duties, douse its lanterns and settle down for the night. Like *Elusive* it had, no doubt, made a run for the Downs, and its captain was relieved to have secured a safe anchorage. It was likely though that the merchant's master would be frustrated, after a journey lasting many months, at being delayed so near home.

'I shall go to my cot, Mr Smith. Wake me immediately should the slightest thing disturb you. And pass that message to Mr Parry when he comes on deck.'

As he turned to go inside, he felt a breath of wind. It teased his face as coquettishly as the flick from a lady's fan. It slid across his twisted hand with the smoothness of a gossamer silk gown. But these gentle allusions brought nothing but feelings of foreboding. They were dangerous in the extreme if roused by association with any other woman than a man's wife.

Oliver shook his head. The frigate would ride out the night and hopefully in the morning there would be sufficient wind to carry them around the North Foreland. If so, they would weigh anchor early and slide out of this maritime bottleneck and head for the Thames. He did not intend to wait for his escort.

As he left the deck, the young midshipman raised his hat. Oliver Quintrell was aware he was leaving the care of his ship in the hands of a pair of midshipmen – one being a fourteen-year-old lad.

The urgent knocking woke him. He recognized the voice. It only seemed a matter of minutes since he had swung his legs into his cot and listened to the creak of footsteps on the poop deck above his head. He was sure he had not slept, yet the motion of the ship had changed considerably. No longer was he being lulled by the gentle lapping of the waves. Now the ship was pitching and rearing like a startled stallion.

'Didn't I say to tell me of any change?'

'It blew up all of a sudden, sir, and Mr Mundy thinks we're dragging the anchor.'

'Damn!' he cried, fighting to find the armhole in his coat. 'Wake Mr Parry!'

'I'm here, sir,' Parry said from the shadows, moving closer while Oliver adjusted his eyes to the darkness. 'I'm afraid it's as Mr Smith said. That blast hit us just a few minutes ago. It almost threw me from my bunk. The wind has turned right about. It's a westerly coming off the land and it gave no warning. I've got men on the staysails and the yards.'

Oliver looked through the rattling rigging to the lights of the other ships moored along the coast. 'We're drifting!'

Mr Mundy's voice bellowed from the darkness. 'The cables have been cut, Capt'n. Both anchors have gone!'

'Someone will answer for this!' But the clap of thunder deafened everyone to his voice. 'Get the helm over. Staysail haul. Man the braces. We must get her around. Mr Mundy, see to it the marines check for boarders and tell the lookout to watch for any luggers nearby.' He turned to his lieutenant, tilting his head slightly as lightning flashed brighter than any broadside from a triple-decker.

'Over there!' Simon pointed. 'Breakers!'

'I see them. How close are we?'

The first lieutenant was about to answer when the sky burst into a majestic performance. Peel upon peel of thunder was accompanied by flashes of searing white light. What they saw on the stage before them was the subtle horror of the Goodwin Sands. Not the black, angry, needle-sharp rocky protuberances which rose from the disfigured body of an active volcano but soft mounds of sand dunes lying as still as a sleeping woman covered by a silken sheet. This was surely Neptune's Temptress, who for centuries had lured sailors into her open arms. Now she was preparing for her next victim.

'Beg pardon, Captain.'

'What is it?'

'There's nine inches of water in the well!' Will Ethridge called.

'Since when?'

'Since noon. We had only five inches.'

'Get below and find out where it's coming from.'

'Aye aye, Capt'n.'

'If she doesn't respond soon we'll be aground!'

Turned and tossed like washing in a tub, the officer on deck shouted the orders but could do little more than watch and wait as a dozen men hauled on each of the starboard braces. The sound of the wind was threatening as it whipped the waves higher with every thrust. Across the expanse of sands they could see the waves slithering further and further over the gentle contours, filling the dips and valleys with swirling foam, sucking away its dryness till the shifting sands melted and succumbed to liquid form.

'I swear, I am not going to lose my cargo now,' the captain shouted. 'Nor my ship. Mr Parry, I need your advice. You have been in this situation before. Give me the benefit of your knowledge.'

'How can I help? I lost my ship.'

'Facts, Simon. You must have learned something from that experience.'

'I know there are two channels,' he yelled. 'The Gull Stream is the main one through to the North Foreland. Then there's Kellet Gut. It's a narrower channel midway separating the North from the South Sands.

'Could we get through this middle passage?'

'I didn't, and I don't know that it remains in a fixed position. I do know that at low tide the sands sit thirteen feet above the sea, but I've also heard that like the islands of ice in the Southern Ocean, it's likely that only a tenth of the area is visible. The Goodwin Sands are like serpents. They heave and twist and shift and no one can guarantee from one night to the next where the channel will be the following day.'

'I don't want an oration on oceanography,' Oliver said. 'What I asked is, can we get through it?'

'With a pilot, perhaps.'

'You mean a Deal man?'

'Yes, sir,' he said flatly. He had no other answer or suggestion. The only thing imprinted in Simon Parry's mind was the longest night he had ever experienced – the night he spent clinging to the main mast as his ship and his men were swallowed by the shifting sands, the night he had prayed like he had never prayed before. The night he had been granted a miracle. But Simon Parry knew he could not expect to receive another.

'Tom Wotton my coxswain, and Jo Foss, one of the boat crew, are Deal men are they not?'

'Aye, sir,' Mr Mundy answered. 'But they're locked up below to stop them running like you ordered.'

'Bring them up here, and quickly.'

The word was passed and the bosun dived down the forward hatchway. But his hands were greasy and as the ship heeled he slipped, landing heavily on the deck below.

The storm was intensifying and the wind strengthening, swinging the other ships on their anchor chains in a perilous fashion.

'Keep clear of that Indiaman. I don't want her slamming into us if she drags.'

'See over there, sir!' Mr Parry shouted. 'Skulking in her lee. There's a light and it's moving. A lugger maybe.'

'Keep an eye on it. What I would give to put a twenty-four-pound ball through her hull!'

'I hope he's not intent on cutting her cable also. Are there not enough wrecks on these sands without the men deliberately setting out to create them?'

'All hands on deck, Mr Parry.'

As the larboard watch spewed onto the deck, Mr Mundy returned with the two sailors. Stiff after being confined below decks and concerned about the rolling sea while imprisoned beneath a locked grating, they had been woken from a troubled sleep and were somewhat confused. Unaware of what was happening on deck, they had only heard a rumour that two other Deal men had run. They were not sure of the truth of the whispers. It took a moment for their eyes to adjust to the lack of light.

'Do you recognize where we are?'

'The Downs, Capt'n.'

'But at what point? How well do you know the Sands?'

Thomas Wotton allowed a grin to spill across his cheeks. 'As well as any man born and bred on this coast, Capt'n.'

'Then you will be the pilot. You will take us by the North Foreland or through the middle channel. You will give your instructions to Mr Mundy.'

The smile disappeared as the seaman looked at his mate.

Jo Foss answered. 'It's impossible on a night like this. There ain't no lights, only them few town lights for guidance, and it's fifteen years since we sailed this stretch.'

'Well, you have fifteen minutes to recall those times, mister.'

The men glanced from the deck to the dozens of lanterns swaying haphazardly in the roadstead. There were definite signs of disorganization. Occasional cries carried on the gale confirmed the captain's fears that more than one of the ships' anchors was dragging through the shingle and heading for disaster.

'We must get clear before we collide!'

As the storm flashed overhead its effect was evident. Already four ships had drifted too far to the east to be safe from the pull of the Sands while two others were attempting to run the gauntlet to the north, battling the wind and attempting to make it into the Gull Stream and around the North Foreland.

'I've seen four hundred ships in the Downs when a wind came up and twenty lost in a single night,' Wotton said.

'And the Deal men no doubt clapped their hands with glee!'

Mr Parry squirmed at the sailing master's caustic remark. He remembered the men who had saved him and his crew and a small local boat named *Pegwell*, which had come back three times during the night and eventually taken him off just before the sand swallowed his ship.

Wotton, the coxswain, dared speak his mind. 'Begging your pardon, Capt'n sir, but that's not fair what Mr Mundy said. Most hovellers are honest men who'll risk their lives to help someone. I know it for a fact. I was out there as a lad. I witnessed my father and brothers drown trying to save some ungrateful lubbers.'

Oliver nodded. His grandfather had suffered the same fate. It had long been said that Cornish folk lured ships onto the rocks to steal their cargo. But it was not true. The fishermen took flotsam and jetsam from the water and saved men's lives in the process but they never set out to sink a ship.

'Take no notice of him, Wotton. The wind is trying its hardest to force us back onto the Sands. It must not succeed. Tell me what heading we must take.'

The seaman raised his voice against the rain and thunder. 'You'll not sail north on this wind, Capt'n. It'll carry us onto the North Bank. And it'd be foolish to try for Kellet Gut. That channel could be miles away from where I remember it.'

'Where then? Speak, man, there is little time!'

'Best beat back to the South Foreland and head for Dover. That's my advice.'

'Then the South Foreland it is. All hands ready? Mr Parry, take her around.'

Dashing the rain from his eyes, Oliver listened to the orders relayed along the deck, watched the man on the helm and the sailors standing ready to haul the jibs and staysails across, and like every man on deck waited, counting the moments, willing the frigate's head to come around. As the wind howled and gusted, *Elusive* heeled over. Waves crashed over her bow and white water cascaded over the gunnels.

'Gun deck's awash, Captain!' shouted Mr Tully anxiously, from the top of the companion ladder.

'Check the port lids. Make sure they're fastened. Get the helm across!'

By this time three men were struggling to turn the wheel, but the ship's bearing was not budging. With the wind spilled from the sails, lines and blocks were swinging pendulously, threatening to smash the skull of anyone within their reach. The rattling canvas crackled like musket shots, snapping back and forth like a pack of angry dogs. From the yards, the square sails backed, forcing the frigate closer to the Sands.

'The rudder's not answering!' came the desperate call from the helm.

'Where's the bosun? Find out why she won't respond.'

Mr Tully reappeared from the companionway. 'Gun port lid wedged open! We've taken a fair bit of water.'

'Go back below. Get some men on the pumps.'

'Aye, Capt'n.'

'She'll fill like a bathtub in no time and take us all down!'

Despite the gale of wind, the captain caught his sailing master's mumbled remark. For the present he chose to ignore it.

'Do you think someone is trying to sink us again?' Mr Parry asked.

'God help us if they are,' Oliver replied. 'Mr Smith, break out the weapons. I want every man on deck armed.'

As the midshipman dashed below, the bosun grappled his way forward. 'Captain,' he yelled, 'there's a small rowboat hanging off the stern with her lines wrapped around the rudder.'

'How many men would have been aboard?'

'Two or four at the most.'

'Anyone see them come aboard?'

'Perhaps the two marines on duty, but one's been shot and the other injured. And their muskets have gone.'

Damnation! His ship had no steerage. It was drifting towards the Sands. It was taking water and now there were boarders on board. The situation could not be much worse.

'Get some men over the taffrail and cut the lines from the rudder. Then put a ball through the bottom of that boat.'

'With pleasure, Captain.'

'Captain! We're boarded!'

Oliver recognized the voice. The news it carried was no surprise.

Will stumbled along the deck, blood running from a gash on his head.

'Where? How many?' Oliver asked.

'Two on the gun deck. One man jumped from a gun port before I could stop him. There's another down there but I need some help.'

'Simon, the ship is yours. I trust you to keep her off the sand. If you lose her, we are all dead!'

It was obvious from a quick glance around the deck that few men could be spared from the sheets or lines. 'You waisters with me!' Oliver called, heading for the companionway to the gun deck.

'Shall I get your pistols, Capt'n?' Casson called.

'No time!' he replied, grabbing a cutlass.

'Here, lad,' said Bungs, thrusting a weapon into Will's hand.

'I don't know how to use it,' the young shipwright cried.

'You'll learn quick enough. Stick with me.'

Moving as fast as they dare, the pair followed the captain while Casson, Froyle and two marines followed closely behind.

'Show yourselves!' Oliver shouted, aiming his pistol at the figure squatting behind one of the twelve-pounders.

'Don't shoot!' a man called, cautiously lifting his right arm in the air. Once upright, everyone recognized the face of the Deal sailor who had run the previous day. From the bundle enlosed in his left arm, it was obvious he had not been satisfied with only twenty pounds of ambergris.

'Put the gold down, and step aside! Marines, bind this man. You others, follow me below!'

A near-palpable veil of odour greeted the men as they stepped onto the ladder. A combination of damp worm-infested timbers, foul urine-soaked ballast washings, salt pork and beef, wine, sweat and empty grease-streaked barrels containing particles of rotted whale blubber was tinged with the sensual, musky aroma of raw ambergris.

Descending into the hold, the captain monitored every sound: the familiar groans and creakings of any ship at sea, the dull thud of the bow as it buried itself into the waves, and the relentless roll and thump of the barrels which had broken loose from their lashings.

The light was dim but no more so than on deck. A pair of swinging lanterns flickered, casting shadows forward and aft, but the amidships' lantern had smashed against the deck beams and extinguished itself.

'Surrender your weapons!' the captain shouted, unsure if any other boarders were hiding there.

His answer came loud and clear in an explosive flash of light. The musket ball thwacked into the deck beam close to his head, bringing an involuntary sneer to Oliver's lips. Now he knew exactly where his adversary was.

The captain jumped down with Bungs one step behind him. 'Show yourselves, you cowards!' he cried.

As he spoke, the frigate pitched and rolled and the swinging lantern threw its light across the face of the man holding the musket. Oliver was shocked.

'Guthrie!' he breathed. 'You dare show your face aboard my ship after what you did to Percy Sparrow!'

For a split second there was silence. Will's breath was snatched from his throat. He could neither speak nor cry out. It was the first he had heard of the culprit who had murdered his friend. It was the same for the cooper, but from deep within Bungs' chest came an involuntarily roar like the bellow of a wounded beast. But before Bungs could rush forward, Oliver leapt towards Guthrie, aware of the musket being levelled towards him, aware of the movement of the man's fingers then conscious of the empty click as the hammer dropped. But the only flash was that of fear across the sailor's face when the powder did not ignite.

'This one is mine,' the captain cried, swinging his cutlass beneath the musket and driving it out of Guthrie's hands. With a flash, he brought the blade down cutting into the man's collar bone an inch from his throat.

Guthrie squealed like a stuck pig and dropped, blood streaming from his shoulder, blubbering like a baby.

The cutlass poised in Oliver's hand quivered for a moment. How easily the point would slide into the sailor's belly.

'Finish him,' Froyle yelled.

'No,' Oliver replied. 'For what he has done, he doesn't deserve a quick death. Marines! Take him away. Guard him and don't let anyone near him for I'm sure every man aboard would be happy to finish him off.'

The instant Oliver stepped aside, Guthrie's mate scuttled from between the barrels. But for Bigalow there was no escape either from the ship's hold or from the cooper who had regarded the ship's carpenter as his friend. Bungs was waiting. And while Will and the other men were eager to join in, there was room only for one man at a time.

After wrenching the knife from Bigalow's fist, Bungs locked both hands around his neck, tightened his grip and squeezed until every ounce of breath had gurgled from the sailor's throat and his knees had collapsed beneath him.

'Leave him, Bungs,' Will pleaded. 'Leave him be. Let the pair hang for what they did to Chips.'

But Bungs hands were still clenched around Bigalow's throat and it took all Will's strength to prize his fingers free. Once released, Bungs fell back against a barrel. 'Poor Percy' he said, tears rolling down his cheeks.

Suddenly the ship juddered violently, throwing the captain and his men off their balance.

'We've run aground!' Oliver yelled. 'Quickly men, with me!'

On deck, lightning flashed and the sound of the stern chaser's discharge coincided with the clap of thunder. A cheer rang out from the gun crew signifying that the small boat had been sunk, but Mr Parry ignored it. His main concern was the line of breakers and the ship was drifting closer. Once the tide rose to its full there would be no warning breakers creaming the sand, and soon there would be no indication where either the North or South Goodwins began or ended. Soon all that would be evident of the twelve-mile hazard would be the illusion of a troubled lake under which a seething sea monster lay in waiting for any unwary ship foolishly attempting to sail over it. How well he remembered.

'And what of the local luggers?' he asked Wotton.

'They'll wait till first light, then they'll sail out, searching for any ship that's fallen foul. They'll take off any survivors but they'll not say no to helping themselves to the cargo before it goes under. It's only flotsam after all.'

Simon was about to answer when the ship jerked and shuddered, and the dull scraping of copper plates on sand resounded through the ship's timbers like an alarm bell. Beneath the hull *Elusive*'s keel was dragging on the sand, grinding itself deeper into the bottom. Skin tingled. Hair stood on end. Hearts pounded. And every man aboard said a silent prayer. Would the next wave lift them free or push them further onto the sand? Every jack-tar was well aware of what a confrontation with the Goodwin Sands could bring.

'It has to be a bar!' the lieutenant shouted. 'There's open sea to port and starboard. Get a man on the lead!'

'We're lost if we stick fast. The sea will break us in two.'

'I don't need to be reminded, Mr Mundy.' But as Mr Parry spoke, *Elusive* heeled on its lodged keel and spun gracefully in an arc forty-five degrees. Canvas crackled. The staysails luffed and filled. Then the frigate launched herself forward into deeper water, raising a resounding cheer from the men on the yards.

'We're off!' Mr Mundy announced jubilantly, as the frigate's head turned, the sails filled and *Elusive* made way.

'This time you had the upper hand,' Oliver said, as he joined his first lieutenant on deck.

'Indeed,' said Mr Parry, with a sigh of relief. 'And you, sir?'

'Three prisoners taken who we will return to London to be hung. In the meantime, I trust they will appreciate the rest of this cruise surrounded by one million pounds' worth of ambergris, for it is the last they will ever see of it.'

'And they'll surely make the finest-smelling corpses when they are dangling from the gallows.'

'Indeed, Mr Mundy. But for now let us get out of here. Take her as close to the wind and as near the Kent coast as possible. Then south and into the Channel again. It is time we were reunited with our escort.'

Stepping aside, Mr Parry gazed back into the darkness.

'Am I right in thinking you will have no regrets leaving this place,' Oliver asked quietly.

Simon Parry sighed. 'Indeed you are.'

CHAPTER 25

Greenwich

Although the Downs was reputed to be one of England's safest havens, Oliver was not convinced, and with the events of the previous night still fresh in his mind, he was relieved when they sailed out past the South Foreland. But it was not until the garrison town of Dover came into view that he allowed himself to relax and accept a cup of coffee from his steward on the quarter-deck. With the ship in the lee of the white cliffs and a sense of security knowing they were within range of the castle's recently improved fortifications, he decided it was safe to heave to and drop anchor until the following day.

Morning came slowly with the sun battling for recognition through a thick sea-mist. The storm winds had settled, the air was still and in the mess the crew were able to sit down to breakfast at stable tables.

After an half-hour nap, Oliver stepped on deck, relieved to see that the mist had lifted. He was greeted by a cry from aloft.

'Sail ho!'

'Where away?'

'Three English frigates off the starboard quarter.'

He turned and saw the escort ships. They too were lolling on the still Channel waters.

'They're signalling, Captain.'

'I can see that.'

The midshipman hurried aft with his board. '*Captain requested to go onboard flagship*,' he read.

'Acknowledge, Mr Hazzlewood. Tell them I will be delighted.'

'Aye aye, sir.'

Then, after a moment's consideration: 'Belay that comment, Mr H. Just acknowledge.'

For Oliver Quintrell and Simon Parry, it was an interesting meeting on board the flagship, *Foxglove*.

After an excellent luncheon, the young commodore boasted quite blatantly how he had teased the French. He described how he had approached the man-of-war near the French coast and fired a warning shot from his forward deck carronade. Registering no response from the warship or the corvettes travelling with it, he had assumed his action had scared the French off. Later in the conversation, when he commented that the French ninety-eight-gun appeared to be riding high in the water and was without its full complement of guns on the upper deck, Oliver and Simon exchanged glances but said nothing. To the pair it seemed likely the ship had been converted to a troop carrier and if that was the case it had more urgent business in northern Europe and did not have time to waste in petty pranks in the Channel.

When Oliver was asked to relate what had transpired in the Downs, he spoke firstly of the weather and then of two men who had jumped ship and of the cable that had been cut. He further advised that the deserters had been captured and were currently under guard in the ship's hold and that they would face court-martial when *Elusive* docked in London. He purposely said nothing of the nature of his cargo or of the quantity which had been taken, and provided no details of his revelations about Mr Sparrow's death and the subsequent events on board. This information was for the attention of the Lords of the Admiralty and was already documented in the ship's log.

All in all, the meeting was pleasant if only for the wine and excellent cold pheasant. He enjoyed listening to the three other captains relating details of their recent cruises on the North American coast, but Oliver was not sorry when the meeting was over. He was eager to proceed to the mouth of the Thames, at which point the young commodore's naval leash would be removed.

Two days later, *Elusive*, in company with her three escorts, left Dover and sailed back through the Downs, navigated the Gull Stream without incident, and cleared the North Foreland before noon. From there they headed west past Sheppey Island and the broad entrance to the Medway before encountering the littered murky waters of the Thames estuary. When the four vessels reached the point where the river narrowed to half a mile in breadth, the ships parted company. After a brief exchange of signals and salutes, *Elusive* continued her journey alone.

The wharf at Woolwich where the powder and shot was unloaded was a welcome stop though Quintrell and his officer remained ever-cautious of prying eyes and sensitive noses. With the danger of explosion making it impossible to burn pitch for an odorous effect, the crew were again ordered to douse the decks with liberal quantities of vinegar, much to the amusement and interest of the dockside workers.

'Kills the fleas,' said one of the sailors cockily, when asked the reason for his labours.

Throughout the unloading, Oliver remained on deck making sure no one slipped aboard and that none of the special barrels and crates were accidentally or deliberately transported ashore.

'Begging your pardon, sir,' said Will, knuckling his forehead as he approached the captain at the gangway. He spoke in a whisper.

'Speak up, Will, I can hardly hear you.'

'I fear we're still taking water, Captain.'

'How much?'

'Twenty inches in the well.'

'Since when?'

'It's not gone down since we took that swamping in the Downs. The bosun says the pumps are not coping.'

'Have you checked for damage?'

'Aye, Capt'n. There's nothing obvious. Just seepage. I think she's just plain tired, sir, and that last pounding squeezed her to the limits.'

'Like some of the crew, if I'm not mistaken. Keep an eye on her, if you please. I'll ask Mr Tully to change the men on the pumps every ten minutes; that may help a little.' He looked forward along the sweep of the Thames. 'I do not wish my ship to sink in the heart of London.'

'I'll check it right regular, Capt'n.'

Oliver walked back along the deck and joined his first lieutenant. 'My instructions are to offload our cargo at the hospital wharf at Greenwich.'

'A strange location, if I might say.'

'My thoughts entirely, but it is not for me to argue.'

'Once the cargo is discharged, the ship will be decommissioned. From there she will be taken into the naval yard at Deptford.'

'Do you think she will be refitted?'

'It's hard to tell. In times such as these, it's likely she'll be sent to the breakers yard or maybe converted to a coal hulk. But who knows what will happen if times change. . . . However, one thing is certain, we will not be taking her to sea, and in her present condition that is for the best.'

'It's back to half pay then.'

'Indeed. But what of you, Simon? Will you be returning to Portsmouth? If so, you are most welcome to share my carriage.'

'I think I will stay in London for a week or two. I can pay my respects at Whitehall and remind the Lords Commissioners of my situation. Plus there are other matters I would like to attend to.'

'You never spoke of a wife or sweetheart.'

'No, I never did.'

'Then I shall not press you. Needless to say, should you ever feel inclined to take a wherry across the Solent and visit Bembridge you would be most welcome to stay with us. My wife would be delighted to make your acquaintance.'

As the words tumbled from his lips, he remembered the letter from his wife's physician. He had placed it inside *Elusive*'s logbook so he would be reminded of its contents daily.

The journey from Woolwich to Greenwich, though only a short distance, was tediously slow. Assisted by the flow of the incoming tide but under very little sail, the frigate navigated the final stretches of the River Thames. On board, the crew, with little to do, wandered the deck gazing out across the marshy swamps and fields interspersed with new wooden wharfs and clusters of redbrick warehouses rising gauntly from the waterfront.

Overhead the sky was clear and the morning sun warm. A group of young ladies promenading along the grassy bank near the Lea River showed little interest in the dowdy ship on the busy waterway. They ignored the grubby faces of the sailors leaning against its rails. But for the seamen the sight of the females in their fancy hats and flowing skirts stirred more than their imaginations. Apart from the fishwives on the Portsmouth foreshore, these were the first women the men had seen in many months. They were aware that very soon they would be going ashore and were eager to do so.

Embarking on the final bend in the river, the gracious buildings of Greenwich's Seamen's Hospital came into view. From a distance the waterfront appeared to be coloured with rows of tall poppies. Oliver wondered how long the marines had been assembled in the sun awaiting their arrival. He doubted their attendance was to celebrate the frigate's safe delivery. A more likely reason was to accompany the cargo of ambergris on its final journey.

Gazing across the water to the palatial hospital buildings, Oliver was reminded of the long months he had spent as a patient there. Much had happened since then.

Once the mooring lines were in place, but before unloading commenced, the three men who had been held in the hold were brought on deck. The instant outburst of jeers and hisses was quickly silenced. Guthrie and Bigalow were closely guarded to protect them from the crew who would readily have strung them up from the main yard. The atmosphere was tense and the business needed to be attended to with due haste.

After signing his prisoners over to a marine officer, Oliver watched them hobble across the gangplank, wrists and ankles shackled. But there was little satisfaction in the knowledge that the pair, who had murdered his carpenter, would soon receive their just deserts.

Oliver wondered how long it would be before a court-martial would be convened. It was an unseemly business but necessary and one he would unfortunately be obliged to attend.

With the prisoners despatched, the offloading of cargo commenced.

Aware that *Elusive* was far from seaworthy, Oliver had ordered the floating gold to be brought up from the hold soon after they had left Woolwich. Since before dawn, containers of cargo had been hoisted on deck and lined up around the gunnels. If the ship was to sink in the Thames, the job of retrieving it from the hold would be both difficult and tedious, and that was one eventuality to be avoided. Furthermore, if the ship went down in the river while still under his command, he would have to answer to a court-martial for the loss of a king's ship. The sooner the cargo was unloaded and the sooner the frigate was decommissioned the better.

In Oliver's estimation everything possible had been done to maintain her and no amount of oakum, pitch or paint could remedy rotten timbers. Now his only wish was that *Elusive* stay afloat long enough to be sailed or towed into the Naval Dockyard at Deptford. It was a distance of only a few hundred yards.

The colonnades and pathways surrounding the elegant white buildings of the Greenwich Seamen's Hospital were abuzz with patients, attendants and visitors, while noisy onlookers lining the riverfront were kept at bay by the vigilant marines.

But it was not the shore activity which attracted Oliver's immediate attention. It was the smell of the place. How well he remembered it. The whiff of old and dying men, of human excrement and infected wounds masked beneath an aromatic veil of mixed perfumes – lavender balms, salves and potpourris. What a contrast it was to the smell of tar, turpentine, vinegar and ambergris – but he doubted any of the other men would notice.

On the lane running between the four main hospital buildings, a convoy of dray wagons was drawn up ready to receive the ship's cargo. Waiting patiently, the Shire horses grazed contentedly on the spring grass.

It did not bother Oliver that he had received no hint of the onward destination of his cargo. Suffice to say, his main concern was to have the ambergris removed from *Elusive* in order that he could officially complete his commission and return to Admiralty House to deliver his report.

Leaving was a fulfilling yet somewhat moving moment for Oliver Quintrell. Before departing he went below to check on the state of the frigate which had served him well.

Much to his relief, the acting carpenter, Will Ethridge, had volunteered to stay with the ship until she was safely delivered into the Deptford yard.

'And what of you when you leave, Will?' the captain asked. 'Do you intend to go home?'

'Yes, sir. I'll finish my apprenticeship – just a few months left. But one day I might sail again as a carpenter if I can get a warrant.'

'Then I wish you well. I have mentioned your name in my report and written a letter of recommendation to the Admiralty on your behalf.'

'Thank you, sir.'

'Just one word of warning. When you pick up your wages, be careful where you find lodgings in London. Your face still carries the colour of a man who has sailed to the tropics – it is hard to disguise.'

Will thanked the captain and bade him farewell.

On deck the captain offered his misshapen hand to all of his officers. They grasped it in turn. Simon Parry was the last in line. As first lieutenant, it was his duty to attend to the paperwork necessary in discharging the crew.

Stepping from the gangplank onto the hospital wharf, the side-boys' whistles shrilled for the final time as Captain Quintrell left the ship. For a moment there was silence then a cry went up for three hearty cheers. Oliver turned and raised his hat. He wondered if he would see any of the men again.

Ambling up the pathway to a waiting hackney coach, he thought about the ambergris and how uninspiring it appeared to the casual observer. Its fragrance however, was unmistakable. How many of the sailors' seachests would carry traces of the distinctive scent? he wondered.

Little had changed in the Admiralty building since his last visit to Whitehall.

Sitting on the wooden bench in the corridor, he studied the young clerk who bustled back and forth cradling a bundle of letters. He was the same youth he had seen the previous July and the worried expression on his face had not mellowed. Only the whiskers escaping from beneath his powdered wig were longer and fuzzier and the furrows in his brow deeper.

What could possibly lie in the Navy's private cabinets which could torment a young man so? For the past nine months the clerk had been navigating a sea of offices, sailing down corridors of polished mahogany and daily fathoming nothing more than where he would dine that evening. In the same period *Elusive*'s common seamen had travelled to the end of the earth, faced unthinkable physical dangers and not known at the dawning of each day if they would live to see the sun go down.

Strange, Oliver thought, we all serve king and country but how different the colour and intensity of our lives.

The interview with the first lord was short and formal and the word ambergris was not mentioned once. That was no surprise. Oliver was grateful to be congratulated on the success of his mission but the glossy words seemed little more than a polite veneer. Once again he was reminded there would be no mention of his cruise in the *Gazette*, although he was assured he would receive some form of recognition – in due course. However, he was given assurance that the recommendations he had put forward regarding members of his crew would be noted and acted on accordingly. That was all.

As he stepped from the room, the clerk dressed in his fine velvet livery and lopsided wig was waiting for him.

'Captain Quintrell of His Majesty's ship *Elusive*?'

'I am Captain Quintrell, but *Elusive* is not a ship, she is a frigate. You would do well to remember that, young man.'

'Thank you, sir. I will.' The youth blushed and looked more worried than ever. 'I have a letter for you which arrived only this morning.' After handing it over, he bowed awkwardly and retreated, seeming unsure of whether to walk forwards or backwards and instead diverting to the nearest doorway which fortunately was open.

Oliver stared at the letter and immediately recognized the handwriting. It was written in his wife's bold, rounded hand. What a relief it was to know she had survived the illness and was well enough to write. That was good news indeed, but at the same time he dismissed a tinge of disappointment. He had hoped to receive word from Susanna, but there had been insufficient time for a letter to be returned from Madeira.

His steward, John Casson, was waiting for him at the Whitehall steps.

'I trust you will be happy to resume your role as a gentleman's valet,' Oliver asked. 'At least for a short time.'

'I couldn't think of anything better, Capt'n.'

'Surely you would prefer to be at sea?' he said, with the hint of a grin on his face.

'Of course, though I don't think *Elusive* will be sailing for quite some time, sir. When your cabin furnishings were being loaded on the wagon, I noticed how low she was sitting in the water. But the hull was empty, the powder and shot had been offloaded, the water used up and most of the stores exhausted. She should have been bobbing like a cork.'

Oliver shook his head. 'Let us pray she makes it into the dockyard.'

'Aye, Capt'n. She was a good ship, wasn't she?' Casson said, bounding along the pavement half a step behind his master.

'Indeed she was. You will share a glass with me when I am home. We will drink a toast to *Elusive* and to a successful voyage. Am I correct in thinking there is a bottle of Madeira amongst my dunnage?'

'Two bottles, Capt'n. I made sure they were stowed safe and sound.'

'Excellent. Then take me to this carriage you have hired. I wish to go home with all haste.'

'The driver promised he will have us in Portsmouth by tomorrow morning and I reckon we'll be at Bembridge soon after noon.'

'Where I will have a time to relax and soak in a hot bath. And you will have time to replenish your sea chest.'

Casson looked puzzled. 'Why is that, sir? Are you shipping out again?'

'Quite soon, I hope. There are murmurs in the corridors of power that the peace with France is coming to an end and that King George is about to sign a declaration of war.'

'Huzzah!'

'If that happens, every able-bodied seaman, and officer from midshipman to admiral will be called upon to return to the sea.'

The steward was hard pressed not to throw his arms around his captain. 'They'll give you a ship-of-the-line next time, Capt'n. I'll bet my last shilling on it.'

Oliver Quintrell smiled. 'Patience, Casson. We must wait and see.'

Author's note

The island described in *Floating Gold* is Deception Island.

It lies at 62° 57' S and 60° 38' W in the South Shetland Islands off the Antarctic Peninsula.

Deception Island is the caldera of an ancient but still active volcano which last erupted in 1969.

Every year, for a few months during the southern summer, Deception Island is visited by cruise ships and expedition vessels.

Today it is the permanent home to Spanish and Argentine Antarctic stations.

In December 1819 the island was first surveyed and mapped by Lieutenant Edward Bransfield aboard the *Williams*, a ship chartered by the Royal Navy. It is thought, however, that the island had been visited previously by some of the early explorers and navigators.

Whaling activities began on the island in about 1820 and the ruins of the whaling station, which was built on the cinder shores of Whalers Bay, are still visible today.

From the sea, the island appears almost circular – however, the enclosed lagoon measures 5.5 miles (9 km) long by 3.6 miles (6 km) wide. The narrow break in the caldera's wall, which provides access for ships, is known as Neptune's Bellows.

Submerged at a depth of 8 feet (2.5 m) below the surface of the channel is a rocky outcrop named Ravn Rock. Over the years, this rock has claimed several ships.

In 2004, I had the opportunity of visiting Deception Island and witnessing the strange and unusual features which I have described in *Floating Gold*.

In 2006 a lump of ambergris (floating gold) was washed up on a south Australian beach.

It weighed about 32 pounds (14.75 kilos) and was reputed to be worth $1 million.

Learning about this unusual find inspired me to write this book.